***Rick let*** *they wel*** *quaking shoulders.***

She turned and stared up at him silently.

Even with the purple bruises that had darkened along her left cheek and jaw, Eve Paris was a stunning woman. But the longer he stared, the more he noticed the emotional ravages of the day.

In the end, it was her eyes that did him in.

They were puffy and red from crying; the emerald irises seemed darker now, larger...and silent tears were still streaming from the corners of her eyes. Mesmerized, he reached out and smoothed his thumbs up her cheeks, catching the damp warmth as tears continued to trickle steadily down.

Before he could stop himself, Rick was leaning down. Closer and closer, until he was breathing her scent. He caught her tears with his lips, absorbing the salt with his flesh. Even as his actions stunned him, they seemed right. *This* seemed right.

And a moment later, it only seemed natural to cover those soft lips with his own....

Dear Reader,

Once again, Silhouette Intimate Moments starts its month off with a bang, thanks to Beverly Barton's *The Princess's Bodyguard,* another in this author's enormously popular miniseries THE PROTECTORS. A princess used to royal suitors has to "settle" for an in-name-only marriage to her commoner bodyguard. Or maybe she isn't settling at all? Look for more Protectors in *On Her Guard,* Beverly Barton's Single Title, coming next month.

ROMANCING THE CROWN continues with *Sarah's Knight* by Mary McBride. An arrogant palace doctor finds he needs help himself when his little boy stops speaking. To the rescue: a beautiful nanny sent to work with the child—but who winds up falling for the good doctor himself. And in Candace Irvin's *Crossing the Line,* an army pilot crash-lands, and she and her surviving passenger—a handsome captain—deal simultaneously with their attraction to each other and the ongoing crash investigation. Virginia Kantra begins her TROUBLE IN EDEN miniseries with *All a Man Can Do,* in which a police chief finds himself drawn to the reporter who is the sister of a prime murder suspect. In *The Cop Next Door* by Jenna Mills, a woman back in town to unlock the secrets of her past runs smack into the stubborn town sheriff. And Melissa James makes her debut with *Her Galahad,* in which a woman who thought her first husband was dead finds herself on the run from her abusive *second* husband. And who should come to her rescue but Husband Number One—not so dead after all!

Enjoy, and be sure to come back next month for more of the excitement and passion, right here in Intimate Moments.

Leslie J. Wainger
Executive Senior Editor

Please address questions and book requests to:
Silhouette Reader Service
U.S.: 3010 Walden Ave., P.O. Box 1325, Buffalo, NY 14269
Canadian: P.O. Box 609, Fort Erie, Ont. L2A 5X3

# Crossing the Line
## CANDACE IRVIN

Silhouette®

INTIMATE MOMENTS™

Published by Silhouette Books

America's Publisher of Contemporary Romance

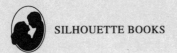 **SILHOUETTE BOOKS**

ISBN 0-373-27249-9

CROSSING THE LINE

Copyright © 2002 by Candace Phillips Irvin

This edition published by arrangement with Harlequin Books S.A.

® and TM are trademarks of Harlequin Books S.A., used under license.
Trademarks indicated with ® are registered in the United States Patent
and Trademark Office, the Canadian Trade Marks Office and in other
countries.

Visit Silhouette at www.eHarlequin.com

**Printed in U.S.A.**

**Books by Candace Irvin**

Silhouette Intimate Moments

*For His Eyes Only* #936
*In Close Quarters* #1078
*Crossing the Line* #1179

## CANDACE IRVIN

is the daughter of a librarian and a sailor, so it's no wonder Candace's two greatest loves are reading and the sea. After spending several exciting years as a U.S. naval officer sailing around the world, she decided it was time to put down roots and give her other love a chance. To her delight, she soon learned that writing romance was as much fun as reading it. A finalist for both the coveted RITA® Award and the Holt Medallion, as well as a two-time *Romantic Times* Reviewers Choice Award nominee, Candace believes her luckiest moment was the day she married her own dashing hero, a former U.S. Army combat engineer with dimples to die for. The two now reside in the South, happily raising two future heroes and one adorable heroine—who won't be allowed to date until she's forty, at least.

Candace loves to hear from readers. You can e-mail her at candace@candaceirvin.com or snail mail her c/o Silhouette Books, 300 East 42nd Street, New York, NY 10017.

For my favorite soldier and forever hero, David.
Thanks, honey, for fielding a thousand and one questions
on everything from fast-roping to small arms
tactics...even at three in the morning.

Acknowledgments

As a former Squid who barely survived Army basic
training before transferring to the Navy's ROTC
program, I was forced to pester several ground-pounding
buddies to pull this plot off. I'm grateful to you all. I'd
like to send a special thanks to Captain Norton A.
Newcomb, U.S. Army, Ret., Special Operations
Intelligence.
Tony, I always appreciate your continuous,
unstinting generosity regarding Special Forces
and the way it "really" is.

Also, to AZ2 Julie A. Thornton, USN;
ABH2 Steve Mark, USN; and Mr. Ken Knowles—
I appreciate the crash courses on the intricacies of
helicopter flight...and especially how to crash them <g>.
I bow to your devious brilliance
and can only hope I did it justice.

Finally, to Damaris Rowland, Allison Lyons
and CJ Chase—thank you so much for being there,
professionally and personally, when I really needed you.

# Chapter 1

*You have never lived until you have almost died. For those who have fought for it, life has a special meaning that the protected will never know.*
                    —U.S. Special Operations motto

She was on top of the world—literally.

Eve grinned as the newborn sun finally seared up through the dense canopy of trees that formed the Central American jungle below, igniting the world with swaths of emerald green, fiery red and burnt orange. She tightened her grip on the chopper's joystick and leaned forward in the cockpit, drawn in by the Black Hawk's panoramic windows and the spectacular view below. There was no doubt about it. She'd finally made it into heaven and she wasn't even dead.

"Takes your breath away, doesn't it?"

Another shot of adrenaline pulsed through Eve's veins, matching the rhythmic thunder of the chopper's blades. She grinned across the cockpit to her copilot. "You got it. The question is, how can you give it up?"

Carrie's answering laughter bubbled though Eve's ear-phones. "I'm not giving it up, exactly. I'm just trading it in for a hot bath back in the old U.S. of A. with enough bubbles to soak the sweat and grime off my face and restore my complexion to manageable." Carrie swept her hands toward the dense trees two hundred feet below. "It's all yours, honey. For the next six months, anyway."

"I'll take it." Eve nodded crisply, then cocked her mouthpiece toward the aerial map spread out on Carrie's lap. "But first, find my blasted landing zone, woman!"

Once again laughter bubbled above the thundering blades as Carrie turned her sparkling blue gaze to the map she'd been using to supplement the Black Hawk's malfunctioning global positioning system for the last thirty minutes. Carrie was all business as she glanced up and pointed dead ahead. "Keep it steady. The LZ is just over that ridge."

Two minutes later they were there.

Eve nudged her stick and swooped the Black Hawk down into the tiny clearing. Even before she felt the gentle thump as the bird touched down into the six-foot elephant grass, the squad of San Sebastián soldiers and their two U.S. Special Forces advisors were storming out of the chop-per and melting into the perimeter beyond. Eve didn't bother taking off but peered into the dense foliage.

Nothing but early-morning shadows and trees.

Where was the American soldier she was supposed to pick up and fly back to the San Sebastián presidential com-pound? Eve glanced at the clock on her instrument panel. The man had better show soon. His briefing started in less than an hour.

"Relax. He'll be here."

"Me? I'm not the one blushing like a sophomore waiting for the school jock to cruise past my locker."

"I am *not* blushing."

But she was and they both knew it. Just as they both knew why. Or better yet, *who* Carrie was hoping to see.

Eve waited until their crew chief bailed out of the bird to scan the perimeter for their next set of passengers before she powered the chopper's engine down to idle. As the roar eased, she switched off her mouthpiece and pulled off her helmet, running her fingers through the tangles on her head as she scrounged up the courage to voice what had to be said. She might have only been in San Sebastián a couple of days, but she knew Carrie well enough to know that this time the woman was in over her head.

Eve finally sighed. "He's enlisted."

Evidently, Carrie had been waiting for her pronouncement, because she just shrugged. "He's a hunk."

"You could lose your wings—and your commission."

"I don't care."

Damn. It was worse than she'd feared. Eve glanced out the side door of the chopper. The jungle was eerily silent beyond, no doubt due to the recent man-made intrusion. She turned back to Carrie, but Carrie still wouldn't meet her gaze. For once she wasn't sure how to respond to her best friend. Though they'd spoken regularly on the phone, they hadn't seen each other in two years.

Evidently things had changed.

She swallowed hard. "Carrie, do you realize what you're saying?"

Carrie turned then, pulling off her own helmet and running her fingers through her inky curls as she shrugged. "Yeah, I do."

Oh God.

Now what?

Fortunately, she didn't need to worry about a comeback, at least not right then. Because, as Eve tipped her head to the left and stared past her friend's olive-drab flight suit,

she spied two camouflaged soldiers with fully-loaded rucksacks on their backs stepping out from the trees beyond.

Two?

She must have stiffened, because Carrie turned around
to stare as well. Her friend was smiling as she swung back.
''It's him. I was hoping he'd have to tag along. But I
couldn't be sure.''

Eve's heart sank. Though there'd been more men in Carrie's life than either of them could count, she'd only seen
that beatific smile once before. It was during their senior
year of college. During the reign of Jake-the-Great. Her
heart sank even further. Carrie hadn't been pretending. Her
friend knew darn well she was playing with fire.

And she didn't care if she got burned.

Eve flicked her gaze back to the men as their crew chief,
Sergeant Lange, joined them. A couple yards more and they
were close enough for her to make out their camouflage-
greased facial features, though not the flat black ranking
insignia on their collars. It didn't matter. Her heart sank to
her toes as she studied the taller of the two Green Beret
advisors. If that was Sergeant Turner, it was too late for
Carrie or the woman's career. Heck, even she'd be tempted
to rip off her wings for a night with the man.

*Hunk* was an understatement.

With those dark forbidding brows beneath the man's
field cap, strong cheeks and firm lips, combined with that
mouth-watering physique beneath his jungle fatigues, the
Army could skip the Be All You Can Be recruiting logo.
For the women, anyway. Just slap a poster of this guy up
in the halls of America's high schools and they'd be signing
up in droves.

As he drew closer, Eve sucked in her breath—and realized she'd been staring. A split second later, she caught the
twin bars on his collar. They matched hers. Thank heaven.

At least she hadn't been ogling the man her best friend thought she was falling in love with.

If Carrie wasn't already beyond saving.

Moments later, Eve knew she was. Before Eve could stop her, Carrie had vaulted from the cockpit and headed out to meet the men. The blinding grin still on her face as she turned back confirmed it. Jake-the-Great and every lover after was nothing more than a distant memory.

Against her better judgment, not to mention standard procedure, Eve climbed out of the cockpit as well. She rounded the front of the bird as her crew chief tossed the soldiers' rucksacks into the rear of the chopper and climbed in after. Carrie stepped forward and grabbed her arm, practically ripping the sleeve of her flight suit off as she hauled her toward the men.

"Eve, this is Sergeant Turner. Bill, Captain Paris."

Eve winced.

Not only had Carrie lost her head, she'd lost her manners, at least her military ones. It was bad enough for Carrie, also a captain, to be on a first-name basis with the enlisted man while in uniform, but did she have to advertise the fact before Turner's commander?

Maybe the man would let it slide?

The deep frown on his face said otherwise.

Anxious to ward off a set-down within earshot of their crew chief, Eve nodded to the sergeant and stuck out her hand toward his commander. "Captain Paris. You must be Captain Bishop."

If anything, Bishop's frown deepened as he ignored her outstretched palm. "I am. Now, if social hour's over, perhaps you soldiers would do me the favor of getting this damned bird off the ground before I miss my briefing." He flicked his steel-blue gaze into the belly of the chopper. "Where's my headset?"

Eve stiffened as the jackass stepped crisply past, dismissing her as curtly as he'd ignored her hand.

"*My* spare headset is on the fritz."

Bishop spun about, the swift arch in his deep black brows clearly voicing his suspicions.

Too bloody bad.

Her crew chief would support her, as would Carrie.

In fact, behind Captain Marvel's very back, Lange was already calmly slipping the extra headset with its perfectly functioning two-way communications link into its storage slot. From the way her chief snapped the door shut, she wasn't the only one who'd taken offense at Bishop's brusque comments.

Eve shrugged. "Global positioning is down, too. Fancy that." She turned her back on the man before he could answer and strolled around the front of the chopper to climb in.

Captain Marvel wanted to play drill sergeant?

Fine with her. But she'd be damned if she was going to give him the courtesy of listening in while he did it.

Of all the lousy luck.

Rick bit down on his scowl as he studied the two pilots who had been tasked with ferrying him to the presidential compound for his briefing. He had no idea who the blonde was—and if she was anything like her copilot, he didn't care. But the dark one, he knew that one all right. Better than he wanted to. Carrie Evans was going to cost him the best sergeant he'd ever had if he wasn't careful. Dammit, he should have requested a set of male pilots. He would have, too, if it wouldn't have led to questions.

Questions he couldn't risk answering.

Still, he should have kept a tighter lid on his disappointment, not to mention his anger. After all, it wasn't Captain Paris's fault.

Well, it was too late now.

The crew chief slid the chopper's side door shut as the officer he'd snubbed settled in the pilot's seat and powered up the Black Hawk. Rick tugged off his field cap and scrubbed his hands through his shorn hair as he sank down into the webbed bench at the rear of the bird.

Another bad move.

His sergeant promptly took advantage of the forward empty seats, commandeering the one directly behind the pilot's. In doing so, Sergeant Turner had afforded himself a choice view of the copilot—the same copilot Turner had been preoccupied with for five of the last six months. Rick tried scowling at the man as the chopper's crew chief moved to the rear instrument panel to busy himself with the takeoff checks. Unfortunately, Turner's attention was already focused on Carrie Evans.

As usual.

The bird took off smoothly, thundering over the trees where Rick had spent the last eighteen months training San Sebastián's soldiers. He allowed his gaze to stray to the back of Captain Paris's helmet. Eve. A good two inches of dark-gold curls spilled out from beneath the bottom edge of the Kevlar bucket, curls that were a shade lighter than the smooth brows framing those striking emerald eyes. He'd seen them for all of five seconds as the woman initiated their introduction. Thickly lashed, her eyes were unusually large…until her gaze had narrowed.

For the first time in a long time, he pushed aside regret.

In the end it wouldn't matter how professional the woman was. In twelve years in the Army, he had more than enough experience to know that a woman that stunning was nothing but trouble out in the field. Take Carrie Evans. The captain was already paying more attention to his sergeant than to the aerial map spread out on her lap. It'd be a miracle if they reached the presidential compound on time. If at all.

Just then, Paris turned to say something to her copilot. Unfortunately, Rick couldn't make the words out over the pounding of the chopper's blades. If only the extra headset wasn't down. What he wouldn't give to listen in on that conversation. Rick had the distinct impression Captain Paris hadn't been any more thrilled with Carrie's familiar behavior toward his sergeant back at the LZ than he'd been. The suspicion bit into him again as the curve of the woman's jaw tightened. Especially when Carrie jerked her gaze from his sergeant's and fused it to the aerial map.

*Way to go, Paris.*

Evidently an apology was in order when this bird landed because at least one of the women was intent on the mission at hand. His sergeant, however, had an ass-ripping coming as soon as he shifted that blasted lovesick-puppy gaze of his to the rear of the chopper long enough for Rick to catch it.

Of course, his sergeant didn't.

Nor did Paris's reproach last.

In the next fifteen minutes, Rick caught Carrie Evans's gaze sneaking back to his sergeant's at least that many times. And given Paris's concentration on her own tasks— that of flying this blasted thing, she didn't seem to be aware of the majority of the glances. That last gaze, however, she did catch. It sent her head snapping to the right once more and, this time, that delicate jaw locked. Again, Rick couldn't make out the words, but from the slump in Carrie's shoulders as she refocused her attention on the map, they weren't any kinder than the ones he'd have fired off.

Unfortunately, Paris's latest rebuke was too late.

Rick was certain the second he glanced out of the chopper's oversized side windows. Differentiating one section of jungle canopy from the next was about as easy as squeezing a platoon of soldiers into a one-man foxhole. But even he knew from that fifty-foot waterfall they were now flying over, the chopper was a good eight kilometers off course. If they didn't get back on course soon, there'd be hell to pay—from San Sebastián's neighbors.

"We're losing power!"

Rick jerked his gaze forward, certain he'd misheard the crew chief's shout. After all, it had barely registered above the roar and vibration of the chopper's blades before the chief spun around to his instrument panel.

But he hadn't.

By the time Rick snapped his gaze to the cockpit, both women were frantically flicking levers and switches. Once again he found himself wishing the spare comm headset wasn't busted.

Suddenly, he didn't need to hear their frantic words.

The choke of the engine as it cut out altogether confirmed his suspicions, as well as the sudden fisting in his gut. Especially when the comforting roar of the chopper's blades gave way to the chilling whoosh of a rotor no longer under man-made power, but that of Mother Nature.

This was it, then.

It was time to kiss their boots goodbye.

It didn't take a degree in rocket science to know that seven tons of Army steel were about to drop out of the sky with all the aerodynamics of a slick brick.

Pain.

No…not pain, piercing agony. It sliced into Eve with each breath she took. Her lungs were on fire.

No, not her lungs. It was her ribs that seemed to be splitting asunder. But her lungs were screaming too.

Why?

On her next breath, she knew why. The air searing through her nose and mouth contained the wrong ratio of gasoline fumes to fresh air. The jet fuel was way too pungent.

Oh, God—they were leaking fuel.

Eve forced her eyes open and struggled to focus.

Shattered glass, shredded steel.

Trees. The distinctive dark green of jungle undergrowth. Patches of dirt.

Where the devil was the sky?

Someone groaned. It wasn't until Eve inhaled again that she realized the rasping sound had come from her own mouth.

Good Lord, what had happened?

And then she remembered. The crash. The chopper's engine had stalled before cutting out altogether. She'd tried to pull pitch to soften the landing but then—

Carrie!

Eve twisted her head to the right and nearly threw up.

Her crew chief was dead. His right arm was flung limply between the seats of the now-crumpled cockpit, his gut impaled by the thick tree limb that had punctured one of the windows imbedded in the side door of the chopper's skin. Death had captured the stark horror of the crash within Sergeant Lange's glassy gaze with eerie perfection. If she ever got out of this chopper alive, she would never forget that bottomless stare.

She forced her gaze from her crew chief's and struggled to scan what was left of the rear of the chopper. She couldn't see Captain Bishop or his sergeant.

Had the two been thrown clear?

Had anyone else survived?

Her answer came in a whimper and then a rasping choke. *Carrie.*

Eve cried out as she pushed the chief's arm into the rear of the chopper in order to see Carrie's battered body. Her helmet had fallen off and the left side of her dark, gorgeous curls were now matted and soaked with blood…as was the torso of her flight suit. With each breath Carrie took, Eve could hear the tell-tale gurgling, sucking sound beneath.

*Sweet mercy.* Carrie had punctured a lung.

Eve wiped the tears from her eyes only to discover they were mixed with her own blood. She didn't bother seeking out the source, just wiped her hand on her sleeve and gritted her teeth against the agony in her chest as she reached out to smooth her fingers down the side of Carrie's frighteningly pale neck, automatically checking her pulse.

It was thready, but it was there.

*Thank God.*

She swallowed firmly, nearly choking on her relief as she prayed her friend was conscious. "C-Carrie?"

Nothing. Not so much as a groan. Just the soft scratching of a thousand rustling leaves and branches scraping against the outside of the chopper.

"Carrie?"

*"Hmm?"*

Relief seared through Eve again. "Carrie, wake up. We have to get out of here. I smell fuel—" Eve winced as she risked a deeper mouthful of air. It hurt just to breathe. "The chopper must be leaking." And given the twisted wreckage surrounding them, there was no way she'd be able to reach the fuel cutoff switch. "Carrie?"

"You…go."

The whisper was so low she almost missed it. Carrie's lips moved again, but she couldn't make out the words that followed. Eve braced herself as she took another agonizing breath, this one cautious and shallow.

Yes, shallow was definitely better. Manageable.

Her chest still hurt like hell, but not nearly as much. "Carrie, please. The chopper could blow any second."

*"Go."*

Dammit, she didn't have time to argue.

*They didn't have time.*

Eve struggled to ignore the rasping gurgle coming from Carrie's lungs as well as the agony slicing her own as she reached out to unlatch Carrie's harness. She'd just have to find the strength to drag her friend out. Her slippery fingers found the buckle to Carrie's harness. But just as she was about to release it, Carrie's icy hands closed over hers.

"Carrie, please. I can't leave you. I won't."

"Must…doesn't m-matter. He's dead. It's dead. F-feel it."

He?

Sergeant Turner.

Eve raised her hands to those dark, silky curls she'd always envied, desperately trying to ignore the blood as she smoothed them from Carrie's cheek. "You can't know that. He could be okay. I don't see the passengers, just the chief. They must have been thrown free."

"W-was. See him…th-there."

Eve braced herself against the pain and turned to follow Carrie's tortured gaze, and understood the deep keening within it. Sergeant Turner was five, maybe six trees away.

Dead.

Given the sickeningly odd angle in his neck, there was no way the man could be otherwise.

*Bishop.*

But Eve couldn't see him. She could only pray the captain had been thrown free as well—and would live to tell of it. But right now, she had to get Carrie out of the wreckage. The searing stench of fuel had taken on nauseating proportions. At least, she was pretty sure the reaction in her stomach was due to the leaking fuel and not her own injuries.

Either way, they had to get out.

"Honey, I'm sorry he's dead. But you have to live. You

have to try. Sergeant Turner—Bill. Bill would want you to. You have so much to live for. You know you do.''

But her friend just blinked back her tears.

''Carrie, please.''

''T-told you. It's d-dead…gone.'' She coughed. ''I c-can…feel it.''

''Don't talk like that—''

''The b-baby…ours…it's gone.''

*What?*

Eve hadn't realized she'd breathed her shock out loud until Carrie answered her. Or maybe Carrie had read her mind.

''So s-sorry. I didn't know h-how to…tell you. Please, m-make sure we're b-buried w-with him.''

No!

Dammit, *no*. Carrie was not giving up.

She wouldn't let her.

But before she could argue, Carrie started coughing again—and this time, she began hacking uncontrollably. Eve forced the panic down and held her friend's hand until the coughs eased. ''One m-more thing, p-promise m-me…'' Oh God, Carrie's whispers were getting weaker. The rasping gurgle in her lungs, louder. Frothy blood had begun to bubble and seep from the side of her mouth. She was losing her.

She had to act.

Now.

Eve ignored Carrie's gasps as she grabbed the buckle again. But again, Carrie's hands found hers. They were beyond icy now. Almost white.

''P-promise…me.''

''Anything.'' She'd promise anything in the world if Carrie would just let her help.

''Don't…h-hate me.''

Eve's mind and heart shrieked in unison. No! Dammit, *no*. This was not happening. Her best friend was *not* dying.

But she was.

Eve could feel it even as those icy fingers lost their grip and slipped away from her own hands altogether.

*Just do it.* Promise her. Let the woman die in peace.

Lie.

She smoothed Carrie's matted curls back one last time and kissed her shattered cheek. ''I promise. I won't hate you.''

Carrie managed a smile, and then she was gone.

Eve screamed.

The loss was excruciating. Unbearable. So intense, she couldn't even feel the agony wracking her ribs anymore. She wasn't sure how long she sat there, shaking Carrie's shoulders, begging her, shouting at her to come back, not to abandon her. But eventually, reality set in.

The *smoke* set in.

The sweltering flames.

The leaking fuel had finally ignited. The Black Hawk was burning, its searing metal creaking and bubbling around her. The sweet stench of melting rubber filled her nostrils.

She had to get Carrie out of here.

Their crew chief, too.

Dead or alive, she was not leaving them to roast in this fiery shell of buckling steel. Determination seared into her, giving her the strength to unlock her own harness and bash her aching shoulders and splintered ribs into the chopper door. She fell out into a whimpering heap on the jungle floor.

But again, determination forced her to overcome the agony. She lurched to her feet and managed to stagger several steps. But in the pain and confusion that followed, it took several more before she realized she was moving away from the chopper and not toward it.

The next thing she knew, something hot and hard slammed into her body, shattering her eardrums and ripping the very breath from her lungs as she went flailing backward into the choking gray mist. But the moment she smashed into the tree she also knew that, dead or alive, it was too late for Carrie or anyone else in that chopper.

Because it had just exploded.

# Chapter 2

C hrist Almighty, his *head.*

Rick groaned. He hadn't had a hangover like this since he and his brother had polished off half a bottle of Jack Daniel's back on their father's farm in the tenth grade. Ah, cripes, he was going to throw up. A second later, he almost did. Rick thrust his hands out, searching for something to grab on to as he worked to steady his aching, spinning brain. He pushed himself up from what appeared to be a rock to suck down a mouthful of air, but what he got along with it was the distinctive sear of smoke.

This was no hangover.

*The crash.*

He tried scrambling to his feet but ended up on his knees, cradling his forehead as he struggled for balance...and something was wet. But why? It wasn't raining. He pulled his hands down and forced his gaze to focus on his shaking fingers. They were covered in blood.

His?

It had to be. He didn't see anyone else around him.

Sergeant Turner.

Where was he? Where was the chopper for that matter?

Once again Rick used his hands to steady his throbbing skull as he twisted his battered torso about, searching. If his eyes were cooperating as well as he hoped, those were trees wavering in and out of his view. Hundreds of trees.

But no chopper.

The smoke. *Follow the smoke.*

He could still smell it.

He braced himself against the nausea and lurched to his feet, grateful he managed to remain upright despite his drunken weaving. At least his vision seemed to be clearing. Wary of his tenuous grip on his balance, he began a slow, systematic three-hundred-and-sixty-degree search of the dense jungle undergrowth. He made it to the one-ninety mark before he spotted the small clearing Paris had tried landing the chopper in. It was a good twenty yards into the brush. He caught a flash of something else through the trees, too.

Was that red? Or orange?

He couldn't be sure. It was just a flicker.

He advanced anyway, determined to check it out. Grasping vines and thick foliage snapped back at him as he moved, lashing around the legs and sleeves of his jungle fatigues with enough tenacity to topple him. He definitely could have used his machete because twice they succeeded. In the end, it was the red that kept him going.

Flames.

He was sure of it now.

He could hear them consuming the chopper, devouring the steel with a vicious rumble that kept him staggering forward until he was almost on top of the tiny clearing. But as he stumbled past the final trees, it wasn't the chopper that brought him to his knees.

It was his sergeant.

Rick swallowed the roiling bile as it threatened once again, knowing it was hopeless even as he slid his fingers down his sergeant's throat and pressed them into the man's carotid artery. The soldier he'd entrusted with his life for nearly three years was gone. Given the angle of the break in Turner's neck, it would have been a miracle if the man had been otherwise. Guilt seared through Rick, burning the pain from his head, leaving only the anguish in his heart as he cupped his hand to his sergeant's face and gently closed those dark, unseeing eyes.

Dammit, why had he brought Turner along?

As soon as he realized Carrie was on that chopper, he should have sent his sergeant back to the rest of their men. Sure, Turner would have figured out the real reason Rick had ordered him to come along this morning. But even that would have been better than this.

Rick stared at the almost peaceful expression on Turner's face, remembering. The good of the last three years far outweighed his sergeant's distraction these past five months. Turner had saved his ass more times than he could count. In training and in the real thing.

What a waste.

*His* waste.

Dammit, there was no time to mourn.

The chopper. Her crew.

Once again, Rick hauled himself to his feet, grateful his strength was coming back. He'd need it. For himself and whoever else had survived the smoldering hell thirty feet away.

*Please, God, let the rest have survived.*

He murmured the prayer over and over, holding fast to the mantra as he crossed the clearing and reached the blackened, shattered shell on the other side. The prayer died on his lips as he spied the remains of the two forms inside the wreckage.

Carrie Evans. The crew chief.

Like Turner, both were beyond hope.

He sent up another prayer for each, saving his last for the soldier he'd yet to find.

Eve Paris.

Had she been thrown free as well? Her chopper door was open. There was a chance. He caught the impression her body had made in the grass beneath the dangling door and set about tracking her uneven footsteps. Ten feet away, the depressions suddenly stopped. It wasn't until he raised his gaze and scanned the area beyond that he understood why. She must have managed to evacuate moments before the chopper exploded because there was nothing by way of a trail until he spied her body sprawled out a good twenty feet back.

The blast had blown her smack into a tree.

Despite his still-spinning head, he reached her limp form in record time and checked her breathing and her pulse, relieved beyond words to find both present, if a bit weak. Twelve years of combat training kicked in and he carefully checked her over before he dared to move her head and spine. Other than the bleeding knot at her temple and the swollen lump at the back of her skull, she appeared fine. But as he skimmed his hands down her torso, she groaned.

"*Don't.* Hurts."

"I know, Paris, I know." Despite her protests, he unhooked her survival vest and unzipped the front of her flight suit, then peeled her T-shirt up her ribs. There was no blood, but she was sporting one hell of a vicious set of bruises across her right side. Most were already turning purple. He eased her shirt down. "It looks like you've cracked a couple of ribs. Any other injuries you're aware of?"

"Isn't that enough?"

Despite everything that had transpired, his lips twisted at her sarcasm. True enough. Given the devastation behind them, not to mention the journey ahead, cracked ribs were definitely enough.

She coughed and then gasped as he helped her into a sitting position. Tears began streaming from the corners of those huge green eyes, mingling with the blood streaking down her cheeks.

From the ache in her ribs, no doubt.

But he'd bet most were a result of the ache in her heart.

Dammit, now was not the time to soften, let alone give in to the ache in his own. "Paris, we've got to get those ribs wrapped. Then we need to get out of here." He held her down as she tried to stand. They definitely had to get moving.

He glanced at the chopper.

As soon as he buried the bodies.

He swung his gaze from the wreckage as Paris touched his temple. "What?"

"You're bleeding."

Considering he had to keep blinking to keep the blood from dripping into his eyes, he figured it was an understatement.

"You need stitches."

"No time. I'll wrap it." Just as soon as he figured out what they were going to wrap her cracked ribs with.

She looked ready to argue with him.

He turned his back on her frown and took stock of their surroundings. By the time he'd turned back, she was staring at the remains of the chopper. Her eyes were red.

"Your crew's dead, as well as my sergeant. I'm sorry."

From her stiff nod, he wasn't sure she'd really understood. She seemed a bit too controlled, too contained.

Almost cold.

Then again, it wasn't like he knew the woman. Nor had the local rumor mill had a chance to circulate its findings. Eve Paris was too new in country. From her professionalism in the chopper as well as the way she'd appeared to stay cool during the crash, cold could well be the woman's normal mode.

Just as well. They had three bodies to bury and a two- to three-day trek ahead by his estimate. Given who was likely to be dogging their boots the entire way, it was past time to get started. But as he reached out to ease off her flight suit, she stiffened. In deference to her shock, he knocked back his impatience. "Please, I need to get a better look at your ribs, and then I'll need to wrap them. You won't make the journey otherwise." He waited for a response.

Nothing.

She still wouldn't even look at him.

She just kept staring at that damned hulk of blackened steel.

"Paris?"

"I'll do it."

For a moment, he considered arguing.

What the hell. He'd probably insist on the same thing in her place. He nodded curtly. "I'll see what I can salvage from the wreck. Then I'd better get started on the bodies. No—" He nudged her down again. "I'll take care of them. You need to conserve your strength."

Another nod. This one even more stiff.

Frankly, he wasn't surprised. Cold or not, he knew full well she had to be taking the crash personally, just as he knew why. But there was no time for guilt.

Hers or his.

They had to get moving. "Eve?"

Again, nothing.

He continued anyway, "That waterfall we flew over. Did

your copilot have a chance to tell you about it before the crash?''

She shook her head slowly.

Great. One more piece of crappy news to lay on her head. Even as his heart went out to her, he hauled it back and crammed it firmly inside his chest. The woman was a soldier.

*So, treat her like one, dammit!*

''That waterfall was on the wrong side of the border. By my estimate, we're about four, five kilometers to the west of the San Sebastián border—*inside* Córdoba.'' He paused, waiting for his words to sink in, not bothering to add that the communist country was probably searching for the crash site as they spoke. Or that they'd be lucky to escape with a bullet to the brain if they were captured. Not to mention the fact that his radio, as well as her own, had probably gone up in the same explosion that had roasted the chopper.

Then again, maybe he should have. Because again, she didn't seem fazed. He touched her shoulder. ''Did you hear me?''

She nodded slowly.

Shock.

He wasn't surprised. His own brain was still rattling around in his head. Unfortunately, there was no time to waste. If she didn't snap out of it soon, he'd have no choice but to wrap her ribs for her and toss her hind end over his shoulder and carry her whether she liked it or not.

He'd give her an hour—or until he was done.

But as he stood and turned away, she finally spoke.

''Bishop?''

He turned back and waited. She dragged her gaze up to his and focused. ''Thank you.'' Her whisper was soft, hoarse. There was a wealth of gratitude in the simple words.

And even more pain.

It was his turn to nod stiffly. Then he turned back to the morbid task he'd performed too damned many times before.

Snap out of it!

That was just it. She couldn't.

Eve continued to stare at Rick Bishop in a fog as he covered the graves of their fellow soldiers with the stones he'd gathered. His sergeant, her crew chief, her copilot. Her friend.

Her fault.

But she hadn't just ended three lives, had she?

A baby.

For God's sake, why hadn't Carrie told her? She'd been in country catching up with the woman for three days now. Despite the succession of near-constant briefings, surely Carrie could have found the time to discuss something that monumental?

But she hadn't.

Hell, Carrie hadn't even alluded to her pregnancy. Not this morning when they fired up the Black Hawk before dawn, nor the night before when they'd stayed up way too late filling each other in on everything that had happened since college and flight school.

Why had Carrie kept this secret from her of all people?

Except…she knew why, didn't she?

Friends or not, had she known about the baby, she never would have let Carrie fly. Certainly not two kilometers away from hostile airspace. And not when there was a chance they might end up in that hostile airspace…like they had. Of course, an immediate and detailed explanation would have been required from the brass on why she'd had Carrie pulled from the flight roster. The resulting scandal would undoubtedly have affected her friend's career. But surely that would have been preferable to this?

Eve forced her gaze back to Bishop.

He was marking the graves now, each with a small makeshift cross. Evidently the man was religious. How would
he feel if she asked him to add a smaller cross to the grave
on the far right?

Or did he already know?

Is that why he'd been scowling at Carrie from the moment he'd approached the chopper? Maybe it hadn't been
her imagination earlier out on the landing zone. At the time,
she could have sworn he'd been brusque with her because
she'd tried to divert his attention from Carrie's behavior.
Either way, it didn't matter now.

She wasn't breathing a word about the baby to Bishop.

If she did, the pregnancy would only come out during
the accident investigation—and what would be the purpose
of that? All it would serve would be to tarnish two records
that were already about to be closed forever. Even if the
knowledge did explain Carrie's distraction during their
flight, it wouldn't have changed anything, least of all what
had happened. Yes, Carrie's preoccupation with Sergeant
Turner had allowed the chopper to fly into hostile airspace.
But even if they'd gone down on the San Sebastián side of
the border, they would still have gone down. And that fault
was hers, and hers alone.

"Ready?"

Eve flinched.

"Sorry. Didn't mean to startle you."

"That's okay." Eve eased out her breath as she stared
down at the single rucksack that had been thrown free along
with Bishop. From the bulging seams and rear pouch, she
could tell he'd already added the extra supplies she'd managed to scrounge up from the scorched hulk of steel that
had once been her chopper.

Thankfully, water was abundant in the area.

They also had a rain poncho between them, as well as a
two-day supply of food. Rick had gathered his extra

T-shirts from the ruck and shredded the brown cotton with
his pocketknife, turning them into makeshift bindings for
her ribs. After she'd wrapped herself, she'd gone back to
the chopper and managed to locate the sergeant's blackened
but still razor-sharp machete. Unfortunately, Bishop's radio
was hopeless. As was the PRC-112 survival radio and bea-
con she carried in her flight suit. Whatever had slammed
into her ribs during the crash had cracked the Prick-112 as
well.

They truly were on their own.

But at least they weren't blind.

Bishop adjusted the dark-green cravat he'd wrapped
around the gash on his forehead, then pulled a battered map
out of the cargo pocket on the right thigh of his jungle
fatigues. He hunkered down beside her. The Green Beret
was obviously good at his job as well as a natural choice
for training San Sebastián's troops in their own backyard.
He'd already reduced the azimuths of the two visible Córdoban mountain peaks down to lines on the map and used
them to mark their location. He extended his index finger
and tapped the resulting X, then traced the route he'd already plotted out.

Their route.

He sighed. "The good Lord didn't totally blow us off
this morning, because we went down in a fairly remote
area."

Meaning that since they'd yet to encounter any sign of
the Córdoban army canvassing the area from overhead or
searching on foot, they had time. But even she knew that
how much time remained to be seen. Eve stared at the dirt
and grime still staining Bishop's hands. Strong, capable
hands that had just buried three of their fellow soldiers.

Friends.

One even more so. To her anyway.

Eve pushed aside the mindless torrent of tears that had

been threatening to drown her for the past two hours and raised her gaze. She focused on that collection of imposing, yet still camouflaged facial features beneath the knotted, blood-stained cravat, and waited for the rest. Dark-brown eyes stared back, their gaze razor-sharp and much too steady.

"Well? What's the bad news?"

Those firm lips only tightened further.

"Don't hold back on me now, Bishop. I know I look like I'm about to break, but I swear I won't." At least, not until they reached San Sebastián—and she reached a private room with a locked door and bucket large enough to hold her tears and grief.

Hell, maybe they should head for the Pacific Ocean.

Bishop held her gaze for several moments longer, then finally nodded. He glanced down at the map and traced the zigzagged line he'd added, the one that would take them well around the steep incline of the waterfall they'd flown over. "We've got a good six kilometers to cover."

"How long will it take?"

He frowned. "Given the density of the undergrowth as well as the condition of your ribs?" His dark gaze found hers again. If it contained compassion, she couldn't see it. But neither did it contain reproach. He shrugged. "We're looking at two days, maybe three. Depends on what we encounter along the way."

Natives.

Fortunately for them, at least half the locals were rumored to support the political freedoms of their San Sebastián neighbors.

But which half would they encounter?

Eve studied Bishop's eyes as well as his body language, trying to gauge his mindset in the silence that followed. Unfortunately, it was impossible. The man could have been born a rock. A large, stubborn rock at that. She slid her gaze to the bandage tied about his head. Just as she'd warned him, the exertion of digging had already taken its toll. The center of the dark-green cravat was now soaked with blood.

Red blood, not brown.

Fresh.

She reached out, but he intercepted her hand before she could check the bandage. Startled by the warmth in his fingers, she jerked her hand to her lap. "You still need stitches."

"There's still no time."

"I disagree. You said yourself, we've crashed in a remote area. It looks as if we've gone unnoticed for the time being. We should at least have ten more minutes to sew up your head."

He shook that same damned stubborn head.

As if on cue, a thin river of blood spilled out from beneath the bandage and trickled into his right eye. She raised her brow as he swiped at it with the back of his hand. "If I don't stitch it, you'll just continue to lose blood during the journey. How long do you think you'll be able to keep up with me and my cracked ribs if that happens?"

Apparently she'd chosen the one argument that had a chance of working, because that dark gaze finally wavered. But his frown deepened. "My sergeant's medical kit was charred beyond salvage."

Eve shrugged as she reached into the right pocket of her flight vest and pulled out her first-aid kit. Unlike her radio, the kit had survived the crash intact. "I guess you're lucky you're stranded with a pilot." She flicked her gaze to the canteens he'd already topped off. "Now why don't you wash the grime and camouflage off your face while I thread the needle? You might just save yourself an infection."

Bishop nodded curtly, but at least he complied.

By the time he'd rummaged through his rucksack and

located his stash of alcohol wipes and used them to clean his face, she'd managed to thread the needle and ready her disinfectant.

He turned back. "Ready."

Sweet heaven.

Her hands froze as she took in the man's features without the olive-drab and brown grease paint smeared into his skin. Her initial instincts at the landing zone had been right on. Rick Bishop's face was as commanding as his lean, muscular body. Perhaps even more so. Without the grease paint to break up the planes of his face, he was uncannily handsome. Not in the blond, pretty-boy way that had attracted Carrie to Bill Turner, but in a dark, pure male and very rugged fashion. The only thing remotely soft about this man were his thick brown lashes. But those curling wisps were deceptive.

This was no tin soldier.

Neither was Bishop a man to be toyed with.

Each and every one of those deep lines carved about his eyes and mouth had been earned, etched in over the years spent in Special Forces. The man hunkered down in front of her was no weekend warrior. Nor was he a man who spent his days merely training for war. This was a man who'd lived it, day in and day out in the deserts and jungles of the world. On covert campaigns that had never made it into the nightly news. Those etched lines served as permanent testimony of a youth squandered on the planning and execution of missions no American mother wanted to know her son had ever been tasked with, let alone accomplished. There was no doubt in Eve's mind, Rick Bishop was one dangerous man.

God help the enemy who dared to cross his path.

God help her.

"Well? What are you waiting for?"

Eve nearly jumped out of her skin as his low growl rumbled between them. But at least it succeeded in forcing her thoughts as well as her breathing back on track. Bishop might have the rugged looks and the mystery to attract a woman's interest, but he didn't have the personality to hold it.

At least not hers.

"I—uh—don't have anything to give you for the pain."

"Didn't ask. Just do it."

Yup, the man was definitely lacking in personality.

Still, she owed him. Bishop might have the manners of a caged mountain lion, but he had spared her the task of retrieving Carrie's body as well as those of her crew chief and passenger, and he'd buried them. For that reason alone, she tried her damnedest to work as quickly and as gently as she could.

It seemed to help.

The only hint of discomfort Bishop gave as she stitched was the subtle clenching of his jaw as well as the occasional tensing of his broad hands. Every now and then he swallowed firmly, but that was it. Had she been in his place, the added pain would probably have sent her over the edge. As it was, anything deeper than the shallowest of breaths still sent an eye-watering ache ripping up the side of her chest.

They made quite a pair.

Bishop must have thought so too, because as she reached the halfway mark on his three-inch gash, he shot her a half-hearted attempt at a smile. To her horror, for a moment the pain in her ribs actually ebbed. Good Lord, what kind of a woman was she—let alone soldier—that she could be re-acting to this man as a man here of all places?

And now?

"You're pretty good with that needle."

She yanked her gaze from his. "Yeah, well, I hear women go wild for the wounded-soldier look. I'd leave a better scar, but then your wife would have to drive them off with a stick.''

*Good one, Eve.*

She picked up the next stitch as the reminder that the man had a life back in the States—one that she wasn't part of—helped to restore her breathing.

''Don't have one.''

She almost dropped the needle.

He must have taken her clumsiness for confusion because he elaborated. ''A wife. That is, I don't have a wife.''

Wonderful.

She forced a stiff smile of her own as she regained control of the slender needle and resumed her stitching. ''Girlfriend then.''

''Fresh out of those, too.'' His smile deepened briefly.

The effect was devastating.

Who'd have thought Super Soldier would have dimples?

''What about you? Husband? Boyfriend?''

For a single, blinding moment, she couldn't respond. She didn't know how. Surely the man wasn't coming on to her?

After the way he'd barked at her?

Not that it mattered. She could not afford to get personal. Not now, and certainly not with Rick Bishop.

She must have sat there gaping too long, because he sighed.

''Look, Paris, I was making small talk. It's bound to be a long trek.'' He might as well have come out and said she wasn't his type.

Despite her relief, she flushed.

What the hell. The man was right, it was going to be a long trip. And since Bishop had an M-16 rifle and a 9 mm pistol as well as a machete to her lonely 9 mm, she might as well stay on his good side. She just might need him for more than company. Besides, the conversation was probably an attempt to take his mind off the pain.

Eve shook her head. "None."

Despite her nearby stitching, his brow furrowed.

She elaborated, "No husband, no boyfriend. No time."

"Ah…I know the feeling."

He probably did at that.

He rolled his shoulders slightly as if to ease his tension as she picked up her last stitch. "So…what happened up there?"

Slick. Very slick.

Small talk, her ass. Rick Bishop wasn't interested in getting to know her at all. Neither had he been coming on to her. He'd been softening her up for an impromptu interrogation session. Or maybe it wasn't impromptu. Either way, she didn't care. While she wouldn't pretend to misunderstand, neither was she in the mood to discuss what had happened.

As if she even could.

"You were there, Bishop. You tell me."

But then, he hadn't been listening up in that chopper, had he? She'd refused him the common courtesy of the extra headset in a fit of pique over his manner toward Carrie.

It all seemed moot now.

Childish.

She tied off the final stitch and clipped the ends before turning away to restow her first-aid kit and tuck it into her flight vest. But before she could scramble to her feet, his hand closed over her arm, stopping her cold.

"Eve…I'm not a pilot. I had no idea what was happening in that chopper beyond the fact that it was about to drop out of the sky roughly four klicks inside enemy territory." The words were quiet, almost gentle, certainly devoid of the accusation and reproach she'd fully expected.

Even deserved.

Maybe that's why she was able to scrape up the nerve

to meet his gaze. "Then congratulations, Bishop. You're one up on me."

She hadn't said a word in eight hours.

Not so much as a passing comment or even a question as to how far they'd traveled or when they'd stop for the night. Rick held up a hand, bringing them to a halt for a moment so that he could gauge the pulse of the jungle. Other than the rustle of leaves, the distant shriek of a howler monkey and the occasional chirp and almost constant buzzing of insects, there was nothing. He lowered his hand, then switched his machete into his left in order to hack another swath of vine-tangled foliage from his path.

Eve followed him through.

Again, but for the soft thumps of her boots, silently.

It wasn't normal, even for him. Sure, they were still well inside Córdoba, but no one was tracking them. He was certain. At first he'd been worried about the trail they were leaving. But given Eve's condition, he didn't have a choice. With her ribs in the shape they were, it would have taken four times as long to cover the same amount of ground if he'd forced her to pick through the uncut undergrowth. Even now she was stumbling more often than not.

The woman was exhausted.

If she fell and damaged her ribs further or, God forbid, punctured a lung, they might never make it back. He should stop. Force her to rest if necessary. As tired as she was, she'd probably sleep through to dawn if he let her. Still, he had to hand it to her.

Eve Paris was one tough soldier.

He'd had plenty of time to consider the woman as he buried her crew and his sergeant, plenty of time to worry. It wasn't long before his guilt over Turner's death had turned to apprehension. Apprehension that his sole surviving companion would fall apart the minute he assumed command of their extraction and pushed her to her physical and mental limits.

Mercifully, she hadn't.

That the woman was about to fall over was no fault of her stamina. It was a direct result of her injuries. Injuries that were in serious need of re-tending.

A swift glance to his flank confirmed it.

Though Eve still dogged his boots, she now winced with every step she took. He'd lay odds her bandages had loosened, given the soft gasp that escaped despite her obvious efforts to hold it back. Rick switched the machete to his right hand and took up the swinging rhythm again. Forty more whacks and he found what he'd been seeking.

He stopped short.

Evidently too short, because he was forced to drop the machete and whirl about to grab Eve by the shoulders and steady her before she went down.

She promptly shrugged out of his grasp.

"Sorry."

He shook his head. "No harm done."

She smoothed the sweat from her brow as he slid his M-16 rifle and rucksack from his aching shoulders, dumping both on the ground at their feet.

"Why are we stopping?"

"Rest." He flicked his gaze to the sweat-drenched T-shirt beneath her matching olive-green flight vest. She'd long since unzipped the top of her coveralls and peeled the sleeves down to tie them about her waist. "You need rest. So do I."

He suspected she knew the last was an exaggeration but she let it pass. He chalked up another point in her favor. Accepting their individual limitations and depending on one another to make up for them would only help the both of them reach San Sebastián in one piece. He unhooked one of the green plastic canteens from his web gear and unscrewed the stopper before he passed it over. She accepted the water without argument, earning another point for not bothering to wipe the spout before she drank. His-and-her germs were the least of their worries.

She passed the canteen back. He polished off the remaining water before dumping the empty canteen down next to his ruck. His web gear followed and she wisely added her flight vest to the pile. She could probably use something to eat. Lord knew he could.

But first, her ribs.

Rick bent down, shifting his rifle off his rucksack so he could open the rear pouch and pull out the extra makeshift bindings he'd stashed within. In his haste, however, the personal effects of their men spilled out onto the jungle floor. He cursed his clumsiness beneath his breath as he tried to gather up the watches, wallets, spare dog tags and additional items before Eve noticed.

It was the least he could do.

Unfortunately, he wasn't fast enough.

She snatched up the ring he'd removed from Carrie's right hand. "What the hell are you doing with this?"

He stood slowly, reaching for her.

She jerked from his touch and stepped back before he could stop her. "Well?" The emerald fire in her eyes had chilled to ice.

He sighed. "That's Captain Evans's ring. She was—"

"I know what it is. I asked what you were doing with it."

He ignored the iron set to her shoulders and stepped closer, grasping them gently as he calmly explained what she already knew. "Eve, be reasonable. Carrie probably has a mother and a father who may be grateful we were able to bring a piece of her back home."

Once again, she tore herself from his touch. But this

time, the chill was gone from her eyes. They were on fire now, swirling, raging. And something else.

Pain.

A pain so deep, he swore he felt it searing into him.

"I don't give a damn what you *thought,* Captain Bishop. Carrie Evans was part of my crew, not yours. You should have consulted me. The truth is, we may never be able to retrieve those bodies and you know it. This ring was supposed to be buried with Carrie. And for your information, Carrie doesn't have any family. *I* was her family. Her *sister*—and with Sergeant Turner gone, the only family she had left!"

What the hell?

Rick stood there, too stunned to move as Eve clenched the ring into her fist and stormed out into the eight-by-eight-foot clearing he'd decided would serve as their bivouac site for the night. Her fury propelled her to the opposite side of the clearing. But there, she ended up tangled in the dense undergrowth as well as the vines hanging between the trees. She lashed out at the vines, but that only seemed to make it worse. He heard her cry out as a thick branch came snapping back squarely across her ribs.

He winced as she cursed.

A moment later he caught her muffled sob. An inexplicable punch to his heart followed, almost as if he'd taken a bullet.

Confusion capped it off.

How could Eve and Carrie possibly have been sisters?

Family members weren't allowed to be stationed within the same command. Unfortunately, now wasn't the time to demand an explanation. Even from where he stood, it was obvious that Eve Paris was devastated.

Rick retrieved the fresh roll of bindings and stuffed them into his right cargo pocket as he stood. He snagged his M-16 next, slinging the rifle over his shoulder as he headed across the clearing. Eve's back was to him, her shoulders quaking silently as she stood staring off into the rapidly darkening jungle. It was obvious she and Carrie had been close. So close, he was beginning to wonder how the woman had held it together for as long as she had. He reached out only to force his hands to halt in midair. Each time he'd touched Eve before, she'd pulled away. There was no sense aggravating her again. Least of all now.

So what the hell was he supposed to do?

Were she one of his men, he'd know exactly what to say, how to handle this. He'd done it often enough. But how did he comfort a soldier he didn't even know? A female one at that? For the first time, Rick experienced a twinge of regret at serving the majority of his career within the Special Forces, one of the few remaining holdouts in this man's Army.

In the end, he gambled.

Reaching out again, he let his hands drop until they gently cupped her quaking shoulders.

As expected, she stiffened.

But then she turned and stared up at him silently.

Good God, how could he have spent twelve hours with this woman and only now be noticing how tiny she was? Even in her boots, the top of her head barely reached his shoulders. The soft gold of her hair still curled about her face despite the heat and constant exertion of the day. Even with the purple bruises that had darkened along her left cheek and jaw, Eve Paris was a stunning woman. But the longer he stared, the more he noticed the emotional ravages of the day.

Her complexion for one.

The ivory shade of earlier this morning was gone. Grief had stained her high cheeks and stubborn jaw bright red. Even her gently bowed lips were flushed, but the effect only served to make her seem even more delicate than he'd first imagined.

In the end, it was her eyes that did him in.

Puffy and red from crying, the emerald irises seemed darker now, larger...and silent tears were still streaming from the corners of her eyes. Mesmerized, he reached out and smoothed his thumbs up her cheeks, catching the damp warmth as it continued to trickle steadily down.

Time froze as her tears mingled with his sweat.

His breath froze.

Seconds later he succeeded in jump-starting his lungs, but it was too late. He was already leaning down. Closer and closer, until he was breathing her scent. He caught her tears with his lips, absorbing the salt with his flesh. Even as his actions stunned him, they seemed right. *This* seemed right. And a moment later, it only seemed natural to cover those soft swollen lips with his.

To his surprise, her mouth parted.

And then he was kissing her.

Softly at first. Lightly. But over and over. Though he knew better, he couldn't find the strength or the sanity to stop. Nor did he want to. He gently grasped her bottom lip with his and caressed it, then slipped the tip of his tongue slowly inside. He used his mouth to draw her in closer until he was drawing her very essence into his own. She tasted of the early-morning sun and of the evening rain—but also of sorrow. A sorrow so heavy and so profound, he could feel it slipping down into his soul. Driven to ease it, to comfort her, he deepened the kiss. But he didn't dare touch her with his hands for fear that he'd injure her ribs. So he used his lips and his tongue instead.

He tasted, soothed and caressed.

And then he tasted again, all the while resolved to take just this kiss and nothing more.

Until it changed.

He knew Eve felt it too. Somewhere deep inside it just…changed. The hunger swelled, ignited, consumed.

And then the kiss changed.

She was clinging to him now, reaching up to rake her fingers into his hair, kneading them down the back of his neck, pulling him in tight, molding her lower curves to his now aching erection until all he could think about was peeling that damp T-shirt from her chest as he had earlier, until there was nothing between them but bare skin and the lace of that tantalizing pale-green bra.

When her fingers grabbed his shirt, he caved in to temptation and did the same.

She gasped—and he cursed.

Her ribs.

But as he jerked back and stared at the shock exploding amid the pain and desire still swirling within those wide green eyes, the reality of his actions slammed into him with the force of an Abrams tank grinding a swath of hothouse flowers down into the dirt.

What the hell had he just done?

# Chapter 3

Eve stood there, her mouth gaping, liquid heat still flooding her body. Heat that had nothing to do with the sweat still trickling down the back of her neck and in between her breasts. It had to do with him.

Bishop.

*Captain* Rick Bishop. Her fellow stranded soldier.

And that steamy kiss.

Why on earth had he done it?

Who was she kidding? She hadn't even tried to stop him. She'd just stood there, like some doe caught in the crosshairs of a hunter's scope. And then she'd kissed him back.

Grief. That's what it was. It had to be.

Shock. Uncertainty.

Yes, even fear.

She'd experienced them all today. They both had. But that was no excuse and she knew it. She and Bishop were trapped behind enemy lines. They had no business engaging in sexual misconduct. According to the Army's code

of professional ethics and morals—hell, according to her
own—that's exactly what they'd just done. From the way
the color had bled from the man's face as well as the terse
working of his throat, he felt the same way.

"Please…forgive me. There's no excuse for what I—"

"It didn't happen."

He reached out. "Eve—"

"No." She jerked away from those dangerous hands before they could seduce her again and strode into the clearing. Perhaps the shadows of the jungle beyond would re-
inforce her sense of exposure and reduce these roiling
feelings that that kiss had stirred within her.

They didn't.

She felt just as safe as she had since the moment Bishop
had implicitly assumed command. She scrubbed her hands
over her eyes and down her cheeks, but that didn't help
either.

She could still feel that kiss.

Dammit, it *hadn't* happened.

She punished herself with a sharp breath, grateful when
the resulting stab succeeded in fusing her thoughts back on
her ribs. Once again, she welcomed the pain. The constant
ache had served to keep her grief over Carrie sealed up and
tucked away until she could risk dealing with it. Until she
could risk dealing with the memories. So far, the throbbing
had kept them at bay.

How long would the reprieve last?

*Promise me you won't hate me…*

But she already did. She couldn't help it. Despite
Bishop's constant presence, the loneliness had begun to
creep back, slowly but steadily. She hadn't felt it in years,
but here it was. Like the cold, familiar companion it was.

Taunting her, stifling her.

"Eve?"

She stiffened, only to feel foolish moments later. After

spending the last twelve hours watching Rick Bishop in action, she shouldn't have been surprised that he'd managed to sneak up on her without making a sound. If they were discovered before they reached the border, it would be her fault, not his. She risked another deep breath to steady her nerves and turned. Her relief bled out. Other than the concern lingering in that dark-brown gaze, it was void of emotion. Bishop obviously agreed—that kiss had *not* happened.

He nodded toward her sweat-soaked T-shirt. "I need to rewrap your ribs."

"I'll do it."

The firm hand on her arm stopped her.

She turned back.

"I will." This time, there was no room for argument in his voice. Unfortunately, he was right. She hadn't been able to get a good enough grip on the bindings he'd fashioned this morning to wrap her ribs as tightly as she'd needed to.

Hence, they'd loosened.

While she welcomed the distraction the pain provided, neither of them could afford the caution that was now part of her every step. What she'd lose in embarrassment, they'd both gain in speed. She nodded. "Fine, I'll just get—"

He held out a fresh set of bindings, already rolled.

There wasn't much she could add, so she just stood there. He finally glanced over to the trees where they'd just been standing. Where they'd just been kissing.

"Over there. It's sheltered."

Was that supposed to help her feel less humiliated?

She nodded anyway.

But once she'd crossed the clearing and eased herself down onto a gnarled root, she realized her mistake. She should have refused. Early evening was rapidly giving way to late. As Bishop propped his M-16 against the tree trunk and hunkered down in front of her, the lengthening shad-

ows magnified the tension between them, giving the small
alcove a distinctly bedroom feel. The intimacy was com-
pounded when he dropped the fresh bindings beside them
and reached out to pull the hem of her T-shirt from the
knotted sleeves of her flight suit at her waist. He'd obviously decided it would be too painful for her to remove the
shirt herself.

Unfortunately, he was right.

Even more unfortunate was her subsequent realization
that she wasn't wearing one of her basic cotton bras today,
but one of her lace ones.

What else could go wrong?

Evidently, a lot.

Eve sucked in her breath as he peeled her shirt up. If he
stripped her any slower, the act would qualify as foreplay.

And his *hands*.

They were so large, he couldn't seem to avoid her skin
as he eased the shirt from her head and set about unwrap-
ping the old bindings. Yeah, her skin was definitely paying
the price. His callused fingers skimmed her waist as he
adjusted his grip, only to slide another trail of fire across
her stomach as he moved around to the front. She forced
herself to lift her arms and stare past his head as he quick-
ened his pace, only to inhale sharply as one of his fingers
bumped into her right breast and scraped the tip.

She flushed as it puckered embarrassingly beneath the
lace.

He cleared his throat. "Sorry."

"N-no problem."

Mercifully, the final layer of cotton bindings disappeared
along with his disturbing hands. She would have welcomed
the pain that followed as he began to rewrap her ribs
tightly—but this time, it was just too intense. Her eyes began to water and soon she was on the verge of whimpering.
She needed a distraction.

Desperately.

"I—ah—I don't know what happened."

His gaze shot to hers. She swore she could see a hundred different questions swirling amid those probing depths. She wasn't sure how, but he picked the right one. "The chopper?"

She managed a nod. "The engine, it just…stopped. Cut out. Almost as if we'd run out of fuel." She risked a deeper breath. "But that's impossible."

"Why?"

"Because the tank was nearly three-quarters full when I took off from the landing zone, *that's* why. Not to mention the blasted fuel exploded." Damn, she hadn't meant to snap. But her ribs hurt so bloody bad. "Sorry."

He shrugged off her apology as he continued to wrap her torso, tucking the free end beneath the bindings. He met her gaze as he began a new strip. "Do you think there was an electrical problem?"

Despite the agony in her chest, she blinked.

"You mentioned your global positioning system was down when I reached the LZ—along with the comm links to the extra headsets. Do you think the problems were related?" He glanced down to smooth the bindings, saving her the humiliation of admitting the headset malfunction had been a fib.

"No."

His gaze shot up. "Are you—"

"Yes, I'm sure." If she was lucky, he'd chalk up the fire in her cheeks to the constant stabbing in her ribs. Despite both, she managed not to shift beneath that dark gaze.

She might not know why the Black Hawk had crashed, but she did know the malfunctioning GPS hadn't contributed to it. Nor had there been a systematic electrical failure. Other than global positioning, all equipment had been functioning correctly until the chopper's engine simply stopped.

Even if she confessed her fit of pique regarding the headsets, what would that explain?

Nothing.

But it would open up a discussion about Carrie.

A discussion she had no intention of initiating with this man, let alone an accident investigation board. If the board discovered Carrie's relationship with Sergeant Turner by some other means and then asked her a direct question, she wouldn't lie. But neither did she intend to volunteer anything that would stain her friend's military record. Carrie was dead. So was her lover. As far as Eve was concerned, the extent of their relationship had died with them.

In more ways than one.

She didn't know how much Bishop knew, but she was fairly certain he didn't know about the baby. Given his time and care with the makeshift crosses, surely he would have added a smaller one if he had? Again, even if he did know, what would it change? Hindsight might have filled in several of the blanks regarding Carrie's behavior during the flight, but it certainly hadn't absolved her of her own actions.

As the pilot in charge, the safety of the Black Hawk's passengers and crew had been *her* responsibility.

And now they were dead.

Eve was holding something back.

Rick stared into that wide green gaze for several moments, hoping she'd tell him what it was, but she didn't. She just slid her gaze from his and resumed that distant, fixed stare beyond his shoulder. He knew exactly what she was looking at. The past.

This morning, to be exact.

Eve Paris knew something about that crash that she wasn't sharing. He'd stake their paltry supply of ammunition on it.

But what was it?

Well, he wasn't going to get it out of her now, not after his inappropriate behavior. He was better off sticking to his makeshift mission. He'd get them the hell out of Córdoba and let the investigation board handle the rest. It was better for Eve and better for him. Hadn't he already proven his objectivity was out of whack with that blasted kiss?

*That kiss.*

Dammit, he was not going there.

Though he'd been willing to apologize for his behavior, Eve was right. It was best to pretend those mindless moments had not happened—and to make damned sure they didn't happen again. Rick jerked his attention to the task at hand, glancing down one last time to check the bindings he'd finished.

Not a smart move.

His fellow soldier might be minus a couple of intact ribs, but she was sporting some seriously healthy cleavage. He ripped his gaze from the generous curves spilling out from the top of her bra and grabbed the T-shirt lying beside them. He stretched the neck opening and eased it over her curls, pausing as she carefully reinserted her arms before he pulled the shirt the rest of the way down to tuck the hem into the arms of the flight suit knotted about her waist. The sigh that followed seemed to fill the darkening jungle.

He wasn't sure if it was hers or his.

Not that it mattered. He suspected her relief was as great as his. Especially when she stood abruptly. He reached out, but she stepped away, evading his hands as she turned.

"I'll break out the food."

He studied her movements closely as she headed across the clearing toward their gear still dumped at the base of the tree on the opposite side. Rebinding her ribs had been a good call. She was walking easier now, her stride almost matching the energy she'd displayed that morning at the landing zone.

Almost.

Well, he'd done the best he could, given the circumstances. If only he hadn't lost his sergeant's rucksack with its medical kit and painkillers.

Hell, if only he hadn't lost his sergeant.

Regret slammed into him for the thousandth time that day.

He slammed it back. There'd be time enough for that later. Eve was right; they needed food. Twenty winks wouldn't hurt either.

Her or him.

Rick shifted his rifle and leaned back against the trunk of the tree, swallowing a groan as he raised his hands to probe the line of stitches Eve had added to his latest soon-to-be scar. This was definitely no hangover. Those ebbed as the day wore on. This headache had only worsened. Since they'd stopped, the throbbing had taken on the cadence of an M-60 machine gun chewing through a belt of bullets, damned near drowning out the subtle sounds of the jungle beyond.

Even when he concentrated, it was becoming increasingly difficult to hear the birds and the insects above the pounding in his skull—and that was dangerous. Any change in their behavior could well signal the stealthy approach of an enemy.

But if he was too tired to hear it...

Rick stood, flexing his aching neck and shoulders before he snagged his M-16 and headed across the clearing after Eve. By the time he reached her, she'd already rummaged through the rucksack and located the MREs, or meals, ready to eat, using her pocketknife to slit open the brown plastic wrappers.

He gestured to the makeshift meal, indicating she should

take her choice, not that there was much of one. As far as he was concerned, one version of MREs tasted as much like wet sawdust as another, especially cold. He leaned his rifle against the ruck and reached for one of the instant coffee packets instead as he settled back against a tree trunk.

"Feel free to take the other coffee, too."

He did. "Thanks."

He poured out a canteen cup of water, dumped both packets in and swished them around for several seconds. She grimaced as he downed the lukewarm contents, but didn't say anything. Cold coffee wasn't on his list of favorite foods either, but they both knew they couldn't risk a fire.

He reached for the Army's attempt at beef stew, discreetly watching Eve as he settled back against the tree. She seemed more interested in studying the moss clinging to the knotted root beside her than she did in consuming the contents of her own MRE pouch. The longer she stared at the moss, the more fascinated he became—with her. He was beginning to suspect that no matter how cool and controlled Eve seemed when she thought he was watching her, she was anything but when she did not. A myriad of emotions continued to sweep through her gaze, each one more intense than the last, until the distinct shadow of grief finally shrouded those deep-green eyes and settled in, turning them even darker.

His gut clenched as her gaze began to glisten.

Tears.

He'd lay odds she was thinking about Carrie and the crash. As much as he felt the pull of compassion, it had to stop. He had to distract her. Frankly, he couldn't afford to watch those tears well up again. Look what had happened the last time.

Dammit, she was a soldier.

*So, think of her as one.*

God help him, he was trying. But in spite of his best efforts to relegate her back to the ranks of fellow officer, he couldn't quite manage it. The truth was, the longer he stared at this particular soldier, the more he became intrigued by the glimpse of pure woman he caught beneath.

Just who was Eve Paris?

Whoever she was, she was seriously hurting.

If she and Carrie were really sisters, it made sense.

He sought out her gaze, steeling himself against those tears and their effect on his sanity. He'd have to deal with them—because she obviously needed to get it out. To be honest, he wanted to know. He gave up all pretense of eating and leaned forward to return the food pouch to the communal space between them, then cleared his throat softly.

"Eve?"

Her wide gaze shot to his. "What is it? Did you—"

He held up his hands. "Relax. I didn't hear anything. I haven't all day. I was just thinking about something you said about Carrie—" He broke off as she stiffened.

Odd.

He swore Eve was more tense now than when she thought he'd sensed someone else's presence in the rapidly encroaching night. If anything, her reaction only made him more determined to get to the bottom of what had happened. But to do that, he'd have to proceed carefully. As much as he disliked the idea, he'd have to treat her as a tactical combat objective to be studied and then overcome.

He gentled his voice as much as possible and took the first step. "Eve, how can Carrie Evans be your sister?"

He knew it was a good call when she relaxed.

But she didn't answer.

A good thirty seconds of jungle silence dragged into

thirty more. Just as he was about to question his approach and revise it, she sighed.

"We went to college together. UT."

"University of Tennessee?"

She shook her head as she reached for the packet of instant cocoa. "Texas—Austin." He poured out a cup of water from the canteen and passed it over. "Thanks."

"I take it you two were in the same ROTC program."

She nodded as she stirred the powder into the cup and took a sip. "A couple of us started an all-women's military sorority our freshman year. We called it Sisters-in-Arms."

That would explain the sisters, then.

Blood wasn't always thicker than shared experiences. Twelve years in the Army had taught him that. Evidently Eve and Carrie had learned the lesson as well. It also explained why she seemed especially devastated. But if they were sisters because of some sorority— "What about the others?"

She blinked. "Excuse me?"

"You said a couple of you started the sorority. How many calls do you have ahead of you when we get back?"

For the second time in as many minutes, she stared at him silently, this time over the cup of cold cocoa.

Her voice finally broke, "Three."

From the depth of the sigh that followed, they wouldn't be easy either. And those didn't even include the calls and personal visits she'd have to make to her crew chief's family.

"Tell me about them."

Her mouth dropped open. Obviously he'd surprised her.

Hell, he'd surprised himself. He actually wanted to know.

When was the last time he'd encouraged a woman to talk just to hear the husky rasp in her voice? Or worse, to get to know her better? Come to think of it, when was the last time he'd honestly wanted to get to know a woman at all outside the bedroom?

The devil with the jungle, *this* was dangerous ground.

Perhaps it was time to rethink his strategy in getting to the bottom of whatever Eve was withholding.

Unfortunately, it was too late.

She polished off her cocoa and set the tin cup down. "Anna's Navy. She's an Intel officer currently stationed in San Diego. Samantha's Air Force. Sam and I met in an engineering class the first week our freshman year. We were both aerospace engineering. Sam's a theater missile systems design expert out of Kirtland, New Mexico."

He couldn't help it, his low whistle escaped.

She chuckled softly. "Don't worry, Sam's the brilliant one. I just fly." Her laughter faded into a soft smile, and he nearly lost his grip on his canteen cup. Even half-formed, Eve's smile had the power to sear straight through a man. The subtle curve was much too teasing and much, much too tempting.

He brought the tin cup to his mouth and forced himself to swallow the remainder of the cold coffee before he dared to risk speech. "You mentioned three. Who's the other one?"

She nodded. "Meg. She's Marine Corps. I'm not sure where she is right now. No one ever is." Despite her shrug, he sensed the admiration in Eve's husky voice.

"Why?"

"Meg works personal protection. Generals, Marine Corps or other visiting military officers, or anyone else she's assigned to protect. Men or women, she watches their backs and keeps them alive—whether they want her there or not."

"I take it she's good."

That tantalizing half smile returned. "The best."

He suspected they all were. Which brought him back to

the chopper. He was beginning to wonder if whatever Eve was holding back had to do with Carrie's actions that morning. Had Carrie done something that directly or indirectly caused the crash? Given the woman's behavior with his sergeant as well as her distraction, it was more than possible. It was also becoming downright probable.

Unfortunately, he couldn't come out and ask.

"So...you and Carrie were close because you were both Army?"

Her lips curved again, but this time down. He suspected the shadows had returned to her gaze as well, but he couldn't be sure. Dusk had settled in, cloaking the jungle in near-total black.

"We both wanted to fly, but it was more than that."

He was sure of the shadows now. He could hear them in her voice. "How much more?"

She sighed. "Carrie's mother died when we were sophomores and she...well, she didn't have anyone else. Not really."

He knew he'd hit a tender spot when Eve failed to continue. He waited, but there was nothing save her soft breathing amid the insects and nocturnal jungle life waking to the shroud of night.

He decided to risk it.

"Eve...what happened to your family?"

Again, nothing but jungle.

He wasn't surprised.

But he was startled by the unexpected knife to his own heart when she wouldn't share her pain. He reached out— but she was gone, scrambling to her knees as fast as her cracked ribs would allow. Eve averted her face and began cleaning up her mess as well as his own with a zeal he suspected she'd rarely afforded another man. Just as he suspected her movements were fueled more by desperation than a desire to conceal their camp site from any Córdobans who might stumble across it later.

He knew the feeling.

A droplet of water splattered onto his face and rolled down his cheek, taunting him almost as much as the tears Eve had shed earlier. He scrubbed it away, cursing to himself as he stared up at the sky through the opening in the jungle canopy. Not a star in sight. The clouds had been forming since noon. They'd finally merged into the thick layer now blanketing the sky. The dark thunderheads combined with the raw emotions still roiling though his gut to close in on him. But it wasn't until Eve pulled the rain poncho from his rucksack that he experienced claustrophobia in a way the jungle had never caused before.

He only had one poncho.

It made one hell of a tiny tent.

And they were going to have to share it.

# Chapter 4

Rick stared down at his web gear, cursing as several more drops of water splattered onto the ammunition pouches attached to the front. Waterproof liners or not, there was no sense taking a chance. He leaned down, sighing as he retrieved the web gear and slipped it on. Resignation locked in as he snapped the buckle into place. If he had to spend the next several hours in purgatory, he'd at least make sure his ammo stayed dry while he was at it.

But as he turned to face Eve, he froze.

He stood there for a full five seconds, silent, straining—his heart pounding against his chest, his nerves damned near screaming, as he worked to convince his brain that the distant but familiar thunder he *thought* he'd just heard had been caused by his imagination. By his need to avoid that poncho. By his need to avoid her.

But there it was again.

His hope surged as Eve stiffened too.

Adrenaline followed.

Her gaze swung to his as she breathed the prayer out loud, "It's a Black Hawk."

Before he could blink, she'd leaned down and snatched up her flight vest. Her flare pistol was out and pointing straight to heaven as he reached her side. He clapped his hand over her wrist with less than a trigger's breath to spare.

*"Don't."*

"Dammit, Bishop, that's our ticket out—"

"Or it could be a Huey." She had to know as well as he did that Uncle Sam had sold off half a squadron of the Army's Vietnam-era UH-1s to San Sebastián and Córdoba before all hell had broken out between the two countries.

Her free hand snapped up, locking down on top of his. "Bishop, listen to me. Trust me. I didn't argue with you once today, because I knew *you* knew what the hell you were doing. Now it's your turn to keep the faith. I know my choppers."

The thundering blades grew louder, drew closer.

But for how long?

If she was right, even this delay could cost them. Even without the thick blanket of clouds, the jungle had its own unique way of buffering sound waves. That chopper could be directly above the canopy, ten yards away—or ten miles.

Unless Eve fired that flare, they'd never know which.

Her short nails drove into the skin on the back of his hand as that emerald gaze burned straight into him.

*"Trust me."*

God help them, he did.

He pulled his hand from the pistol.

Before he could jerk his chin down, the flare shot up, a trail of white phosphorous searing through the canopy.

What the hell.

He grabbed his M-16 with his right hand, Eve's upper arm with his left, pulling her body firmly behind his as he sprinted to the edge of the clearing. He heard her gasp as she stumbled. He forced himself to ignore it as he hauled her up and steadied her. If she was right and that pilot was one of theirs, manna was about to fall from the sky in the form of additional MREs, a fresh first-aid kit, and the blessed black plastic casing of a working Prick-112 to replace the radios roasted in the explosion that took out their own chopper.

And if she was wrong?

The adrenaline surging through his veins matched the pulsing roar of the chopper's blades as it drew closer and closer until, suddenly, the bird was visible.

Eve was right.

Relief seared into him as the distinctive silhouette of an UH-60 slipped into view within the opening in the canopy above. The greenish glow of flailing chemical light sticks whirled toward the earth as the Black Hawk dumped its package and bugged out. Rick nudged Eve down and tucked her amid the sheltering trees.

''Wait here.''

A flick of his thumb and the M-16's safety was off—and so was he. He snagged the bundle in record time and beat an equally low, hasty retreat back into the trees.

Back to Eve.

Rick reset the safety on his M-16 and propped it against a tree trunk before ripping into the bundle. He snagged the Prick-112 and fired up the radio as Eve retrieved her survival strobe with its infrared lens. ''Black Hawk, this is Captain Bishop. I have you at sixty degrees, two hundred yards. Over.''

A burst of static filled the air as the pilot keyed his own mic. ''Roger, Bishop. This is Romeo Six. What's your status? Over.''

Status?

Try three soldiers dead and not a blessed body recovered.

Remorse slammed into him for the countless time.

Rick ordered it aside, determined to concentrate on the soldier kneeling beside him. At least Eve was alive. He had every intention of making sure she stayed that way. He keyed his mic, knowing full well the man on the other end was not going to like what he was about to suggest. "I have one ambulatory wounded. Multiple fractured ribs, possible internal bleeding. Request immediate extraction. Over."

"Do you need a litter? Over."

Christ, they didn't have time for twenty questions. He might not be able to distinguish the distant drone of a Black Hawk from a Huey but he knew damned well Hawks didn't normally carry litters. He could tell by the pilot's tone he wasn't carrying one now. It was a harness or nothing.

"Negative on the litter. A STABO will work, over."

"Negative, Bishop. Suggest you find cover for the night. Will attempt extraction in the morning."

The hell they would. They couldn't afford to hole up for the night. Eve couldn't afford it.

Yes, their position had been compromised. If not by the mile-long swath he'd spent the day carving into the jungle undergrowth, than certainly by the bellowing blades above. Rick flicked his gaze to the right. From the fresh tears streaming from the corners of those fierce green eyes and the rhythmic working of Eve's jaw, their mutual sprint to the edge of the clearing had taken another toll on her ribs.

If the Córdoban army came calling now, there was no way Eve would be able to maneuver effectively.

"Negative, Romeo Six. I need extraction *now*. Over."

Five seconds stretched into ten, then fifteen.

Then twenty.

What the devil was the problem?

Just as he was about to key his radio again and demand an answer, the pilot beat him to the punch. Rick caught the end of a fiery stream of Spanish above the pulsing din and static, but couldn't make out the speaker's words. He could, however, make out the pilot's.

"Roger, Bishop. I only have time for one evac, over."

"Understood, over."

"Roger. Need you to identify your location, over."

"Identify red lens, over."

Eve pointed the strobe toward the canopy as the chopper slipped into view and popped off a succession of flashes.

"Roger, Bishop. I identify your signal. Stand by for STABO harness. Out."

Rick shoved the Prick-112 into Eve's right hand and stood. "Wait here." He left his M-16 at her side as well, drawing his 9 mm as he sprinted around the clearing's near pitch-black perimeter to their gear. He ripped open the outer pocket to his rucksack and scooped out the rings, watches, dog tags and other personal effects he'd gathered prior to burying their men that morning. Thirty seconds later, he was back at Eve's side, his breath coming in short and hard as he grabbed the radio before shoving the personal effects into her hands.

"Here."

He snagged her crew chief's watch as it slipped from her grasp and stuffed it into the left pocket beneath the knotted arms of her flight suit. He should probably help her don the suit correctly, but they didn't have time. He'd already wasted precious seconds in his quest for their men's effects. The Black Hawk moved into the clearing, kicking up a maelstrom of swirling twigs, leaves and decaying jungle foliage into their faces as he helped Eve to her feet.

He shoved his pistol into its holster and slung his M-16 over his shoulder before hooking his left arm around her back. As he guided her into the clearing, he shouted above the pounding din of the chopper's blades. "When you get back to post, call my colonel and tell him—"

She missed a step. "What?"

He tightened his grip on her shoulders and pulled her closer, taking care not to crush her ribs as he nudged her forward again. "I said, when you get back to base, call my—"

This time she stopped dead in her tracks.

On purpose.

"I'm not leaving without you."

"Dammit, Paris, we don't have time to argue. *You* don't have time. Fellow pilot or not, that bird is not going to hang out like a sitting duck, I could hear it in the man's voice."

Rick glanced up at the Black Hawk. Sure enough, he could tell by the luminescent chem sticks that the STABO harness had already been kicked out of the chopper's side door.

They really didn't have time.

Eve stood fast.

"Paris, listen to me—"

"No! You listen to me! I am not leaving without you. I refuse. I've already lost my copilot, my crew chief *and* a passenger today. I will not risk losing another."

"You don't have a choice!" He hadn't meant to bellow, but blast it, the STABO was ten feet from the ground now—and they were still a good fifteen feet away from the bird.

Any other soldier, with any other injury, and he'd have picked the woman up by now and slung the harness around her body himself, discussion be damned.

From the look in her eyes, she knew it, too.

Unfortunately, she also knew he hadn't nursed her ribs along this far only to risk puncturing her lungs now.

Her gaze dropped to his web gear, to the dangling steel D-clip he and every other soldier in his platoon carried for insurance when they were on a mission. "We can go up together. I'll take the STABO. You use your D-clip to latch yourself to the main ring. You've probably done it before."

He had.

"What if I knock into you during the evac? Puncture your lungs? We may not get you across the border in time!"

"That's a risk I'm willing to take, Bishop. But I won't risk leaving—and losing—you!"

Rick stared down into her fiery gaze. He'd known Eve Paris for less than a day. But he knew in his gut she was deadly serious. She was going up with him, or not at all.

"Fine."

Anything to get her in that blasted harness. Besides, he could always hook her up and signal the pilot to pull her up before she had a chance to argue.

"I want your word, Bishop."

Evidently he wasn't the only one who'd learned a thing or two about the other during their trek.

"You have it."

He slung his arm around her shoulder and tugged her across the dark, toward the glowing chem sticks as the STABO hit the jungle floor once, twice, before being dragged through the undergrowth as the chopper played out enough line for them to work with. He grabbed the harness and slipped one of the lower loops over Eve's right combat boot, the other over her left. For a split second, the intimacy of his hands hit him as he tugged the loops up to seat them firmly into the V at her thighs.

"Thanks."

"No problem." He avoided her gaze and quickly guided her bare arms through the remaining twin shoulder loops before locking the STABO into place. Before he could step away, he felt rather than heard his D-clip snap. He glanced down.

Bloody hell.

Not only had Eve not taken him at his word, she'd taken it upon herself to lock him to the main ring. He couldn't decide if he was pissed or impressed. While he'd been momentarily flustered over the location of his hands, she'd taken other matters into hers.

He yanked the Prick-112 from his cargo pocket and keyed the mic. "Romeo Six, this is Captain Bishop. STABO attached. Reel it up, over!"

"Roger, Bishop. Out."

The line went taut as his entire body jerked into the air. He tried to avoid slamming into Eve as her own boots cleared the ground, but failed. He shoved the radio into his cargo pocket and leaned down as she stiffened. Unfortunately, he could barely reach the top of her head. He smoothed her curls as he shouted over the now-deafening roar. "You okay?"

"Fine!"

She had to be lying.

He was certain as she tucked her face into his lower thighs and held on tight. The chopper lurched, sending an eye-watering jolt though his own ribs. A split second later, Eve's arms slackened.

"Paris?"

Nothing but the thunder of chopper blades.

*"Eve?"*

Again, no response.

Worse, her head was hanging limply to the side now. He tried reaching her neck to check her pulse, but couldn't manage it. Panic seared into him as an entire evolution that should have taken under two minutes seemed to stretch into twenty as he waited for the winch to haul their bodies through the dark, inch by agonizing inch, until his shoulders were finally flush with the yawning side door of the chopper.

The crew chief grabbed his torso and yanked him inside.

"Careful! I think Captain Paris passed out."

At least, he hoped that's all it was.

Prayed.

Unfortunately, he didn't get a chance to find out as the crew chief unlatched his D-clip and shoved him into the belly of the bird. Before he could blink, another set of arms hauled him in tight and clapped him on the back.

"*Gracias a Dios,* you're alive!"

Rick jerked back and stared into the dark, backlit by the wide bay of glowing lights and switches from the cockpit beyond. Despite the camouflage paint concealing the man's features, he'd recognize that mustachioed grin anywhere. Ernesto was here?

*Inside* Córdoba?

His buddy nodded. "It's me."

No doubt with one hell of a story to relay, too.

But not now.

Rick spun around as the crew chief stopped the winch for the second time and leaned outside the chopper door to grab Eve's dangling body. "Ernie, help us get her inside!"

As usual, Ernesto didn't have to be asked twice.

He snagged Eve's boots as Rick linked his arms beneath her torso and dragged her limp body inside the chopper. The chief unlocked the main STABO link from the rescue cable as Rick laid her body out on the chopper floor. Unwilling to damage her ribs further, he left the harness attached.

"Paris?"

An ache Rick couldn't explain ripped into him when her eyes remained closed. Damned if his fingers weren't shaking as he slid them down the length of her neck, praying for a pulse. He squeezed his eyes shut and worked to block out the bone-jarring vibrations of the chopper.

*There.*

The ache in his chest ebbed as he located the faint throb

of her pulse. He squeezed his eyes tighter, concentrated harder. Relief seared into him as her pulse strengthened beneath his fingers. Satisfied, Rick opened his eyes and brushed his fingers across her bruised cheek.

"Eve?"

Again, no response.

He tried gently squeezing her shoulder.

Not so much as an eyelash flutter.

The Black Hawk's first-aid kit probably contained smelling salts. But if Eve's body had shut down from the fresh assault on her ribs, who was he to bring her around so she could suffer through another round of splintered agony? He unhooked his web gear instead, peeling it and the blouse to his jungle fatigues down his arms together. He tossed his web gear to Ernesto and quickly folded his shirt before carefully slipping it beneath Eve's head to cushion her skull from the vibrating floor of the bird. Nothing left to do, he slumped down beside her and leaned his back against the metal tubing that framed the Black Hawk's forward webbed bench.

A feather bed couldn't have been more comfortable. Even the stench of fuel mingling with his own sweat and filth didn't faze him.

"Sergeant Turner?"

But that did.

Ernesto slid across the steel floor of the chopper, closing the distance between them to inches to save him from bellowing above the deafening roar. Rick raked his hands through his hair, sighing as the guilt burned through him. "Sergeant Turner's dead." He glanced at Eve, automatically seeking reassurance in the steady rise and fall of her chest. "We lost Eve's crew, too."

"*Eve?*"

Rick stared into his buddy's dark, curious gaze—and the brow rising suggestively above.

Bloody hell.

He needed that slip of the tongue like Eve needed another broken rib. Fellow officer or not, he and Ernesto both knew it wasn't like him to be on a first-name basis with a female soldier he'd just met. But that was part of the problem. It felt as if he'd known Eve for years, not hours.

And then there was that kiss.

Buddy or not, there was no way he was confessing that to Ernesto. Not when he couldn't explain it to himself.

"Captain Paris."

"Ahhh…" Ernesto's tone told him it was too late. He'd already let too much slip. Sooner or later, he'd have to come up with an explanation. Knowing Ernesto, it would be sooner.

Speaking of explanations—

"How the devil did you get your brother's permission to cross the border?"

Ernesto's wry grin flashed in the dark. "I forgot to ask."

*"What?"*

The hell with explaining his own behavior.

Ernesto's half brother wasn't crazy about the U.S. Army's presence as it was. The chopper crash on Córdoban soil was only going to make it worse. And now Ernesto had slipped across the border without so much as a by-your-leave to the Mighty Miguel? Rick shook his head. "My hide was not worth losing your spot in the pecking order, buddy."

Ernesto shrugged. *"El Presidente Pequeño* will get over it. Besides, he has more than me to worry about at the moment." The man he'd endured many a mud bath alongside in Ranger school tossed a grubby sheet of paper into his lap and then clapped him on the shoulder. "And you are worth it."

Easy for his friend to say.

He sincerely doubted Ernesto's older brother would

agree. Miguel Torres might not be president of San Sebastián yet, but it was only a matter of time. Some thought weeks. Their father had entered the last stages of his own personal battle with cancer—and the man was losing. It was a damned shame.

For reasons personal and political.

While Guillermo Torres had passed on his growing fascination with capitalism to both his sons, Ernesto held the concept much closer to his heart than did his elder half brother. In fact, Ernesto had taken it one step further, believing that one day his country would also be ready to make the transition to democracy. As an exchange cadet at West Point years before, Ernesto felt that strong ties between American and San Sebastián armed forces could only help. As a result, Ernesto had worked hard two years ago to convince their father to invite the U.S. Army into San Sebastián to help train her indigenous troops in the art of special warfare. Slowly but surely, real progress had been made.

Until lately.

With their father weakening with each passing day, Rick had begun briefing *El Presidente Pequeño*—or the "little president" as Ernesto's half brother was now commonly called. The chopper's crash this morning had caused him to miss his weekly brief. Miguel had always maintained that an American military presence in San Sebastián would create more problems than it solved. Neither he nor Ernesto needed a crystal ball to know that the next time they all met, Miguel's first words would be *I told you so.*

Rick glanced down at Eve.

She still hadn't regained consciousness.

Her lashes were fanned out over the dark circles beneath her eyes. He smoothed his fingers across her cheek as he had before. Again, not so much as a flutter amid the delicate wisps. He slid his fingers to her neck and checked her pulse.

Steady. Strong.

He breathed a sigh of relief as he turned to stare past the bill of Ernesto's camouflage field cap. Though the crew chief had long since closed the chopper door, its double windows were tall and wide enough that even sitting on the floor, he could make out the distant glow of city lights bleeding up into the cloud-laden night sky. They were now firmly on the right side of the San Sebastián border.

Praise the Lord and pass the ammunition.

"*Captain* Paris?"

Confused, Rick snapped his gaze to Ernesto's. He followed his buddy's pointed stare down—and winced.

*Damn.*

Somehow his fingers had worked themselves into Eve's hair. He couldn't have been smoothing the tangled curls from her temple for long, but it had been long enough for Ernesto to notice. Rick shot a glance at the crew chief as he withdrew his hand from Eve's hair as discreetly as he could.

Fortunately, the man was immersed in his duties.

Unwilling to face his buddy's speculation, much less his own, he locked his hands into his lap, grateful for the rhythmic thunder in his ears as well as the cold steel at his back as he focused his attention on the chopper's windows and the ever-growing glow of city lights beyond. Whatever had or hadn't transpired between Eve and himself before, during and after that kiss they'd shared, was over.

Reality was, Eve Paris was just another soldier.

Once he passed her off to the waiting medical personnel, he probably wouldn't even see her again. It would take her ribs weeks to heal. Even if the investigation board cleared her of any wrongdoing during the crash and sent her back in country, he was on his way out. By the time she was reinserted into the San Sebastián air rotation, he'd be stateside again.

The chopper hit a thermal pocket, knocking his shoulder blades against the steel tubing of the bench behind him. It was a good thing Ernesto had arrived when he had, because there was a devil of a storm brewing. Rick slid his gaze down to check on Eve as another blast of wind buffeted the chopper.

Her lashes fluttered.

"Eve?"

Her eyes opened slowly. For all his prayers, he regretted it as the chopper hit another pocket moments later, this one jolting the bird's entire airframe—and Eve's battered torso.

She groaned.

This time, he didn't give a damn who was watching as he smoothed her hair from the bruises on her brow. "It's okay, Eve. Just relax. We're out of Córdoba. We'll be landing in San Sebastián City any minute. Everything's going to be fine."

The airframe shuddered again.

He was relieved when her lashes fluttered down and she slipped into unconsciousness. Until the next jolt, and the realization that slammed into him along with it. Rick sucked in his breath as the answer to the one question about the crash that had been nagging at him all day clicked sharply into focus. He finally knew what had happened during that crash. Or rather, what *should* have happened—but hadn't.

So why hadn't it?

Unless Carrie had fought for control of the chopper.

He'd heard of it happening before.

Given the haphazard professionalism Carrie had displayed before and during their flight, he had to wonder if it hadn't happened that morning. Rick ignored Ernesto's curiosity as he leaned forward to snag Eve's right hand. He stared at the ring encircling her third finger for several moments. A ring that matched the one he'd removed from Carrie hours before.

Sisters.

Eve had said it herself, she and Carrie were that close.

But were they close enough to cover up for one another?

Before he could ponder the answer, Ernesto nudged his shoulder. ''Are you going to read it?''

Read what?

Ernesto pointed to the floor of the chopper.

The sheet of paper.

*Damn.* He'd been so worried about Eve, he'd forgotten all about it. He retrieved it quickly, adding another layer of dirt to the paper as he smoothed it out on his thigh. Ernesto handed him a red-filtered penlight before he could reach for his own. ''Thanks.'' He flicked on the mini flashlight and skimmed the classified memo and promptly cursed. Córdoba was at war—with herself.

Rick double-checked the time block on the flash message.

Sure enough, less than five minutes before their chopper had crashed, democratic rebels had stormed the capital city of Córdoba. The entire country was hot. No wonder the pilot up front had been nervous about extracting them, and no wonder no one had bothered to track them through the jungle today.

The Córdoban army had been too damned busy.

He was still staring at the message when the chopper touched down on the tarmac. Ernesto nudged his shoulder again.

''You are okay?''

''Fine. Situation report?''

''Patrols along our mutual border have doubled. No doubt because they fear we will choose to send aid.'' His buddy frowned. ''So far, my brother has not authorized any.''

The crew chief slid the chopper's right side door open as the bird's blades began powering down. Two medics reached in and snagged Eve before Rick could stop them.

"Careful! Her ribs are—"

"We know, sir."

He vaulted out of the bird as the medics strapped Eve's still-unconscious body onto the waiting gurney. But as he struck out to follow them to the waiting ambulance thirty feet away, Ernesto's hand clapped onto his shoulder.

He whirled about. "Dammit, I—"

"—know. It is in your eyes, my friend. But she is fine, or will be soon enough. You can see her later. For now, duty calls. I need you. Your colonel needs you. Neither of us have been able to convince Miguel to open our armory to the rebels. Time is of the essence. My brother may not like you, but he has come to respect you these past two years. Perhaps he will listen to you."

Rick spun around, for the first time in his life torn between duty and desire as the medics shoved Eve's rolling gurney across the darkened tarmac. They reached the flashing lights of the ambulance and hefted the gurney in one smooth sweep, folding and locking the frame's wheels beneath the bed as they slid the gurney into the rear of the ambulance. The double doors slammed shut and the siren shrieked to life. Seconds later, the engine fired up as well.

Bloody hell.

Ernesto was right. Friend or not, there was only one reason Ernesto would risk pulling his hide out of a hot zone in the dead of night and in the process risk igniting an already strained relationship between San Sebastián and Córdoba. Ernesto truly needed him. Colonel Robbins needed him.

Soon, his platoon would need him.

With Turner gone, doubly so.

He should be eager to return to the jungle. To return to his men. But as Rick forced himself to turn his back on the flashing but fading pinpoints of lights—on Eve—he was left with the stunning realization that for once, he wasn't.

## Chapter 5

*H*er tummy hurt. Bad.

Eve balled up her fists and pushed them into her belly, but it didn't help. And it made the coughs come back. She grabbed the blanket her mother had wrapped around her before she'd put her in the car and pulled it tighter.

The coughing got worse.

It made her bump into the handle of the car door, right into one of the bruises mommy's new friend had made on her arm. She bit her bottom lip to keep from crying.

At least the coughs stopped.

She stared out the window, scrubbing the tears from her cheeks as the car turned. Except for the tall white light they passed, the street was dark. Scary. She stared at the back of her mother's golden hair and bit her bottom lip harder.

Where was mommy taking her?

She knew better than to ask.

She followed her mother's hair down to the stain on the back of the front seat. It was red and blotchy. Kinda like

*Mr. Tim's face when she'd tried to crawl into bed with mommy tonight. Just thinking about Mr. Tim made her stomach hurt again but she didn't tell mommy. There were lots of things she didn't tell mommy now. She didn't tell her when her toes hurt from the cold or when she was hungry. It just made mommy cry and drink. And then she'd find a new boyfriend.*

*Someone like Mr. Tim.*

*Eve pulled the blanket tight and leaned against the car door as she yawned. Whatever she did, she mustn't let mommy see the new bruises....*

"Evie?"

*She rubbed her eyes and forced them open.*

*The car had stopped.*

*Her mother's door slammed shut and hers opened. She gasped as her mother lifted her out of the car.* "Oh, baby, I'm sorry. I didn't mean to hurt you."

*Yeah, mommy always said that.*

*She wrapped her arms around her mother's neck and buried her head into her hair anyway. Even when mommy made the bruises herself, she didn't mean it. It was the beer.*

*Isn't that what Father Francis said?*

*She was too scared to lift her head and see where her mother was taking her this time. At first she thought they were going to the shelter, but the street didn't look right. There were lights on the street with the shelter. She didn't see any light here. Besides, mommy didn't like the shelter.*

*Eve winced as her mother shifted her against her hips. She opened her eyes and stared down at the steps her mother was climbing. Stone steps. She'd seen them before.*

*The church?*

*Eve tightened her arms as her mother reached the big wooden door. But instead of knocking, her mother pulled her arms from her neck and tried to put her on the ground.*

*"Please, mommy—"*

*"It's okay, Evie. I just need you to sit here for a few minutes."* Her mommy pushed her down onto the prickly mat with the big white cross. *"I want you to promise me you'll wait right here for Father Francis, okay?"*

Alone?

But it was so dark. So cold.

*"Mommy, I w-want to go back to Mr. Tim's."*

*"I know, baby, I know. But right now, you can't."* Her mother pulled her close and gave her a quick hug, but then she pushed her away and tucked the blanket under her chin. *"I'll come back for you, Evie, okay? I promise. Until then, you wait here for Father Francis and you be good."*

She swiped at her tears. *"I will, mommy. I promise I'll be good."*

Her mother smiled, but she didn't look very happy.

When was mommy ever very happy?

Eve shivered as she huddled onto the mat. She could feel tears streaming down her face again, hot and wet. This time she didn't wipe them. She didn't bite her bottom lip to stop her sobs, either. Mommy couldn't hear them anyway.

She'd left.

Eve tried to get comfortable, but the mat was too prickly and it was too cold. And dark. She leaned against the wooden door but it didn't help. The mat and the cold made the bruises on her legs and arms hurt worse. Soon they hurt so bad, she couldn't feel her tummy anymore—or her toes.

And then suddenly, she started to get warmer.

Her bruises stopped hurting—and her tummy and toes.

There was light, too, burning away the dark. It shone around the prettiest angel she'd ever seen. Prettier than the picture in Father Francis's office. The angel wore a long white dress like the one she'd seen in the window of the *wedding store next to the alley she and mommy slept in one night. The dress shimmered as the angel glided closer.*

*She could see the angel's eyes, now.*

*They were bright blue and she had lots and lots of short, black curls and pretty pink lips. The angel was so close, she could have reached out and touched her if she'd tried.*

*She didn't dare.*

*What if she made the angel mad? She might go away like mommy. But the angel didn't go away. She glided closer and closer and smiled as she leaned down to touch her cheek.*

*"You're not alone."*

*But she was.*

*This time she really, truly was.*

He should have called first.

Rick jerked his gaze from the apartment door and stared down at his rumpled jungle fatigues. Bloody hell.

He should have showered.

What made him think he could climb off a C-130 troop transport after ten hours in the air, turn in his weapons and field gear, call the Fort Campbell post operator while his men were turning in their gear and then drive across Clarksville, Tennessee, without making sure he was even welcome?

What if Eve wasn't home?

He should have planned this better.

He would have, if he wasn't so exhausted.

For the past six weeks, he hadn't had the time or the energy to give much thought to anything beyond keeping his men alive. Less than a minute after Eve's ambulance departed, he'd climbed into Ernesto's waiting jeep and headed in the opposite direction. Unfortunately, he hadn't been able to convince Miguel to assist the Córdoban rebels—even discreetly. So he and Ernesto had done the only thing they could. They'd headed back to the airport and climbed aboard another chopper. Ten minutes later, his bird was hovering over the same landing zone where it had all started that morning.

The moment the chopper had touched down, he'd forced himself to push Eve and his sergeant from his mind and concentrate on the job at hand. It had been easy enough to do while he and his men picked their way through the jungle undergrowth, readying San Sebastián's newly trained forces in the event that Córdoba's exploding civil war spilled over their mutual border. It was much harder to do once he was on his way home.

Especially when he'd landed.

Watching his men as they greeted their wives and kids had gotten to him. He'd known then he wouldn't be getting any sleep until he found out what had happened. Not that he'd gotten much anyway. Rick stared at the brass knocker on the apartment door. Besides, stopping by would allow him to check up on Eve while he was at it. He'd have taken the time to do the same for any soldier with whom he'd survived a crash.

So why had he brought flowers?

Rick stared into the froth of green tissue in his right hand. The daisies he'd settled on had seemed innocuous enough in the shop down the street. Now they seemed…eager.

He should have left them in the truck.

But as he turned to do just that, he caught the sound of footsteps on the opposite side of the door. The taps were soft, but they were definitely headed toward the door.

Best to drive on through.

He turned back to the door and raised his hand.

Unfortunately, his knuckles didn't get a chance to connect, because the door opened.

"Hi."

The deep-emerald gaze that had been haunting his dreams these past six weeks widened with shock. Before he could blink, it dropped to the daisies in his hand and narrowed. From the ice that crystallized within, he knew what she was thinking. He opened his mouth to explain—

He never got the chance.

Eve's fist plowed into his gut so hard and so fast, that if he hadn't watched it happen, he'd have sworn he'd been knocked on his ass by a man twice her size, with four times her strength. He staggered backward, the daisies raining down around him as he gasped for air. A second later, the apartment door slammed shut, the force of it echoing down the breezeway.

He didn't think; he reacted.

Rick lunged for the doorknob and wrenched it open before Eve had a chance to throw the lock or the security bolt above it. At the same time, he braced his shoulder into the door and heaved against it with all his might.

He needn't have bothered.

She hadn't been bracing the door. He went flying across her kitchen, plowing into the protruding ledge of the breakfast counter, directly into his groin.

White-hot pain exploded inside him.

He hung there for an eternity, doubled over the counter, his eyes watering, his jaw locked against the whimper clawing up his throat as wave after wave of the most intense agony he'd ever experienced ripped through him. The bullet he'd taken in the Balkans had nothing on this. By the time he regained his composure—hell, his *breathing*—and peeled himself up from the counter, Eve was standing beside him. Not a single ounce of pity in her frosted glare.

*"What the devil did you slug me for?"*

She shrugged. "Next time, knock."

"The bloody door opened before I could!"

The curls at her temple flattened beneath his roar.

The sight stopped his fury cold.

He'd never yelled at a woman before in his life. Not like that. What on earth had possessed him to do it now? Despite her sucker punch, he opened his mouth to apologize, only to snap it shut when her arms crossed defiantly.

Her chin kicked up a notch.

"What did you expect, Bishop? A medal?"

What?

He understood the source of his own anger—namely his still throbbing groin—but what in God's name was driving hers? He yanked off his field cap and raked his hands through his filthy hair as the hurt in Eve's gaze cut into him more deeply that her fury had. He balled up his cap and tossed it onto the counter. It slid down the length, coming to a halt just shy of a small framed photograph propped at the far side.

The glass was cracked in several places, as if it had been thrown against a wall or the floor. Even so, he could make out the faces of five smiling women. Though the picture was too far away for him to be certain Eve and Carrie were among the women, he'd bet his Ranger tab they were.

And suddenly Eve's anger and hurt made sense.

The crash investigation.

"*Get out.*"

He faced her reluctantly. "I'm sorry. I guess they showed you my statement. I know you're upset but—"

She stiffened. "Upset? Mister, you don't know the meaning of the word." She marched over to the counter and snatched up his field cap before spinning around to thrust it at him. "I said, *get out.*"

Rick stared at the camouflage fabric. From the way her fingers were clamped at the very edge of the cap's bill, it was obvious she wanted no part of him tainting her or her home. What had he expected?

He'd tarnished Carrie's reputation. Her career.

''Eve, I'm sorry. I know Carrie Evans was your friend, but the fact is, she panicked. Out of respect for my sergeant, I'd decided not to volunteer anything. Unfortunately, I was asked under oath. I had to tell the truth.'' There wasn't anything he could add, so he retrieved his hat and turned to the door. It was still gaping open from his fiasco of an entrance. He stared at the daisies crushed and scattered beyond.

He'd never brought a woman flowers before.

He doubted he'd ever attempt it again.

''Wh-what did you say?''

The shock in Eve's whisper stopped him in his tracks. He turned around slowly, afraid he'd misheard out of desperation. Afraid she hadn't spoken at all. He wasn't sure she had until she moved. She laid her hands on the counter carefully, as if she didn't trust herself to do anything else with them.

She kept her stare fused to her hands as she dragged in her breath. ''What are you talking about? *Who* panicked?''

''You mean…you haven't read my statement?''

Her gaze snapped up. Fury smoldered once again as she stared hard. ''If I had, would I be asking you to clarify it?''

No.

He took a step toward her. ''Eve, are you—''

Her hands shot out. ''Stop right there, Bishop. Let's get one thing clear right now. The only reason your ass isn't smarting from the weather-side of my door is because I need information. Information you apparently have. If you're willing to share it, fine. You can stay right there until *I'm* done asking the questions. Understand?''

The hell he did.

He had a few questions of his own. Questions that had been simmering in his brain and in his gut for six weeks now.

Evidently, they'd have to wait a bit longer.

He jerked a nod.

"Good. Now, as long as you've bothered to show your lying face, I'd like you to do me the courtesy of starting at the beginning. Right about the time you decided to destroy my career."

He blinked.

"Oh, don't look so indignant. Innocence does not become you. Much less when it's phony as hell."

That's it!

Grief or not, he'd had enough. She wasn't the only one who'd lost someone in that crash. He'd be damned if he'd let her get away with calling him a liar—especially when he had no idea what he was supposed to have lied about. He stepped up to the counter, well into her personal space, and slapped his camouflage cap down next to her. "Where do you get off impugning my integrity?"

To his surprise, she didn't give an inch as she matched his searing glare. "Me? Where do you get off, showing up at my door dripping with apologies and flowers? Frankly, I'm surprised you're not out celebrating. Then again, I was told your company finished its tour of duty and was headed home. Maybe you haven't heard the news. If so, let me be the first to congratulate you. You got your revenge. You'll be thrilled to know my wings were stripped. I've been grounded as of yesterday—because of *you*." She reached past the photograph and grabbed the portable phone from its base unit. "Now get out of my apartment before I call the police."

He didn't budge.

She slammed the phone onto the counter. "Dammit, Bishop! Unless you've gone deaf since I saw you last, you heard me!"

"I heard you."

Given the fact that the front door was still yawning open behind him, half the apartment complex had probably heard her. He opted not to mention that as he studied her—really studied her—for the first time since he'd arrived. He took his time, noting everything about her from the tangled curls she'd yet to comb, to her pale complexion, to the gray Army T-shirt and shorts that seemed to swallow up her too-petite frame.

She looked like hell.

Grief had exacted a relentless toll on the woman's features these past six weeks. While Eve still wasn't wearing makeup, frankly, she needed it. Then again, he wasn't even sure a stick of cammo could disguise the dark circles that had taken up residence beneath her eyes. He knew it would take more than grease paint to conceal the rest of the hollows he saw. She'd lost quite a few pounds, too. Pounds she could ill afford. The woman he'd met out on that LZ had been stunning.

This one was nothing but hollows, cheeks and eyes.

Stark, shadowed eyes.

She was hanging by a thread. A thread she truly believed he'd helped fray. That bothered him most of all.

So much so, there was only one thing to do.

Eve sucked in her breath, stunned, as Rick severed his stare and finally turned around and headed for the door. Stunned not because he was leaving, but at the disappointment that shafted through her as he reached the tiny foyer. It was as unexpected as he'd been unwelcome. Or was he?

Dammit, what *had* she expected?

After all, she'd ordered him to leave.

And now he was doing it.

She turned her back on him and abandoned the kitchen, crossing the apartment's small but open floor plan before she could change her mind. She reached the living room all too soon and sank into her couch, sighing as she buried her face in her hands. She flinched as the front door clicked shut.

The sound was so...final.

It was all so ironic it wasn't even funny. Rick Bishop had been on her mind more than she wanted to admit these past few weeks. From the moment she'd regained consciousness in that screaming ambulance, she'd been thinking about him. Especially when she'd learned that he'd returned to the jungle.

She'd wondered if he was safe.

She'd wondered if the gash on his head had healed properly.

She'd wondered if his heart had healed at all.

She'd known Rick for less than a day but, somehow, she didn't think he was the sort to pour out his grief over losing his platoon sergeant to just anyone. If he shared it at all, it would be with someone special. Unfortunately, from their conversation while she'd been stitching his head, she gathered he didn't have anyone. At least, not at the moment.

She'd thought about contacting him after everything settled down—until she'd realized which way the investigation board was leaning. And why. From that moment on, she'd prayed that Rick would contact her and soon. She'd secretly hoped he'd show up like some long-lost white knight of old, riding onto post at the last minute to save the day or in her case, her career.

He'd shown up all right.

A day late and a recanted statement short.

With flowers, no less.

As if a bunch of daisies would ease the humiliation of having her wings stripped and, worse, being offered some half-assed, out-of-the-way job to quietly serve out the remainder of her military commitment. She'd joined the Army to fly choppers, not sit at a damned desk. Eve sighed.

First Carrie and now this.

*You're not alone.*

Really? Then why did it feel like she was?

Except, it didn't.

Just as she had when she'd wrenched herself from that damned dream hours before, she swore she could feel someone's presence. But this time it wasn't Carrie's. Certain her imagination was playing tricks on her, she forced her eyes open and faced her empty apartment. It wasn't empty.

And that was no angel.

"I thought I told you to leave."

Either Rick Bishop really had gone deaf these past weeks, or he'd chosen to ignore her yet again—because when he'd left the rectangle of oak that served as her apartment's foyer, it was to step into the apartment, not outside it.

Of all the nerve.

She stiffened, determined to vault off the sofa and knock him down and drag him out by his combat boots if that's what it took. A split second later she froze as something hot and wet slid down her cheeks.

Tears.

She wasted precious seconds scrubbing them from her cheeks as discreetly as she could. By the time she lowered her hands, his boots were directly in front of her running shoes, the cuffs of his sweat-stained jungle-fatigue trousers still perfectly bloused despite a ten-hour flight in a C-130.

"Eve?"

She stared at the deep gouge cutting into the toe of his left boot before shifting her attention to the right. The shine on both had succumbed to San Sebastián's damp jungle undergrowth during the past month. She studied the remaining nicks and scratches on the leather uppers before moving on to the meshed green nylon side panels. If she stared long enough, he just might take the hint.

He finally sighed.

She ignored that, too.

Camouflage filled her view as he hunkered down to one
knee. "Eve?" He tipped her chin and trapped her gaze. He
searched silently for several long moments as she tried her
damnedest to ignore the heat in his hand as well as the
concern in those deep-brown eyes. "What happened?"

She sighed. "You know what happened. Stop pretending—"

His thumb covered her lips, pressing in softly as he
shook his head. "I don't. Tell me."

She stared into the truth burning steadily in his gaze.

He really didn't know.

But how?

According to the senior officer on the investigation
board, it was Rick's statement that had sealed her fate. She
closed her eyes again as he withdrew his thumb from her
lips, swallowing hard as she felt his hand settle on her
shoulder.

Gently, encouragingly.

She drew her breath in slowly and forced the words past
the lump of betrayal and shame clogging her throat. "The
board ruled that I caused the crash. That it was pilot error.
They based their decision on your statement."

"But I never said that."

She opened her eyes. "You may as well have. You told
the investigator who tracked you down at the San Sebastián
border that Carrie must have fought for control of the chopper and that that's why I never pulled pitch." It was the
latter comment that had sealed her fate. "The board believes that if I'd pulled pitch in time, the subsequent auto-
rotation of the chopper's blades would have softened the
landing enough to have given my crew and passengers a
chance at survival."

In other words, pilot error. Her error.

Her fault.

He shook his head. "Eve, the statement I signed said I

believed it was copilot error. *Carrie's* error, not yours. I know what I saw. You two were arguing—''

''Yes. We argued.'' It was something she'd never forget.

Just before the engine quit, she'd yelled at Carrie and dressed her down about her friend's attention to detail—or rather, her attention to Sergeant Turner. Her last words before the crash had been spoken in anger. It didn't matter that Carrie had forgiven her with her dying breath. She would never forgive herself.

''Why did you cover up your argument?''

*Because of the baby.*

She stared at the photo taken their senior year, minutes after their commissioning. Even now, she couldn't afford to let the truth out. Especially now. Telling Bishop or the board about Carrie's pregnancy wouldn't save her career. But it would destroy Carrie's memory and her reputation. It would also prevent Eve from fulfilling her best friend's final wish.

Carrie had asked to be buried beside Turner.

Unfortunately, Eve wouldn't be able to accomplish that any time soon. The same attempted coup that had kept the Córdoban army from searching for her Black Hawk after the crash—and had kept Rick and his platoon patrolling the San Sebastián border afterwards—had also prevented the American ambassador from retrieving the bodies. If the U.S. Army brass learned about the baby and decided to make an example of Carrie and Sergeant Turner after the fact, she'd never be able to honor the request. Not with Turner already scheduled to be buried near his father in a military cemetery outside Midland, Texas.

''Eve?''

She tore her gaze from the counter. Maybe Rick hadn't noticed she'd been staring at the photo. Maybe he didn't know there was more to that crash than she could ever share.

*Right.*

She had a feeling nothing escaped that dark, steady stare. A stare that was focused solely on her. It rattled her nerves so badly she didn't dare risk opening her mouth. She sat there on the sofa, instead. Just as she had before the board yesterday morning, praying it would all go away.

Praying he would go away.

He didn't, any more than the board's decision had.

In fact, the longer she remained silent, the more closely he watched—and the deeper his fingers bit into her shoulders. She didn't care. Impatience she could handle, even anger.

Hell, she could have even dealt with abuse.

But not his pleading.

"Don't you realize I can see what's going on inside you? How much this has you tied up in knots?" He pulled his hands from her shoulders and slipped them beneath her chin, once again trapping her. "I just wish I could see into your mind."

For a moment, she swore he could.

Unable to bear that commanding mix of pain and persuasion a moment longer, she shifted her gaze, only to collide with the jagged pink scar he'd earned that fateful day six weeks before. This close, she could see the tiny holes where her thread had been. The gash had healed well. But the scar was obviously still new. Raw. As if the nerves beneath hadn't quite managed to heal.

She knew the feeling.

His thumbs smoothed the skin at her jaw, eroding her resolve. "Tell me what you're hiding, Eve. Let me help you. *Please.*"

She closed her eyes and shook her head.

"If you don't care about your career, then do it for me. You owe me. I lost the best sergeant I had in that crash. I also lost a friend. I've already sent his mother a letter. Now that I'm home, I've got a follow-up call to make. Give me something I can tell her. Someone deserves to sleep at night.''

*A grandchild.*

A baby with Carrie's dark curls and Turner's blue eyes. Eve pushed the sight from her mind. She had to.

For Carrie and for Sergeant Turner.

She pushed Rick's hands from her shoulders and sprang up from the sofa, rounding her coffee table before he could stop her. There, she filled her lungs with desperately needed air. Air that didn't carry Rick's subtle woodsy scent.

Only then did she turn to face him.

''I told you in the jungle. Carrie did nothing wrong. Yes, we argued. We both know her head wasn't into flying that day, but that had nothing to do with the crash. I swear it. Once I initiated crash procedures, Carrie did exactly as I ordered. Her behavior might have had a lot to do with where that chopper went down, but it didn't have a thing to do with how.''

''Then why didn't you pull pitch?''

''I *did.*''

''Eve—''

''Dammit, Bishop. They told me what you said. I don't care what you think you felt—or rather, what you think you didn't. I pulled pitch.''

He tracked her around the coffee table, stopping short when she backed away farther, this time all the way to the kitchen. He raked his fingers through his hair and pulled them down to knead the base of his neck as he sighed. ''Sometimes in the heat of battle soldiers do things they later swear they didn't, mainly because they don't remember doing it. Maybe the reverse happened to you. Maybe you've just trained to crash-land a chopper so many times that when it actually happened—''

''Read my lips! How many times do I have to say it?

Without that bird I can't prove a blasted thing, but I *know* I hauled back on that collective. *I pulled pitch.*''

Rick stared at Eve, stunned by the absolute conviction burning within her gaze. The devil with her gaze, it burned within every inch of her body.

It practically radiated off her.

She truly believed she hadn't screwed up. He knew it as surely as he knew she was withholding something crucial about Carrie Evans. Until their rescue chopper had hit that thermal pocket over San Sebastián's capital, he hadn't realized what had been missing from the crash. But from that second on, he'd been positive he hadn't felt her Black Hawk pull pitch.

Was he wrong?

Was he the one who couldn't remember what had really happened during the heat of the moment? His heart had been pounding fairly fast and furious as they'd screamed down into the trees. Had he truly missed the sudden, cushioning lift seconds before they'd hit? Or was it possible that the crack to his skull had left more than another scar?

Had it left a faulty memory?

"You don't believe me."

He blinked. Until that moment, he hadn't realized he'd been staring at the group photograph on the counter beside her. He jerked his attention from the cracked glass and stared into her eyes. The resignation he found cut him to the bone.

"Yes—no." He shook his head. "I don't know."

*Damn.* He hadn't meant for it to come out that baldly.

She stiffened. "Wh-what did you say?"

The hope in her eyes cut almost as deep. It would have been so easy to give her what she wanted. So much so, it scared the daylights out of him. He forced himself to choose his words carefully, determined to give her what she deserved and nothing less. The truth.

"I believe that you believe you pulled pitch."

She stood there for several moments, silent.

And then she nodded. "Thank you. I'll admit, that's not the ringing endorsement I'd like, but I'll take it." She slid her hand across the counter and retrieved the picture. His heart tightened inexplicably as her neatly filed nails traced the silver vines that framed the photo. She sighed. "A lot of good it'll do. What I really need is proof." Her fingers traced the frame again but this time they trembled.

Before he realized what he was doing, he reached out, his own fingers closing over hers before he could stop them. When she didn't recoil from his touch, he squeezed gently, struck silent by the sudden, intense need to see these too-slender hands as they'd been less than two months ago. As Eve had been. Confident, capable.

Content.

The moment she'd fired up that chopper back on that LZ, he'd known that Eve Paris was a woman who'd found her calling in life and gloried in it. The woman standing two inches in front of him was not the real Eve. This was an empty shell.

Dammit, he wanted her back.

He might never be able to breathe life into his sergeant again, but he just might be able do it for Eve.

She needed proof? "Go get it."

The photo clattered to the floor. "What did you say?"

"You heard me."

"I heard you. I just can't believe you're suggesting what I think you're suggesting."

"I am."

She pulled her hands from his and stepped back as she gaped up at him. "You're nuts."

He had to grin at that. "No, I'm Special Forces. Though I have heard it's the same thing." He stepped up to the counter, committing himself to the rapidly forming plan in

his head even before he had a chance to think through the
details. He'd planned enough missions over the years to
know it would work.

It was also the only way.

"You said it yourself, Eve. Without examining that bird
there's no way to prove anything. So let's go do it."

"*Let's?*" She shook her head. "Uh-uh. No way. Even
if I do decide to put my ass on the line, there is no way
I'm letting you do the same. My career is already over.
Yours isn't. But it will be if you get caught."

He cracked another grin. "If you have so little faith in
me, why'd you let me lead you out of there the first time?"

"Dammit, Bishop, this is serious!"

So was he.

He'd also made up his mind. "Trust me."

"I already did." From the pain shafting through her
whisper, she wasn't talking about the jungle anymore.

"Eve—"

"I said, *no*."

He did what any Special Forces soldier would do under
the circumstances. He changed his tactics.

"You need me."

Unfortunately, all that earned him was a snort. "The hell
I do. You might be able to rig a bridge to blow up at
precisely five seconds to midnight with your hands tied
behind your back, but you don't know squat about examining the remains of a charred chopper."

"I do know how to survive in the jungle undetected."

Silence.

When it deepened, he knew he'd managed to sway the
battle with that one. It was time to turn the tide on the war.

"Sergeant Turner."

She flinched.

As anticipated, the man's name drove home the obvious.
He might not have quite as much of a stake in the outcome

as she did, but it was close. Rick ignored the fresh stab of pain and guilt at using his platoon sergeant like this. Of all men, Turner would have understood. There was no way he was letting Eve go back into that jungle without protection.

*His* protection.

Nor was this mission about her alone.

Rick reached down and snagged the picture from the floor. Carrie Evans grinned up at him as he laid the frame on the counter between them. He'd told the truth. He needed to know why Bill Turner had died. For reasons Eve would never know.

"Okay."

He snapped his gaze to hers, relieved at what he found. She was serious. Committed. To the mission and, for the moment at least, to him. "Good. I signed out on three weeks leave shortly before I showed up at your door. You?"

"Two weeks starting yesterday, ostensibly to finish healing." She scowled. "I'm really supposed to be making up my mind about a desk job. I can call in and extend if I need to. I've got two more weeks on the books."

"Take one, just to be safe. Gear?"

"The usual."

He nodded. He'd take care of the unusual. He retrieved his field cap from the counter. "I've got a couple of buddies I can look up. I should be able to arrange a country outside the States for us to pre-stage in." Somewhere he could obtain the unusual…no questions asked.

"No."

"Eve—"

She shook her head. "This is a joint op from the start or it doesn't go down at all. That means I handle the actual insertion and extraction, if it comes to that." Her brow lifted. "Unless you have a problem with me at the stick?"

Given the circumstances, he figured she had the right to

ask. "Not at all. But I am curious as to how you plan on obtaining a chopper on such short notice, along with a pilot willing to risk his or her neck."

She turned the photo around so he could get a better look. Five women in dress uniforms stood arm-in-arm, grinning into the camera on what was probably commissioning day. The founding members of the Sisters-in-Arms. He studied the three faces he didn't recognize and placed his bet on the woman on the far right. She was closest to Eve's height, but as dark as Eve was light. Definitely Hispanic.

He didn't remember her name.

She tapped the woman in dress whites. "Meet Anna Shale. Lieutenant, U.S. Navy. She's half Panamanian. She spent half her childhood there. I thought Anna was still in San Diego, but she's not. When I got home, I called to tell her about Carrie and learned she'd been transferred to Panama. Temporary duty as a military attaché with the embassy in Panama City. If I remember correctly, Anna has family there, too. I'll know more by tonight, including how much she can help. I'll call you."

"Agreed."

He donned his field cap. If this was a go, he had a lot to do. Better get started. He was amazed at how easily they fell into sync with one another as Eve turned to follow him to the front door. It was as if they'd never left the jungle.

It should have scared him, but it didn't.

In fact he was so at ease with her, he didn't think twice about bending down to pluck one of the daisies that had survived its trip to the cold concrete on the opposite side of the door. It wasn't until he held it out to her that he realized his mistake. He held his breath as she stared at the flower, knowing full well she, too, felt the sudden undertow that swirled around them. What if she didn't accept it?

What if she did?

He'd meant for the bunch of flowers to comfort her. To help ease her pain over losing Carrie. To ease the guilt he knew she still bore. What did this single daisy mean?

He had no idea.

Hell, he wasn't fooling anyone. Least of all, himself.

He might have told himself all the way to that blasted floral shop that his sole purpose had been to ease Eve's pain, but he was lying. Yes, he'd wanted to cheer her up. But he'd also wanted to see her. Needed to. Maybe then he'd be able to get that kiss out of his head, to get her out.

He'd failed.

As much as he should not want this woman, he did.

More than he'd ever wanted another.

Her hand came up, only to halt in midair. He swallowed his disappointment as she glanced up at him and flushed. While the color warmed her skin, her wariness and reluctance were painfully obvious. To his relief, she reached out again, her fingers brushing his as she took the daisy from his hand.

"Thank you."

His breath hitched, caught somewhere between confusion and desire as the petals skimmed the pulse beating at the base of her neck. He cleared his throat.

"Sanitize everything."

She blinked. But then she nodded briskly.

Relief flooded him as he realized that she'd slipped into sync with him once again as they returned to familiar, military ground. It was for the best.

They were soldiers.

Soldiers about to depart on a private, unauthorized mission. If they were caught inside enemy territory, they'd damned well better have picked their gear and clothing clean, removing anything and everything that could tag them as U.S. Army—or worse, give away their individual identities. It was the only way to ensure that no one knew they were ever there.

Whether or not they made it out alive.

# Chapter 6

The room screamed honeymoon suite.

The doorknob slipped from Eve's jet-lagged fingers, clicking shut behind her as shock reverberated down her spine. She stared at the cozy alcove for two tucked neatly into the far corner of the room, the silver champagne bucket—bottle already on ice—resting atop an accent table beside the cherry armoire, the matching intricately carved king-sized four-poster that dominated the room. There was no doubt about it. This was a bridal chamber if there ever was one. Even the mosquito netting cascading down from the twelve-foot ceiling had been spun so finely it resembled a wedding veil.

What on earth was going on?

When Anna had offered to make all the arrangements on her end in Panama, Eve had clearly told her sorority sister to make the hotel reservations for separate rooms—twice.

Eve stared at the key card in her hand.

This had to be the right room.

If it wasn't, the magnetic strip wouldn't have deactivated the door's lock. Her gaze slid to the white eyelet bedspread and pristine heart-shaped pillows that completed the virginal effect. God only knew what Bishop would think when he arrived. While they'd managed to schedule the same departing flight from Nashville earlier that morning, they'd been forced to take separate, connecting flights from Houston this afternoon to Panama City. The flights should have arrived within minutes of each other. Unfortunately, hers had been delayed. Maybe Bishop's had been, too. Eve spun around. Maybe she could change the rooms before he—

Too late.

She'd been so stunned she hadn't noticed the sound of running water until that moment, much less the suitcase sitting atop the valet chair beside the bathroom door. Both were open. The suitcase, all the way.

The door, roughly two feet.

It was far enough for her to catch a glimpse of Rick as he shaved the last, narrow strip of shaving cream from his neck. He tossed the disposable razor to the back of the marble sink before twisting the left knob, reducing the amount of steam rising up from the flow of water. The muscles of his back rippled as he leaned over to splash a handful of water onto his face. She stood there, seared to the spot by the unexpected rush of desire that swept through her.

Curiosity fanned the flames as he straightened.

If the man's chest was half as impressive as his back...

Reality slammed into her, cold and hard, as he reached for his gray dress shirt and pulled it on. What was she thinking, standing here, ogling this man? They were returning to Córdoba for answers, not to engage in a bout of steaming jungle sex. But before she could clear her throat and make her presence known, he glanced into the oval mirror.

His gaze met hers.

She swore his fingers fumbled on the buttons of his shirt. It must have been her imagination, because he snagged his tie from the towel rod, looping it around his neck as he turned smoothly about. He pushed the door wide as he stepped into the bedroom.

"We're late."

"I know." She swallowed her lingering shock and crossed the room to dump her suitcase on the bed. "My plane sat on the runway in Houston for almost an hour and then I got stuck in customs on this end."

His hands froze in the middle of buttoning his left cuff. "Why?"

"Relax. Everything went fine." She slipped off her sandals, staring at the pile of pillows at the headboard as she dug her toes into the carpet. What she wouldn't give to crawl up under the covers and sleep for a week. Rick had finished buttoning his cuffs and was tucking his shirt into the waist of his black trousers as she turned around. "The ID your buddy dropped off didn't even raise a brow. It was more a case of screwing with the little woman—or trying to."

He frowned as he knotted his tie. "I told you we should have waited for another flight. A woman with your looks was bound to attract attention in this part of the world."

Her looks?

From the way he'd gruffly ordered her to eat before he'd left her apartment yesterday, she didn't think he thought she was capable of attracting anyone's attention, much less holding it. Especially his.

"Blond."

"Of course." She squelched her disappointment as she turned to unzip her suitcase. Hadn't he as much as told her in the jungle all those weeks ago that she wasn't his type?

Yes, they'd shared a kiss.

Okay, one hell of a soul-torching kiss.

So what?

She wasn't some naive kid. Adrenaline did funny things to people. So did grief and shock. They'd been riding a roller coaster forged of all three for a good twelve hours by the time he'd covered her lips with his. If the man kissed her again right here, right now, she doubted the contact would carry half the electricity their first kiss had.

Not that he'd want to.

But for a single, blinding moment yesterday she'd thought differently. As he'd held out that daisy at the door to her apartment, she could have sworn he was considering it, considering them. But then it was gone.

The flower had been a peace offering, nothing more.

To her surprise, the disappointment cut deeply.

"Eve?"

The daisy disintegrated from her view as she blinked. Her suitcase assumed its place. She whirled about. "I know, I know. We're late. You've seen Anna's picture. The restaurant is supposed to be across the street from the main lobby. Go on ahead. I'll meet you in ten minutes, fifteen tops."

His brow shot up at her rumpled T-shirt and jeans.

"I promise. Now go—and hurry. I spoke to Anna during my layover. Something's come up. She can't stay long."

His scar furrowed as he frowned. "Why?"

"I don't know, but it has nothing to do with us."

"How can you be so sure?"

"Because she told me." She knew he wasn't comfortable letting Anna handle the arrangements, but this was ridiculous. Not to mention unwarranted. "Dammit, Bishop, we don't have time to revisit twenty questions. Will you please leave?"

She held her breath as his gaze captured hers. Probed.

He finally nodded.

She waited until the bedroom door closed before she returned to her suitcase and that god-awful bed, a bed that had obviously been designed with sex and not sleep in mind. A bed so spacious, she would be obligated to suggest they share it. She had no idea if Bishop would agree. If she was lucky, Anna would be waiting for them with their supplies and gear already good to go—before she was forced to find out.

"You're sleeping with her."

Rick jerked his gaze from the retreating waiter and fused it to the woman seated across from him. He hadn't even had a chance to pull his chair up to the table and get comfortable. Just as well. Anna Shale's statement had killed any chance of that. He masked the suspicion that had been eating at him since he discovered he and Eve had been booked into one of Panama's premiere honeymoon suites and reached for the bottle of spring water waiting beside his goblet. He raised his brow as he twisted off the foil cap.

"I beg your pardon?"

To his surprise, the woman flushed.

"I'm sorry. I didn't mean for it to come out that crudely. It's just, we don't have a lot of time. *I* don't have a lot of time. But I do have a lot I need to tell you—and Eve." She glanced past his shoulder and scanned the room behind him.

Suspicion flared again.

She might want him to think she was searching for Eve, but she wasn't. For one thing, that dark, tense gaze had shifted to his right, away from the double doors that marked the entrance to Enrique's restaurant and well into range of the smaller doors of the connecting bar.

Who was she looking for? And what was she so afraid of?

Because she *was* afraid.

Though Anna was actively working to conceal her fear, it was there. It was more than the fact that she'd bypassed the chair the waiter had offered in order to take the seat at the far side of the table instead—the seat that offered the choicest view of the restaurant behind him—it was the way she'd taken it. Like a cop or an undercover agent, or an operative on or off the job. Not like a woman about to be reunited with an old college friend.

And then there was the matter of her bodyguard—a local—looming not quite discreetly two tables away.

Military attaché, his ass.

Something was going down and it had nothing to do with Eve or him. Sorority sister or not, he settled into his leather chair, determined to find out what it was before he entrusted his safety and Eve's to this woman. "Eve will be arriving shortly. Until then, why don't you save time and fill me in? You can start with your comment…and that room."

Her gaze swung to his.

He knew immediately she hadn't found whoever she'd been searching for.

"It was the best I could come up with on short notice."

"Best?"

"Cover." Her attention slipped past his shoulder for the briefest of seconds, then returned. "I'm assuming you two would rather conceal your intentions."

He nodded. "Of course." He was definitely in favor of protecting their careers if at all possible.

"I thought so." She slipped a strand of dark hair into the loose twist at the base of her neck and leaned into the table, for the first time affording him her complete attention since they'd met in the foyer. She lowered her voice until it skirted below the strains of the classical guitar floating out from the dance floor in the corner of the room. "It'll go down like this. You and Eve came down here for one reason and one reason alone. Hot, passionate sex. I want your hands all over her from the second she arrives. Touch her, kiss her, dance with her, whatever it takes. By the time you two head back to your room, we need every person in this restaurant to believe you both want nothing more than the chance to hole yourselves up on that bed and spend the next two weeks setting the sheets on fire. Can you handle that?''

Handle it?

His temperature shot up sixty degrees just thinking about it. It had been far too long since he'd had sex.

He swallowed firmly. ''Done. Why?''

''Because someone *will* be in your room. As you two leave by the maintenance elevator minutes before 0400 tomorrow morning, he'll be arriving. The first thing he'll do is hang up the Do Not Disturb sign. It'll stay there the entire time you're gone. He'll order for two and eat for two, leaving the empty bottles of wine and champagne and the trays outside the door along with enough used towels for the maid to believe you and Eve had sex in the tub at least twice a day.''

Eve Paris wearing nothing but bubbles.

His temp shot up another sixty degrees.

He bypassed the thick green goblet beside his linen napkin and took a long pull on the water bottle instead.

It didn't help.

Who was this woman? And how the hell had she managed to plan—and staff—*this?* He was about to ask when Anna shot to her feet, her smile mile-wide and downright beaming.

''Eve!''

Rick came to his feet, turned—and stiffened. He didn't know which stunned him more. That Eve had managed to sneak up on Anna despite her succession of furtive glances, or the absolute shock that rocked through him at seeing Eve in a dress and heels for the very first time.

Dress, hell.

That black sheath Anna wore was a dress.

The stretchy scrap of flesh-colored fabric Eve had donned was little more than a backless slip with sleeves. It didn't cover her, it clung to her, finding curves and dips that a day before he'd never have believed existed. Even her face had filled out since he'd seen her in the hotel room—though he suspected that was an illusion drawn and shaded in by the touch of makeup she'd applied to her eyes and cheeks and the pink gloss she'd slicked across her lips.

"You look *gorgeous*."

For a split second, he was afraid he'd breathed the words aloud. A moment later he realized that by God's grace, he hadn't. They'd come from Anna as she threw her arms around Eve and hugged her as tightly as he'd wanted to the moment Eve had opened her apartment door the day before. The memory of her response slapped him down hard.

He might be experiencing an intense and thoroughly inappropriate case of lust, but it was an act.

Or so Eve would have to believe.

Determined to get the worst of the charade over with, he stepped up to the women and reached out, slipping his hands around Eve's as she stepped away from Anna's arms. He pulled her smoothly into his own arms and leaned down to press his lips intimately to her temple. Before she could flinch, he slid his mouth to her ear, his breath much too hot for his own sanity as he whispered, "Relax. We're lovers."

"We're *what?*"

At least she hadn't shouted.

He spun her gently around and guided her into the leather chair to the right of his. Anna sat as well, leaning into Eve's opposite ear as she quickly filled her in on the plan. He knew she'd reached the crucial part when Eve stiffened. Her eyes met his in total and almost emasculating disbelief.

"You honestly think people are going to believe we flew down here just so we could hole up for a marathon session of sex?"

"By the time we leave tonight, they will." He covered her hand with his, smoothly linking their fingers. "Now *relax*." He punctuated the command with a quick squeeze before nudging their hands beneath the table. Unfortunately, their bodies were so close, his fingers came to rest on her thigh, not his.

Her *naked* thigh.

Logically, he knew the dress still covered her body because this close up he could see the flecks of green and burnished gold that had been woven into the fabric. Unfortunately, he couldn't feel it—and his hand was damned high up on her thigh. Which meant the hem of her dress had ridden higher.

The heck with Eve, he was the one who needed to relax.

He turned to Anna, doubly anxious to get this over with.

"The chopper? Our gear?"

Anna leaned forward, adjusting a gold necklace as she got down to business. "It's all set. A taxi will pick you up at the staff entrance at exactly 0400 tomorrow morning. You'll be driven to a private airstrip. From there, you'll be given the gear you requested and then you'll board the Huey. Once the chopper inserts you both at the position you've requested, the pilot will head home and wait. You'll have seventy-two hours to check in at the number keyed in on the cell phone he'll provide you with. Don't worry, it's encrypted. You can fine-tune your extraction then."

"How?" He didn't bother elaborating for either woman. They both knew exactly what he was asking.

Anna stared at him for several moments, as if gauging how much she should tell him, how much she could.

She finally nodded.

"I'm sure Eve told you I've been staying with my cousin while I'm assigned down here. What she couldn't have told you, because she didn't know, is that my cousin has connections. Connections that aren't exactly…respected. Once I downloaded the file containing the list of your requirements, it was obvious the best way to help you was not to go through the regular but obscure channels we discussed, but to go through my cousin. He's agreed to help."

His earlier suspicion snapped back. A hundredfold.

"Why?"

Anna held his gaze steadily for several more moments, then shrugged. "Good question. Unfortunately, it's one I can't answer at the moment. What I can do is fulfill your request." Her gaze narrowed, steadied. "Are you still interested?"

He felt Eve's thigh tense beneath his hand. She was afraid he was going to walk. He might. If he didn't get the answers he needed. "What do we owe your cousin in return?"

"Nothing."

He felt more than saw Eve blink.

He just smiled. "Try again."

Anna glanced at Eve. "Is he always this suspicious?"

"*Yes.*"

He flicked his gaze to Eve, not so much surprised they'd answered in unison, but at her certainty. She flushed beneath his stare and shifted, sending his hands precariously close to the one spot it had no business seeking.

Her flush deepened.

So did the silken heat beneath his hand.

As he inched his fingers away from the danger zone, he was aware that Anna's wandering stare had once again moved beyond his shoulder. Had she anticipated his distraction when she formed her plans? Did she need it?

If so, she'd gotten it.

While he'd played this game many times before, he'd never done it with his hand a hair's-breadth from the apex of Eve's thighs. It was playing hell with his concentration.

Eve *was* playing hell with his concentration.

He shifted his hand once more, this time executing a full retreat. He hooked his arm around Eve's shoulders instead and trailed his fingers down the curve of her neck. She tensed as he moved to trace her collarbone, as if absently. Her flesh was softer here, smoother, but cooler.

His concentration returned.

"Expecting someone?"

Anna's dark gaze shot to his. "Of course not."

"Then answer my question."

"Rick, *please*."

He ignored the hiss. Sorority sisters or not, even Eve couldn't believe that some absentee cousin of Anna's would be willing to front their entire mission without expecting something in return. He sure as hell didn't. "Look, lady. I don't care how good a friend you are. This guy may be your cousin, but he's still a man. He's not sticking his hand into a puddle this deep and this muddy without knowing he can fish out something he wants in return. Now, *what* do I owe him?"

"I told you, nothing."

He tugged his arm from Eve's shoulders and grabbed her arm, pulling her to her feet along with him as he stood. Just as he was about to reject Anna's help and supplies, he caught sight of the sudden panic that snaked through her eyes.

It must have been instinct.

Before he realized his intent, he'd released Eve's arm and spun around. Shock ripped through him as he stared.

Recognized.

There might be fifty feet and thirty-some-odd tables between them, but it was him all right. Just inside the bar, mingling with natives and tourists alike, stood the man Anna had been searching for all evening—Captain Tom Wild, U.S. Army. He was certain of it when Tom stared back.

Openly.

What the devil was Tom Wild doing here, in Panama City, with his hair five shades lighter than the color the good Lord had given him? Just *don't* let him be on the job.

But he was.

The subtle twist of Tom's hand confirmed his worst fears. Delta Force had a deep and abiding interest in the one woman to whom he'd spilled his plans to reinsert Eve and himself into Córdoba. Bloody hell. What was he going to do now?

"Rick?"

He ignored Anna's query and turned to Eve. "I need to use the latrine. Be just a minute."

Eve stared in disbelief at Rick's departing back.

The latrine?

They were finally in Panama, in the middle of solidifying plans that would either reinstate her career—or kill both of theirs—and he had to go to the bathroom? She watched, amazed as he reached the restaurant's foyer and hung a left through the doorway that led to the rest rooms she'd noticed on her way in. She turned, only to become even more amazed at how much the man's departure had transformed her friend.

Though they hadn't seen each other in two years, Eve could have sworn Anna had been on edge since she'd arrived.

Was it coincidence?

Or had Rick said something before she'd arrived that set her friend off? She knew Anna didn't dislike him. She'd have picked up on that. Maybe Anna was suddenly nervous

with how far she'd stuck out her neck on their behalf?
Except, that didn't make sense either. Anna had offered her
help willingly.

At any rate, she seemed fine now.

But definitely concerned as they took their seats. "Are
you sure you trust that man to guide you to your chopper?"

"Yes."

She might have serious doubts about Rick's sanity at the
moment, but of his professional skills, she had none. It was
strange. Her innate trust of the man on that level was as
much a mystery to her as he was. Evidently it was a mystery to Anna as well, because she shook her head in disbelief.

"Wow. I never thought I'd see the day—"

"You haven't."

Anna's brows arched at her too-quick response, but she
remained silent. Unfortunately, that secret smile Eve had
gotten to know all too well in college spoke volumes.

Eve frowned. "I mean it."

"Did I say you didn't?"

"No, but you were thinking it."

If anything, Anna's smile deepened. "Wrong. I was
thinking how much he wasn't like your usual type."

There was no way she was going to touch that one.

Mostly because it was true.

She'd learned a long time ago to stick to guys who were
overtly footloose and fancy-free. The ones who went into
a relationship knowing they had no intention of staying and
were honest about it were even better. It tended to save
wear and tear on the heart when they lived up to their word
instead of breaking it. She smiled brightly as she shook out
her napkin and laid it on her lap. "So, what does a tourist
have to do to get a menu around here?"

Anna wisely took the hint. "We already ordered." She

lifted her hand. Moments later, a waiter appeared at their table, his bow slight but innately respectful.

Odd.

Especially given the way most of the native women had been treated by customs at the airport.

*"¿Señorita?"*

*"La comida, por favor."*

Another bow, and the man retreated.

"I asked him to bring dinner." Anna lifted the bottle of spring water beside her plate and winked as she cracked the seal. "I know I said we ordered. I should have said he. Either your tastes have changed or this new guy of yours is desperately trying to fatten you up. Not—" She swept Eve's face and torso frankly. "—that you couldn't use a few more pounds."

Yup, Anna was definitely back to normal.

"My tastes haven't changed, and Rick Bishop is not my guy." Eve shifted her scowl across the room to avoid another of those blasted secret smiles.

Still no sign of Rick.

Just how long did it take a Green Beret to powder his nose, anyway?

Long enough to put this one in a better mood, she hoped.

Speaking of the man's mood, there was only one thing that stood a chance of improving it. An answer. She waited while Anna leaned over to retrieve her purse before asking the question. But as her friend straightened, she no longer needed to ask. As Anna adjusted her necklace, Eve spied the charm dangling from the end of her stunning gold necklace. With it, came her answer.

She gasped.

Seconds later Anna tucked the gold charm beneath the understated neck of her dress, but not before the ruby winked at Eve—a single telltale ruby that dripped like blood from the tip of a scorpion's deadly stinger. The sight was more than enough to confirm her worst fears. No wonder Anna rarely mentioned her cousin. If she was wearing that scorpion, the man didn't just have connections. He *was* the connection.

Sweet Mother in Heaven. "Rick was right. We're going to owe—"

Anna's hands shot out, encircling her wrists. "No."

"But—"

"Honey, I swear to you on Carrie's grave, you won't. I meant what I said. You two owe him *nothing*."

"But...why? How?"

Anna smoothed her hand down the neck of her dress, the determination in her eyes as black as the fabric beneath her fingers. "Because Luis owes me."

Eve swallowed the bile threatening at the base of her throat. "Then why do you wear that—that—thing."

"Protection."

Eve couldn't help it. She scanned the room quickly, praying she was searching discreetly.

"Don't worry. My shadow finally left."

"Don't worry?" Eve twisted her hands around until she was gripping Anna's. "I call you up out of the blue, spill out my woes without even bothering to pick up on yours and you're worried about me?"

"I'm glad to help. Right now, frankly, I need to. Eve, you've got to believe me. I'm fine. Nor are things as they seem right now. That's all I can say. You have to trust me."

Anna she trusted.

It was the woman's cousin she didn't.

Anna must have sensed her reluctance, because her hand took on the strength of a death grip. "Remember how you were there for Carrie when her mother passed away in college, no questions asked? Well, now I'm here for you. We all are. Samantha, Meg, me. I'm just the one in the position to help. All we needed was to know that you needed us. Now we do. *I* do. I have to leave soon to take care of something. Don't worry, your gear will be ready as promised. The Huey will be fueled and fired up. All you and Captain Bishop need to do is board that chopper. I'll take care of the rest from here."

"Who will take care of you?"

Anna stared at their hands for what seemed like an eternity. When she finally looked up, a light Eve had never seen before burned fiercely within her eyes. "You'd be surprised if I told you. But I can't. Can you trust me?"

"Always."

"Then go save your career and bring Carrie home."

*"She was pregnant."*

Anna stiffened.

Before her friend could open her mouth, before *she* lost her nerve, Eve forced the rest out. "The father was enlisted—and one of her regular passengers."

This time Anna just sat there, gaping at her.

Eve knew exactly how she felt.

She let go of Anna's hand and reached past her own empty water goblet and the fat, flickering candle in the middle of the table to grab Rick's full goblet. She wrapped her hands around it, somehow comforted by the thick heavy glass as she settled into her chair. "I'm sorry, I didn't mean it to come out like that. I wasn't even sure I should tell you. I didn't want to put you in the position of ever having to lie."

The tears that had been welling up in her friend's eyes slipped free as Anna finally closed her mouth. She sighed heavily. *"Bring them both home."*

"I will." If it was the last thing she ever did. She lifted her goblet and stared into the candle's flame as she drank, wishing the water could wash away her own tears.

"Eve?"

She set the glass on the table. "Yes?"

"Don't be careless with your life. We can't lose you, too. We all love you, you know. You're not alone."

Eve froze.

For a moment, she swore it was Carrie's whisper searing through her. But when she looked up, she realized it couldn't be. While Anna's hair was black, it wasn't short, and it wasn't layered with curls. And those soft, shining eyes weren't blue.

This wasn't Carrie Evans. This was Anna Shale.

Her *other* Sister.

With that realization came another, more startling one. One she should have made weeks ago. While this Sister sitting beside her might not have been her best friend in the world, she was a pretty damned good one just the same. Anna was right, just as Carrie had been. She had Meg and Sam, too.

She really wasn't alone.

For the first time in weeks, Eve could feel the heaviness easing from her heart.

Oh, it was still there.

The grief was still there. But she also knew that it was time to move on with it, not in spite of it. That it truly was okay to smile. To laugh, to love.

To live.

She scrubbed the tears from her cheeks and did just that. She reached out and wrapped her arms around her sister and felt the pure release of joy as Anna hugged her back just as tightly. The world seemed clearer as she pulled away, crisper. She was still trying to process the sounds of music, laughter and muted conversations that had somehow been dulled to her a mere minute before when Anna's stare snapped behind her.

"Is it—"

She shook her head. "It's your guy. He's coming back."

No! Not now.

She wasn't ready.

Even in the deepest, mind-numbing throes of her pain and grief, Rick had somehow managed to reach through and touch her. What would it be like now? How would she survive the onslaught of pure, naked sensation without the buffer?

Before she could blink, she found out.

His scent enveloped her first, then his heat as he leaned over the back of her chair. His breath swirled into the curve of her neck providing a split-second warning before his lips pressed softly into her flesh. Goose bumps rippled down her arms as he drew out the caress, leaving her grateful her dress had long, concealing sleeves. She locked her fingers around the linen napkin in her lap, holding on for dear life as blood surged through her veins at breakneck speed before flooding into the most embarrassingly intimate places.

*Get a grip.*

This was a charade. An act.

She stiffened her resolve, determined to see the mission through for Carrie's sake and her passengers', if not her career. She could do this. She could spend an hour in Rick's company, even stare into his eyes and graze her fingers down his shoulders and across his jaw every now and then. She could even turn her head and meet those dangerous lips ever-so-briefly if that's what it took to cover their tracks. She could do anything, as long as he didn't ask her to—

*"Dance with me."*

# Chapter 7

She was in trouble.

Eve knew it the moment her fingers touched Rick's outstretched palm. The electric shock that sparked between their flesh should have been enough to convince her to remain at Anna's side and hunker down for the count. But it wasn't.

And she didn't.

She did manage to avoid the magnetic pull in his eyes as she stood. Unfortunately, his other hand came up as she turned, compounding the assault on her senses as his fingers splayed out against the small of her naked back. This time, her flesh sparked with an entirely new sort of pain. She considered changing her mind, but it was too late. He'd already guided her away from Anna and the relative safety of their table. It was everything she could do to put one high-heeled foot in front of the other as he escorted her through the maze of tables that led to the small wooden dance floor at the far corner of the restaurant.

Halfway there, the canned music ceased.

She was certain she'd gained a reprieve...until the featured guitarist who'd been playing when she'd arrived retook the small stage.

Great.

Not only was she going to have to dance with Rick Bishop, she was going to have to do it in this dress. She wouldn't even have brought it had it not been for Anna's formal-clothing criteria. None of the others she owned would have made it though a customs inspection without needing a touch-up ironing afterwards.

Rick tipped his head down as they reached the edge of the dance floor. His warm breath filled her ear.

She promptly fumbled.

He snagged her elbow and smoothly righted her before she fell flat on her face. "I said, watch your step."

"Sorry. Couldn't hear you."

She'd been too busy feeling him.

Then again, that's probably what he'd intended.

Yes, he'd agreed to Anna's plan. But that was before he'd argued with the woman over her cousin. Eve sincerely doubted the eternity he'd spent in the bathroom had changed his mind. She was about to question him when his hands slipped around her waist. He drew her into his arms as the opening notes of a Spanish classical number floated across the floor. Trapped, she linked her hands behind his neck as he guided their bodies into a slow rhythm set by the elderly guitarist.

Oh, boy. This was not good.

Not good at all.

If Rick hoped to distract her, he was already succeeding. Her body fit far too easily against the hardened muscles of his chest and thighs for her peace of mind. She cleared her throat in a desperate attempt to clear her thoughts. "So, what took so long? They run out of paper towels?"

His scar furrowed.

"You were gone a long time."

His brow cleared as he nodded. "I stopped to help a couple of college kids place a call to the States."

No, he hadn't.

She wasn't sure how she knew, but she did. Maybe it was his eyes. He seemed to be staring at her too intently, almost as if he was waiting to see if she'd believe him.

Unfortunately, she couldn't call him on it.

Panama City would be in the throes of Carnaval in two days. The hotel lobby had been crowded by kids who'd already kicked off Spring Break. "You couldn't get through?"

"No, I did—they did. Why?"

She shrugged. "I don't know. You seem...distracted."

"You seem refreshed."

A definite change of subject.

Even more damning.

She smiled anyway. "It's amazing what a quick shower can do. And a long talk with a good friend." She glanced across the room toward their table, but several of the couples dancing alongside them obscured her view.

"She's gone."

She wasn't surprised. "I told you she couldn't stay."

Rick frowned. "Meaning you already agreed."

*Here it came.*

Might as well get it over with. Eve nodded. "I did. Look, I know we said we'd make the decisions together. But you also led me to believe you could trust me. Lord knows it's obvious you don't trust her. But *I* do. Frankly, that ought to count for something. I'm the one who's known the woman long enough to know that when Anna gives her word, it's worth something."

Unfortunately, she received nothing.

Just that blasted magnetic silence.

Rick continued to stare down at her. If anything, his gaze appeared darker and more impenetrable than ever.

What was the use?

She should have known better than to think Rick would ever trust her. She sighed. "It doesn't matter, does it? No matter what I said—heck, no matter what *you* said—you're not about to take my word on anything. *Fine.*" She jerked her arms from his neck and stood there in the middle of the dance floor, not moving, as he continued to stare at her.

It wasn't until she noticed that several of the couples dancing closest to them were staring as well that she realized what she'd done. She hadn't raised her voice.

She didn't have to. Her body language said it all.

So much for Anna's meticulous cover.

So much for his trust.

"Look, I appreciate everything you've done. I really do. But maybe it's best if we part company now. People are already paying attention. If we stage a fight, you'll be off the hook. You can tell the Brass you followed me down here to stop me, but that I slipped away from you. Heck, you can tell them whatever you want. They'll never know the dif—"

He swept her into his arms before she could finish, hauling her in so close, so fast, she didn't even see it coming. Before she could blink, one of his hands tunneled into her hair, the other splayed out firmly across her back. The tips of his fingers delved beneath the edge of her dress, his calluses rasping over her tender flesh as he caressed her intimately. She sucked in her breath as he discovered first-hand that there was no bra beneath this dress.

His pupils flared as he stared into her eyes.

A split second later, he lowered his mouth and swallowed her gasp until there were no more secrets between them.

Nothing but slick, hungry heat.

Just like that, she was *flying*.

Unable to do anything else, Eve gave herself up to the joy of it. The thrumming in her ears, the surge of adrenaline as it thundered through her blood. The mind-blowing sensation of shooting through the air at a hundred and fifty knots, climbing higher and higher, followed by the reckless rush of slamming into a sudden thermal pocket and plunging ninety feet in the blink of an eye. If this was what kissing Rick Bishop was like without the fog of grief dulling her senses, she wanted more. She wound her arms about his neck and stretched up to get it—

But he was gone.

She came crashing down to earth with a solid thud as he ripped his mouth from hers, leaving her cold, shaking and strung out on the acrid tarmac of unfulfilled passion as she struggled to hold on to his shoulders and regain her balance. She cursed him a thousand times over in the taut moments that followed. She didn't give a damn that his breath seemed to be coming in and out as short and as raw as hers, or that the callused fingers still fused to her back seemed to be trembling as fiercely as her legs—until she remembered.

Their audience.

She finally found her nerve and raised her head, staring into deep-brown eyes still smoldering with passion. She licked her lips. "We're not…settling anything like this."

"I thought we just did."

She blinked.

He leaned down to nuzzle her neck, before dragging his mouth to her ear. "We're following her plan, aren't we?"

The plan.

Reality seared through her confusion, burning away her lingering passion as he slipped his arms around her waist and once again eased them into the rhythm that had been kept up by the openly amused couples around them. What they saw as a passionate make-up from a lovers' spat was simply an act. That's all this was. What an idiot she was.

A stupid, lusting idiot.

Yes, the man had been turned on. The hard ridge still pressing against her abdomen was proof enough of that. But so what? It didn't mean Rick trusted her, believed in her or cared about her, much less respected her. And it certainly didn't mean he had any intention of sticking around. You'd think she'd have learned that lesson enough times already.

He'd said it himself, right there at the table.

Men simply didn't help someone out with a problem as muddy as hers without expecting something in return. Well, Rick had just proven without a doubt that he was a man. And he did want something in return. He just didn't want her.

What he wanted was answers.

Like her, Rick wanted to bring his sergeant home and lay him to rest without any lingering questions.

Best she remember that.

He tipped her chin, the simmering heat in his gaze at total odds with the seriousness in his low voice. "What's wrong? I didn't hurt you when we—"

"*No.*"

Not physically. She dropped her gaze to his tie, concentrating on the tiny threads of blue woven in amid the silvery gray. It was easier than staring into those smoky eyes and that imaginary seduction.

"Then what is it?"

The music trailed off on a series of what should have been soothingly gentle notes. She waited for him to release her, but he didn't. He kept them moving until the guitarist plucked at the opening notes of another, sultrier, arrangement. Like the others, it was hauntingly beautiful.

"Eve?"

She sighed. He wasn't going to give up, was he?

She finally looked up.

It was a mistake.

His phony desire was bad enough. His concern nearly did her in. She steeled her nerves as his fingers smoothed her hair behind her ears. Especially as his hand slid down the side of her face, its heady warmth coming to rest at the base of her neck. Filmmakers everywhere must have mourned the day Rick joined the Army instead of the Actors Guild.

If she didn't know any better, she'd have sworn he cared.

Especially when his thumb snuck up to graze her lips. "This isn't going to work if we don't trust each other."

That snapped her resolve into place—firmly.

"I guess we're more alike than you'd like to think."

"How so?"

"Oh, come on. You've got some nerve, accusing me of holding out when you're doing the same thing."

His brow shot up.

"Anna?" Eve swept her gaze to the surrounding dancers, quickly ensuring that no one was eavesdropping. "Do you honestly expect me to believe that you're suddenly, miraculously, willing to accept my word that she's on the level about—"

"*I do.*"

"—tonight." She stiffened in his arms. So much so, he had to nudge her legs into motion. "Wh-what did you say?"

"You heard me."

She had. She just didn't believe her ears. She searched his eyes for a good minute, looking for something, anything, that would support her suspicions, only to be completely floored by what she couldn't find. Doubt.

He honestly believed her.

"*Why?*"

His stare remained rock-steady as he picked up on the rest of the words she couldn't seem to form. "You gave me your word, didn't you?"

She had. Right before the kiss. But so what? It's not like her word had been enough before.

Like yesterday, in her apartment.

Again, he seemed to read her mind. "I'm here aren't I? Helping you?" His shrug barely registered beneath her nerveless fingers. "I admit, I still have concerns about the woman. But I'm willing to hold them in check for now." He reached up and covered her hands with his, tugging them down to study her fingers as he cradled them against his chest. "What else can I do to prove myself?"

He fell silent.

She knew he was waiting for an answer.

Too bad, she didn't have one to give him. Not one that would make sense, much less one she was willing to share.

From the deep puckering of his scar when he frowned, she suspected Rick had reached the end of even his superhuman patience. His soft growl as he lowered his forehead to hers confirmed it. "I swear, Paris, you trusted me more six weeks ago when I was a total stranger."

She stared at his mouth.

At the faint lines where his dimples should be. She hadn't seen them once today. But then, he hadn't had much of a reason to smile lately, had he? She closed her eyes as the subtle scent of his shaving cream swirled through her. He was right. She had trusted him more when he was just some unknown soldier on a joint mission. Trusting the uniform was easy. It had never let her down before. But the man beneath?

Trusting that was hard.

Perhaps impossible.

"Eve?"

She knew what he wanted. He wanted her to share ev-

erything he thought she was holding back. She couldn't.
She wouldn't. To do so would betray two friends now. So
she opened her eyes and said the only thing she could.

"You still are a stranger."

Eve Paris had been burned.

Badly.

He didn't know by whom and he probably never would,
but if the bastard were to materialize before him right now,
he'd be hard-pressed not to strangle him with his bare
hands. Rick dropped his towel on the bathroom tiles and
stepped inside the hotel room's blistering shower for the
second time in as many hours. He refused to feel guilty
about the water. Even if he hadn't needed to wash away
the lingering scents of shampoo and shaving cream before
reinserting into the jungle, he'd have needed the steam to
clear his head and assuage the guilt.

Not that that was possible.

He'd walked a fine line out on that dance floor with Eve
tonight and he still wasn't comfortable with the results.
Unfortunately, he hadn't had a choice. Misleading her had
been the only way to preserve her quest and possibly her
life. He only wished Eve's so-called sorority sister was as
concerned with the latter as she'd been with the former.

Anna Shale.

Now there was an actress.

What the woman's true game was, he had no idea. Tom
had been unable to share that with him during their brief
meeting after he'd slipped out through the bathroom window and into the alley behind the restaurant. Nor would he
have time to investigate Anna on his own. Not if he and
Eve were to leave at 0400 as planned. And they *were* leaving. Tom had been able to assure him that although Anna
was into something unsavory up to her neck, it had nothing

to do with the supplies and the chopper she'd managed to procure on their behalf.

That was enough for him.

He only wished he'd been able to share the real reason as to why he'd changed his mind with Eve. Not that she hadn't suspected he was being less than truthful for a while there.

The woman was sharp.

She was also on target more than she knew.

He *had* been holding out on her. For six weeks now.

He'd thought about coming clean at her apartment. He'd even wanted to. But in the end, he hadn't. Why add more to her burden than she already carried? Especially when this load was his to bear and his alone. He shoved his head under the scalding spray and scrubbed the remaining scent of his earlier shampoo from his hair. Eve wasn't the only one suffering from guilt. But at least hers might be vindicated. There was no hope for his. The truth of it was no matter what Eve uncovered in that wreckage, she wasn't the one responsible for his platoon sergeant's death.

He was.

Rick turned and subjected his face and chest to the scalding water as regret lashed through him. Hell, the only reason Turner had boarded that chopper at all was because he'd ordered his sergeant to accompany him to the presidential compound that day. He was the only one needed at that briefing. But Turner had come to him two weeks before the crash, sixteen years into his Army career—a mere four years from retirement—and told him he wanted out.

At the time it had been inconceivable.

To work that long and then throw it all away before the man had even asked Carrie to marry him?

What if she refused?

Even Turner had admitted he wasn't sure she wouldn't. And if she hadn't? With the current crackdown on officer–

enlisted fraternization, a captain openly dating, much less marrying, a recent sergeant would have done more than raise brows. It would have killed careers.

Hers.

Would Carrie have traded in her wings for a wedding ring?

He'd never know.

All he knew was that Bill Turner would never have the chance to find out. Rick turned around and twisted the knobs at the rear of the stall. The scalding stream ceased. He stepped out of the shower and grabbed a towel. It was time to turn the room over to Eve. He hoped she'd finished eating the takeout dinner their waiter had bagged for them after they'd returned to the table, neither of them in the mood for food anymore.

*Damn.* His sweats.

He'd been so rocked by a charade that hadn't quite managed to stay a charade with either of them that he'd locked himself into the bathroom without fresh clothes. His trousers lay at the base of the shower, still drenched from the spray that had shot out from the stall before he'd changed the angle on the nozzle.

Now what?

Should he step out with a towel at his hips? His sweats were lying on top of his suitcase, a mere three feet to the left on the opposite side of the door. Or would Eve worry that he'd decided to carry the charade back to their room?

Not that he honestly didn't want to.

He simply couldn't.

Even if the Army no longer cared how they passed their off-duty hours, he did. It was obvious Eve was still shell-shocked by the crash and the board's decision to ground her. He refused to take advantage of that. He refused to take advantage of her. Rick stared at his soaking trousers and then the dry towel.

Bloody hell.

Eve was a soldier, so was he.

He wrapped the towel around his hips and tucked the trailing end firmly into place before he opened the door. He stepped out into the room—and froze.

Eve was in bed, on her side.

Naked.

In an instant, that kiss came crashing back. His arms damned near ached with the memory of her curves. He could even feel the side of her breast, soft and full against his fingertips. He closed his fists. Banished the memory.

He was a *stranger*.

But even as the insult flayed his pride he knew, strangers shared the same bed all the time.

He ought to know.

But did she?

She stirred, spoke. But with her back to him, he couldn't make out her words. He turned toward his suitcase and reached for his sweats, only to drop them as he heard her again.

Tears?

"Eve?"

Silence.

He checked the tuck on his towel, cleared his throat and tried again. "Are you okay?"

This time the sobs were unmistakable.

The sheet had slipped past her shoulder. He could see the curve quaking softly. He approached the bed slowly, lest he startle her. But as he rounded the foot board, he realized he couldn't. She was sleeping, deep in the throes of a dream.

No, a nightmare.

Tears were spilling freely from beneath her lashes, soaking into the white pillow at her cheek. He stepped closer and discovered she wasn't naked. The sleeve of her dress

## The Silhouette Reader Service™ — Here's how it works:

Accepting your 2 free books and gift places you under no obligation to buy anything. You may keep the books and gift and return the shipping statement marked "cancel." If you do not cancel, about a month later we'll send you 6 additional novels and bill you just $3.99 each in the U.S., or $4.74 each in Canada, plus 25¢ shipping & handling per book and applicable taxes if any.* That's the complete price and — compared to cover prices of $4.75 each in the U.S. and $5.75 each in Canada — it's quite a bargain! You may cancel at any time, but if you choose to continue, every month we'll send you 6 more books, which you may either purchase at the discount price or return to us and cancel your subscription.

*Terms and prices subject to change without notice. Sales tax applicable in N.Y. Canadian residents will be charged applicable provincial taxes and GST.

If offer card is missing write to: Silhouette Reader Service, 3010 Walden Ave., P.O. Box 1867, Buffalo NY 14240-1867

NO POSTAGE
NECESSARY
IF MAILED
IN THE
UNITED STATES

## BUSINESS REPLY MAIL
FIRST-CLASS MAIL    PERMIT NO. 717-003    BUFFALO, NY

POSTAGE WILL BE PAID BY ADDRESSEE

SILHOUETTE READER SERVICE
3010 WALDEN AVE
PO BOX 1867
BUFFALO NY 14240-9952

# GET FREE BOOKS and a FREE GIFT
## WHEN YOU PLAY THE...

*Just scratch off the silver box with a coin. Then check below to see the gifts you get!*

## SLOT MACHINE GAME!

**YES!** I have scratched off the silver box. Please send me the 2 free Silhouette Intimate Moments® books and gift for which I qualify. I understand I am under no obligation to purchase any books, as explained on the back of this card.

**345 SDL DQLQ**

**245 SDL DRNM**
(S-IMA-10/02)

| | | | | | | | | | | | |
|---|---|---|---|---|---|---|---|---|---|---|---|

FIRST NAME                    LAST NAME

| | | | | | | | | | | | |
|---|---|---|---|---|---|---|---|---|---|---|---|

ADDRESS

APT.#                    CITY

STATE/PROV.                    ZIP/POSTAL CODE

| **7** | **7** | **7** | **Worth TWO FREE BOOKS plus a BONUS Mystery Gift!** |
| 🍒 | 🍒 | 🍒 | **Worth TWO FREE BOOKS!** |
| ♣ | ♣ | ♣ | **Worth ONE FREE BOOK!** |
| 🔔 | 🔔 | 🍒 | **TRY AGAIN!** |

*Visit us online at www.eHarlequin.com*

DETACH AND MAIL CARD TODAY!

had simply slipped off her shoulder. A fresh stream of tears poured into the pillow as he tugged the sheet higher and tucked it beneath her chin.

Should he wake her?

She had to be dreaming about Carrie. But that could be for the best. If she was still determined to hold in her grief as she had after the crash, she'd need the release. But damned if each of her silent sobs didn't pierce his heart. He leaned close and smoothed the curls from her brow. When she didn't stir, he leaned closer. Before he realized what he was doing, he pressed his lips to her temple. "Shhh."

She stirred. "Please don't go."

His gut twisted at the odd, unfamiliar note in her voice. If he didn't know better, he'd swear he was comforting a small child, not a grown woman. He leaned down to smooth her brow again and whispered, "It's okay, Eve. I'm here."

"It doesn't hurt, mommy, I promise. Please don't go. I'll be good."

He froze.

Horror congealed along every single inch of his body as she continued to murmur and plead until it was suddenly, completely, seared away by pure, unadulterated *rage*.

How?

*Why?*

Images flashed before his eyes as he staggered back and fell into the chair beside the bed; each picture was uglier and more gut-wrenching than the last. He had no way of knowing which was accurate and which wasn't. He wasn't sure he wanted to. Six weeks ago, he'd seen this woman's body battered and abused. But it had occurred in the line of *duty*.

Not under the guise of love.

He swallowed the bile burning in his throat and cradled

his head in his hands, scrubbing his eyes over and over until the images were gone. By the time he raised his head and focused again, her tears had ebbed.

Eve was resting quietly now, peacefully.

The touch of makeup she'd applied earlier had faded, but her cheeks were still flushed. He suspected she looked much like the child she must have been the first time her world had fallen out of the sky and then exploded around her.

Carrie. Anna.

Trust.

It all made sense now. Or at least, enough of it did for him to know Eve would never trust him. She had no reason to. Not if he continued to press her the way he had six weeks before and then again yesterday and today, much less if he continued to conceal the truth from her as he had out on that dance floor tonight, even if he had thought it was for her own good. If he wanted Eve's trust, he'd have to do what Carrie and Anna and her other two Sisters-in-Arms had done.

He'd have to earn it.

# Chapter 8

She'd always wondered why the grunts were so damned eager to rappel out of a perfectly good chopper.

Now she knew.

They must have flown in this one.

An early prototype model, the Huey rattling around them should have been given a decent burial fifteen years ago. Eve stared at the hefty Panamanian thug hunkered down on the opposite web bench. She wasn't sure if the goon had been relegated to the rear of the chopper along with her and Rick to cut their rappelling ropes after they hit the ground, or to cushion the chopper's eventual crash.

*Lord, did this bird need a tune-up.*

But as bad as the Huey was, she had to admit she'd give anything to be flying it instead of sitting in the dark, a fully-loaded rucksack on her back, waiting for Rick's signal to bail out one of the side doors before whizzing down through fifty feet of pitch-black jungle canopy with nothing more than a slender rope to break her fall.

Or her neck.

Frankly, she had more faith in the Jesus nut atop even these decrepit rotor blades than she ever would in some thin strand of nylon. Eve glanced over her left shoulder and into the glowing cockpit.

No doubt about it.

She was on the wrong end of this operation—or even of the equally illegal one that would be going down after she and Rick inserted into the jungle. She shifted her attention across the moonlit belly of the Huey and studied the ammunition crates stacked beneath the thug's frayed webbed bench. She might not be able to read Chinese, but she knew enough to know those crates contained enough 7.62 mm rounds to supply a private army.

The question was, whose?

And where had the pilot stashed the AK-47 rifles that went with those rounds? But most importantly, exactly how was Anna mixed up in all this? The first two questions might never be answered to her satisfaction, but the last one would. Just as soon as she and Rick returned to Panama.

She owed it to Anna to find out.

"Ready?"

Eve swung her stare to the right. To Rick. His eyes burned steady and brown amid the green and black camouflage grease paint he'd applied to his face. He pointed silently, directing her attention toward the cockpit. The pilot had his right hand in the air, all five fingers splayed wide.

Five minutes to insertion.

Five minutes to experiencing Newton's Law of Gravity firsthand. Joy. If she ever got her wings back she'd never tease another recruit about getting airsick again.

She braced the stock of her AK-47 against the floor of the chopper and stood as high as she could along with Rick.

They took a moment to sling their rifles over their respective rucksacks before shuffling forward, fighting the stiff wind blowing in through gaping holes where the Huey's side doors had been. Rick had already woven separate ropes around both their waists and thighs to form the Swiss seats they'd use to rappel down through the trees several kilometers from the actual crash site. The last either of them had heard, Army Intelligence believed the Córdobans hadn't located the remains of her chopper. Nor did the search appear to be a priority.

Neither of them were anxious to rectify that.

Eve stiffened as Rick leaned close enough to run his hands around her waist and down between her legs. She flushed, grateful for the dark, as she realized he was double-checking her Swiss seat. Her thundering pulse slowed, but not by much.

Dammit, *breathe.*

Relax.

It was easier to accomplish than she thought. Maybe it was the hand that settled firmly on her shoulder.

Rick's hand.

Just as it had during their initial trek through the jungle, the man's mere presence seemed to steady her. She couldn't explain it, but she was grateful for it. Just as she'd been grateful last night—despite the fact that then Rick had been nothing more than a figment of her imagination.

She'd had the dream again.

She hadn't had it in years. Not since college.

It had started up again in the hospital, the night of the crash, and it had been waking her up ever since. It didn't take a student of Freud's to figure out why. But lately, the dream had been changing, almost…evolving.

First Carrie had been in it.

And now Rick.

Last night, her mother had left her as she always did.

But this time, when she'd finally broken down and cried out for her, Rick had appeared. He'd cradled her in his arms and warmed her and comforted her as he promised her over and over that everything would be all right. And for once, it had been. She usually woke up disoriented and crying after the dream. But this time she hadn't woken until 0300.

The alarm had gone off, but Rick was already up and dressed in the jungle fatigues that had been waiting for them when they returned to the hotel, ready to go.

Just as she should be right now.

She glanced forward in time to see the pilot hold up his hand. This time, two fingers.

Two minutes.

Rick passed her a pair of black leather gloves and donned another pair as she jerked hers on. He gripped her shoulders again as she finished, nudging her toward the chopper's left gaping doorway. His fingers tightened, steadying her as the cross wind slammed into her.

It was a good thing.

With the rucksack on her back, her balance was off.

He reached up and clipped both her rappelling ropes through her snap link, then slapped the lead ends in her hands as he kicked the remainder of the coils out the side of the chopper. His breath filled her ear as he leaned close and shouted over the pounding blades. *"Remember, brake no more than ten feet off the ground! Understood?"*

In theory, yes.

In practice?

Hell, no!

Unfortunately, her one-day cliff-rappelling training would have to suffice because as she nodded, Rick moved off. By the time she'd pulled her ropes taut and twisted her braking hand behind her back, Rick had snapped his own ropes into place and stepped out onto the chopper's right skid. He swung straight out from the doorway of the chopper until he was leaning sixty degrees off the skid.

Eve glanced down at her own skid.

The Huey was hovering ten feet above jungle canopy, centered over a tiny clearing. She quickly blessed the pilot and silently thanked his bird as she hooked the heels of her boots onto the skid and used her ropes to swing out into the rotor wash to balance Rick's position. The waiting thug unsheathed his machete and shuffled forward to toss a neon green chem light out each doorway.

She focused on hers as it fell and marked its location.

It was time.

She glanced up and Rick nodded.

And she let go—

Adrenaline shot through her as she fell through the dark, thundering through her veins until it matched the roar of the rotors above. She ignored it and focused on the chem light as Rick had instructed. Moments later, she felt her gloves overheating the way he'd warned and instinctively tugged her right hand low and fully behind her back.

Her entire body whiplashed.

She recovered quickly and shifted her hand forward, loosening her grip enough to slide down the rest of the way. Her boots hit the jungle floor with a thud. Rick was beside her, grabbing her shoulders with one hand, her ruck with his other, steadying her before the force succeeded in knocking her on her rear. A moment later, their ropes rained down around them as the Huey roared off into the night.

And then there was nothing but dark, eerie silence.

"You did great."

"Thanks."

He must have realized he was still holding her because he jerked his hands away. Unfortunately, her nerves had held up better than her legs. Her knees buckled. His hands snapped out again. This time he grabbed her arms just below her shoulders and pulled her close. Close enough for her to see his eyes in the dark as the moon slipped from beneath the clouds, filling the tiny clearing with a soft glow.

"Sorry. I don't know what—"

He shook his head. "Happens a lot the first time. Give the rush time to work itself through." He must have gotten a rush himself because he grinned. She sucked in her breath as his dimples caved in. This second, piercing jolt that ripped through her was much more intense than the first. And it had absolutely nothing to do with adrenaline.

It was desire, pure and simple.

She strangled something embarrassingly similar to a groan—or thought she had. The tail end slipped out.

He frowned. "Your ribs. Did you re-injure—"

"They're fine. They have been for two weeks now."

He nodded, visibly relieved. "I thought so after your apartment. But I figured I'd better make sure."

Her apartment?

Her confusion must have shown, because he winced in memory—and she flushed. The door. She'd slammed her fist into his gut and then when she'd opened the door on him, he'd plowed headlong into her counter. Into his—

Her flush deepened.

To her surprise, his chuckle filled the dark. He tipped her chin. "It's okay. I might have deserved it."

"No, you didn't. It's just, I was…upset."

"I gathered that."

Uncomfortable with the odd mix of amusement and open admiration in his gaze, she took a step back.

He released her instantly.

Who was this man?

With his face camouflaged to match his jungle fatigues, he certainly looked like Rick. He even sounded like him. But the man standing ten inches away was different somehow. She'd felt it from the moment she'd woken. At first she'd chalked it up to their pending insertion. The normal pre-mission excitement and jitters that even seasoned soldiers experienced. Now she wasn't so sure.

For one thing he was too confident, too relaxed.

Too focused.

But on what?

She was still trying to decide when he turned around and set about retrieving the ropes they'd used to rappel down from the Huey. She shook off her confusion and reached down to snag her chem light before heading across the clearing for his. By the time she'd returned, Rick had piled the ropes into a small crevice several trees inside the jungle and was already concealing the snarled coils with underbrush. She handed over the chem sticks and he added them to the pile.

Moments later, he stood.

She froze as he reached out and brushed a large insect with more legs than she could count from the right strap of her ruck, less than an inch away from her breast. She wasn't sure which stunned her more, that she hadn't noticed the creature or the way he no longer seemed concerned with personal space.

Hers or his.

The insect gone, he retrieved the hand-held global positioning unit Anna had provided from his right cargo pocket and checked their location. He must have been satisfied with the result because he restowed the GPS unit and glanced up.

"Ready?"

She nodded.

She should have taken more time with her answer.

She was sure of it when his hand closed over hers as he turned to part the dense jungle undergrowth before leading her through—especially when he didn't let her go. Something told her that this journey through the jungle with Rick would be nothing like her last.

It had taken six hours and some twenty-odd minutes, but Eve no longer flinched at his occasional touch. Frankly he'd thought it would take longer.

Perhaps days.

Fortunately, heat and exhaustion were on his side.

Rick glanced over his shoulder as he parted what had to be his thousandth section of foliage that hour alone and stepped through. He continued to hold the vines, waiting until they were securely in Eve's grasp before he let go. This time when their fingers brushed, she didn't stiffen. He suspected his touch hadn't even registered at all.

He wasn't offended.

If anything, he was relieved.

He'd spent the better part of the night sitting up in that chair beside the bed, awake. Part of the time he'd used to fine-tune the remaining steps of their mission, but the majority had been spent watching and thinking about Eve.

She was right.

They were strangers.

The woman might be following in his footsteps as closely as if she was one of his men, but the fact was, he knew less about Eve than he did any one of them. Even so, she'd managed to reach a part of him he'd thought long since buried. At first he'd tried to blame his own awakening on her dream. But once he'd been honest with himself and really thought about it, thought about her, he'd realized that this odd connection he felt to Eve had started much earlier.

It had even started before that crash.

It had taken root earlier that fateful morning, out on the LZ, at the precise moment Eve had extended her hand. He knew now why he'd refused to take it, and it had nothing to do with Carrie Evans or his sergeant. He'd been protecting himself. Unfortunately, by the time Eve turned her back on him, he was already hooked. The only question was, what was he going to do about it?

That, he didn't know.

But he did know he had no intention of remaining a stranger to this particular woman. Unfortunately, there lay the crux of his current dilemma. Getting to know his men had been easy. They simply talked and he listened.

Eve Paris didn't talk.

Not to him.

He was beginning to suspect she'd never really talked to anyone other than her sorority sisters. Not about anything that mattered. Not about herself. Hell, she'd been more alive and more animated talking to Anna Shale in the minute it had taken him to return to the table at the restaurant last night, than she'd been with him the entire time he'd known her. He pushed the bittersweet memory aside and focused on the next section of foliage waiting a quarter of an inch from his face, the next vine, the next step.

The next touch.

Fifty steps later, they reached the edge of a clearing. It was barely six feet, but it would have to do.

"Need a break?"

Eve's gaze shot to his, the exhaustion on her face and in her shoulders as well as her step giving her answer before she could. "Are you sure we have time?"

"You keep a pretty good pace."

She waited several beats. "Go ahead and finish it."

"Finish what?"

"Like I told you in my apartment, Bishop. Innocence does not become you."

He shrugged and complied. "You keep a pretty good pace...for a pampered pilot."

She stuck out her tongue.

He stood there for a full five seconds, stunned—and then

he flat-out grinned. The heck with talking. If physical exhaustion worked this well on the woman's barriers, he'd keep her moving until sundown. Eve stalked past. He was so intent on his relief he missed the movement of her hand. The vine she'd taken from his snapped back at his face.

He grabbed it with barely a centimeter to spare.

This time, she grinned.

He sucked in his breath as her smile transformed her face. Despite the cammo paint smeared into her cheeks and the dirt and sweat streaked across her jaw and down her neck, the field cap pulled low on her forehead, concealing all but the very ends of those soft gold curls, Eve Paris was absolutely mesmerizing. And her eyes...they glowed with life.

*She* glowed with life.

Right then and there, he knew his decision to bring her back to Córdoba had been the right one. This was the soldier he'd met that morning out on the LZ. A soldier who was not afraid to work for what she wanted. To fight for it.

A soldier worth risking his career for.

Unfortunately, the moment he shoved the vine aside and stepped into the clearing beside her, everything changed. Eve changed. Even before her smile faded, he could feel her pulling away, withdrawing into herself again. Though he now knew why, it didn't help.

And damned if it didn't hurt.

Determined to ignore this latest setback as he had every one of her subtle flinches throughout the morning, he moved into the center of the clearing and set his AK-47 on the ground before shrugging his rucksack off his shoulders. He dumped the ruck a foot behind him, severely reducing the amount of free space she'd have to place between them. He was almost amused when she began inching backward as expected.

Almost.

"Hungry?" He didn't wait for an answer, but turned and hunkered down to retrieve a couple of the MREs from the main section of his ruck.

"Uh…sure."

He came up with two beef meals. He pulled his K-Bar from the nylon scabbard at his waist and used the tip of the black blade to slit open both main pouches. He passed Eve one. He sorted though his own MRE pouch and pulled out the chocolate bar and cocoa packet and tossed them over as well. She might look better each day, but as far as he was concerned, she could still use the added fat.

"Thanks."

It was as if they'd been transported six weeks into the past. They sat there, awkwardly staring at one another over another set of MREs with yet another humid jungle silence settling in. For every step he took with this woman, he took at least two back. He swore he could feel his morning progress slipping away with each chirp of the insects around them. He opened his mouth—and promptly closed it.

*That* was no insect.

He caught the soft rustle beneath the foliage several inches from her left hand again, but this time it was followed by a distinct slither. Eve must not have heard it, however, much less seen the flash of yellow, brown and orange, amid the foliage because she reached for her canteen.

"You might not want to do that."

"Do wha—Jesus!"

She shot to her feet and jumped to the edge of the clearing before he could tell her it was harmless. He bit down on his grin as he reached out with his K-Bar, slipping the flat of the blade beneath the boa constrictor to lift it up and get a better look. It was four feet tops. A baby.

He flicked it into the trees.

"I suppose you thought that was funny."

He shrugged.

"Let me guess, unlike wimpy pilots—male or female—Green Berets aren't afraid of snakes."

He should probably let that one go, too.

She crossed her arms. "Tell me, Bishop. Have you ever seen a chopper do a barrel roll?"

He nodded. "Once."

Her brow arched. "Have you ever been at the stick?"

Not bad. In fact, damned impressive.

He tipped his field cap. "Point taken." She was right. Every soldier had his moment of valor...as well as his Achilles' heel. He also had his opening.

"Rats."

She blinked. "What?"

"The rodent. Hate 'em. I was five when I came face-to-face with my first one. I wasn't supposed to go in the grain silo alone and I knew it. Never did it again." Not that his dad and his brother had ever let him forget.

"Rats?"

He nodded. "Rats. Nasty, scurvy creatures. Carry all kinds of diseases. Ticks, fleas. Fat bellies with beady little eyes and skinny pink tails." He could still see the damned thing, sitting there, trapping him for what seemed like an eternity, until his screams had finally sent it scurrying away. Hell, he still got queasy just thinking about it. But he was rewarded for his confession when Eve inched her way back to the center of the clearing.

"Rats."

He shrugged.

She just laughed. "I had a pet rat in grade school."

"You're kidding."

She shook her head. "Well, it wasn't really mine. It was the science teacher's. But I got to feed him and play with him. Herbert was white and he had this cute bald tai—"

"I get the picture."

She grinned—and sat.

He *breathed*.

"Grain silos? Just where are you from, anyway?"

"Nebraska."

Again, she blinked.

This time he was actually affronted. "What? You never met a Nebraska boy before? Johnny Carson's from Nebraska."

"I know. I just didn't know there were jungles in Nebraska."

He dumped his MRE pouch beside his ruck and laughed at that. "There aren't. Just miles of cornfields, gravel roads, cows, pigs, a million chickens and an occasional kid or two." At least in the county he was from.

"Your family must miss you." She said it so softly, he almost missed it. The wonder, the envy.

The honest desire to know.

His own honest desire to share snaked through him.

The hell with rats, he was truly queasy now.

And this was dangerous.

He did it anyway. "My brother couldn't wait to get out. It was all he ever talked about. The day Ben graduated from high school, he left for the big city—that would be Omaha for you sophisticated Texans. He lasted a year."

"What happened?"

"Our mom died."

Damn. He hadn't meant for it to fall out quite so bluntly. Who was he kidding? He hadn't meant it to come out at all. He watched her closely. Relieved when she didn't pull away again. If anything, she leaned closer.

"I'm sorry."

For once the words seemed more than a quick platitude. Maybe that's why he actually wanted to continue.

Or maybe it was just her.

He shrugged. "Our dad, he took her for groceries one afternoon. They got caught in a snowstorm on the way back. Dad swore she never saw the semi that hit them. Ben came back for the funeral and never left."

How could he?

Their father might have survived the accident physically, but he sure as hell hadn't in spirit.

"How's your dad?"

"Fine now. He died a year later."

He heard her soft gasp. "I don't understand."

Neither did he. Not really.

Or maybe he still didn't want to understand.

So why did he have this gut-wrenching premonition he was about to?

"Rick?" Her fingers touched the back of his hand.

He flinched.

"Sorry, I didn—"

His hand snapped up before he could stop it, claiming hers before she could retrieve it. He held on shamelessly and forced himself to continue. "It's okay. It's just— I've rarely…talked about it." He had with a buddy once. But he knew damned well if Ernesto hadn't prodded, he'd never have found the nerve. Rick studied the slender fingers in his. They didn't move, didn't flinch. They felt strangely right in his, as if they belonged. In a way, maybe they did.

They'd come this far together.

He took a deep breath and forced himself to finish the story. "It was cold, snowing again. I was at school, Ben was visiting a buddy. There's not much to do on a farm in the dead of winter except repair equipment, so that's what dad was doing." At least, that's what the police report had said. "He was working on his truck, the one he'd bought new after the accident. A tune-up, it looked like. But the garage doors were closed and…" He swallowed the lump in his throat but it refused to go down.

He shrugged. Seemed he couldn't finish after all.

Her fingers shifted in his, until her hand squeezed his. "And he died of asphyxiation."

That's how the cops had pegged it, too. But from the way her eyes were glistening, she knew what had really happened, same as the sheriff had. His father had killed himself.

No, there'd been no note. If there had been, the insurance wouldn't have paid out.

Dad was practical to the end.

Her hand squeezed his. "He must have loved her very much."

"You could call it a family curse." He'd meant it as a joke but she didn't laugh. She squeezed harder.

"How old were you?"

"Almost eighteen. I graduated a couple months later and joined the Army." Hell, he'd have joined the Marines if the recruiter had been in first that morning. He stared at her fingers, still streaked with cammo, tree sap and dirt from their morning trek. He should stop talking, let her eat.

Except now that he had her interest, he couldn't seem to shut up. He wasn't even trying to reach whatever she was hiding anymore. He just needed her to know he understood there were some things that were so painful you just couldn't talk about them. "Anyway, most of the guys I went to basic with were headed for the desert, but I had four years of Spanish and remembered most of it so I was sent to Ranger school and then on to Special Forces."

"How on earth did you find time for college?"

He shrugged. "Not much to do after-hours at Fort Bragg." Not if you weren't interested in marriage or at least shacking up. "Got tapped for an officer slot soon after. Figured what the hell, I like the jungle. Might as well get paid to live here." He stared at the tree trunk behind her, the thick vines and the darker green undergrowth as the silence returned.

He wasn't worried.

It was different this time. Companionable, familiar. He should release her hand though. She really did need to eat. They both did. He tried to, but she refused to let go.

"Eve?"

He searched the shadows swirling through her eyes, the lingering doubts, the indecision. He didn't know what to say anymore, what to do. All he knew was that he couldn't push.

He wouldn't.

She seemed to understand, because her gaze finally cleared, focused. "Remember the headset at the LZ? The one you asked for? The one I told you had malfunctioned?"

He swallowed hard. "Yes?"

"I lied."

# Chapter 9

He knew.

She just didn't know how much. Eve had begun to suspect sometime this morning. But she wasn't certain until now. Why else had Rick exposed his inner self to her? And he *had* exposed his inner self. No man could pretend the pain in his eyes or in the hands that had been locked to hers while he'd been talking. No man would want to. Not even to gain her trust.

Last night hadn't been a dream.

Not all of it, anyway. How much she'd mumbled out loud, she couldn't be sure. She could only hope she'd kept her trap shut about Carrie and Anna. It was ironic. Carrie had discovered her secrets the same way. Once she'd gotten over the shock of waking to find her friend next to her bed, holding her hand during their freshman year of college, she'd realized the discovery was inevitable. When she was under stress, she dreamed. And when she dreamed, she talked.

But that didn't mean she had to explain.

Not even to the man sitting twelve inches away, holding her hand as he patiently waited for her to finish. But she could give him something in return for his silence about last night and for his trust just now.

She could give him that day.

"I was angry with you. No, I was furious."

His brow shot up, but he remained silent.

She appreciated it. She needed time to choose her words carefully. She stared at their hands while she gathered her thoughts. It should have unnerved her to see his calloused fingers still entwined with hers. But it didn't.

If anything, she drew strength from them.

From him.

She drew a deep breath and faced that dark, steady gaze. "You snubbed Carrie. And you did it in front of your platoon sergeant and my crew chief. She was an officer and she was my copilot, but she was also my best friend. I know her behavior was out of line that morning, but so was yours. Frankly, I didn't want you listening in. So I lied. For that, I'm sorry."

He waited several beats, as if he too needed time to corral his thoughts. He finally nodded. "You're right. I was out of line. I was late for my briefing and seeing her didn't help."

Now there was a leading statement.

She'd give a heck of a lot to follow it, but she wouldn't give up Carrie. Unfortunately, short of asking Rick how much he knew about his sergeant's relationship with her friend, there was nothing she could do. She'd gone as far as she could go. It was up to him to trust her.

Or not.

To her surprise, he dropped his stare to their hands and studied them intently. "There's more, isn't there?"

He was right. It was easier this way, not having to look at him. "Yes. But it has *nothing* to do with the crash."

He nodded. "I know." He stroked his fingers down the back of her hand then turned it over to smooth a caress across her palm. "You...need to get anything else off your chest?"

For a blinding moment, she thought he meant the baby. But then his gaze came up and the compassion flowed out. He was asking about the dream. What he'd heard.

What he wanted her to share.

She couldn't.

But not for the reason he thought.

It was simply too personal. Too much a part of her. The real her. She might have dealt with it, but aside from Carrie she'd never, ever, shared it. Much less with some man who'd be leaving just as soon as he got what he'd come for.

She'd never even been tempted.

To her utter shock, she was now. She even opened her mouth.

Nothing came out.

He simply nodded. "If you change your mind, I'm here."

The ray of light he'd managed to locate in the middle of this shadowy jungle glinted off the truth burning in his eyes. She believed him. He truly wanted to be there for her.

But for how long?

Her bird was dead.

There were times over the past six weeks when she'd wondered. Times when it felt as if she was simply trapped in a series of surreal dreams woven within the framework of a larger, more horrific nightmare. She kept hoping that if she hung on long enough, she'd finally break through. She'd wake up and discover that Carrie, Sergeant Lange and Sergeant Turner were still alive. That her career and her chopper were still in one piece. But as Eve stood twenty trees from the edge of the clearing she'd attempted to land in all those weeks ago and stared at the charred remains of her Black Hawk, reality struck home. And it struck harder than the knuckles of some stranger's fist after she'd dared to crawl into bed with her mother all those years ago.

She'd woken up, all right.

Just not to the fantasy she craved.

Six years of her Army career and three-plus lives had been reduced to a shell of blackened steel. Even from here, after all these weeks, she could smell the lingering stench of death, singed metal and vaporized fuel.

What a waste.

Her waste.

Eve tore her gaze from the chopper and searched in vain for Rick, alternately cursing him for forcing her to wait idly by while he scoured the area for any potential booby traps left by the Córdoban army, and yet blessing him for allowing her this time alone with her memories and with her thoughts.

With her doubts.

Oh she had them, all right.

She might not have admitted them to the investigation board or to Rick. But they were there. They'd been burrowing through her brain for weeks, gnawing at her confidence, eating away her resolve. Until this moment, she hadn't known how truly insidious they were. What if the board was right?

Not in their logic, but in the end result.

What if she tore that hunk of cooked steel apart bolt-by-bolt and found absolutely nothing? How could she argue with the board's finding then? Or worse, what if she discovered the crash *had* been caused by pilot error?

Her error.

Hell, even if she was vindicated, would it really matter?

In the end, what would examining the remains of her chopper really solve? Would it silence the what-ifs? Strangle the could-have-beens? Or would she always wonder if she'd done *this* differently or *that* sooner, would three more people be alive today? Would Carrie still be expecting her first baby?

"Eve?"

She nearly jumped out of her boots.

She recovered quickly and spun around. She took one look at Rick's face and reached up to scrub the tears away from her own, then stopped. What was the point? They'd just start streaming all over again when they reached the graves.

Then again, maybe she should have wiped them.

Rick was staring at her as if he was afraid she was about to dive off the deep end. She wiped, if only to stop that gentle compassion before it sent her over.

"Did you find anything?"

He shook his head. "The monkeys have been over it. A puma made a couple of passes around the perimeter, but decided not to enter. Other than that, nothing. Just Mother Nature and entropy hard at work. We're good to go." He stepped up close and smoothed his thumbs across her cheeks, wiping tears she must have missed. "Are you?"

*No.*

She managed a nod.

He didn't move. He just continued to stare. She had the distinct feeling he wanted to say something, something he thought she wouldn't want to hear.

"What is it?" Even as she asked, his debrief sunk in. Monkeys, pumas, and God knew what else. Wild, curious animals.

The graves.

"Did the animals disturb—"

"They're fine. I'm just not sure how you're going to take my suggestion now that we're here."

Fear of the unknown was already bleeding her dry. "Spill it."

He nodded. "It's been a long day. You're tired. We both are. Just seeing the wreckage from here has upset you— not that it wasn't bound to. Dusk hits in less than an hour and we have at least that long to travel before I'll be comfortable setting up camp for the—"

"You want me to wait."

"Yes. Just take a look at it now. It'll be here in the morning and we'll be rested. Thinking clearer."

"Okay."

He tipped her chin. "You're sure?"

"No. But you are. That's good enough for me." After everything he'd sacrificed to make this happen, it had to be. She drew in a deep breath. "Let's do it."

He nodded and turned to hoist his ruck on his shoulders. His hand shot out as she reached for hers. "I'll get it."

The hell he would. Her ribs were fine now. She could carry her own gear, thank you.

She reached out again.

This time, his stare cut her off. It was a stare designed to put the fear of God into combat-hardened soldiers when necessary, a stare that demanded obedience.

Expected it.

"Fine." She grabbed her rifle and took off on point toward the clearing, automatically threading her way through the thinning undergrowth as he'd taught by example during the day. She reached the tree line all too soon. By the time she reached her chopper she knew exactly why Rick had insisted on carrying her gear. She could barely carry her rifle, much less her own body. Her legs turned to lead as the world faded from view. All she could see was that blackened hunk of metal.

Shattered windows, buckled steel.

A vacant, lifeless shell.

Tears scalded down her cheeks again before she could stop them, and this time the pounding in her chest could have put a live artillery exercise to shame. Her breath ripped through her lungs short and hard as every nerve in her body screamed at her to turn around, go back. Leave the way she'd come.

*Run.*

She couldn't do this. Dammit, she *couldn't.*

She was dimly aware of their gear hitting the ground behind her, but she was perfectly, blessedly, aware of Rick. His hands settled on her shoulders. He nudged her forward.

"Take a deep breath and get it over with."

She did.

She reached out her hand and let his strength propel her forward. Before she knew it she was there, her fingers splayed wide, touching, smoothing, caressing the singed skin of her bird. The sobs ripped free, consuming her with a ferocity that terrified her. She couldn't stop shaking. The agony she'd been fighting for so long slammed through her once again. She fell against the chopper to keep from collapsing, clinging to the door she'd managed to smash open before the chopper exploded all those weeks before as she sobbed against the injustice of it all. She cried for everything that had happened and everything that would never have a chance to happen.

And then she cried some more.

She cried for Carrie and she cried for Sergeant Lange. She cried for Sergeant Turner and she cried for the baby. She wasn't sure how long she stood there sobbing, but eventually she realized she'd run out of tears. She was bone-dry.

Parched. Drained.

And she was in Rick's arms.

He held her close and stroked her hair as the cloud of grief continued to dissipate. As the last of it burned off, she forced herself to scrape the dregs of her strength together and pull away. His arms fell to her waist as she stared up at him. She had no idea what to say, how to explain what had happened. When she opened her mouth to try, he shook his head.

"I know."

He did.

He'd lost a man here, too. In the throes of her misery, she hadn't even noticed his.

She did now.

She reached up and smoothed the silent tears from his cheeks, frowning as the salt smeared the day-old grease paint deeper into his flesh. She had nothing to dry him with; his T-shirt was soaked and they'd already stowed their fatigue blouses in their rucksacks hours before. She reached down and pulled the hem of her own T-shirt from the waist of her trousers. She tore off a strip from the bottom and used that, drying one cheek and then the other. It wasn't until she finished that she realized how stupid she must look.

He didn't seem to mind.

He retrieved the scrap of cotton and closed his hand over hers. "Thank you."

She managed a nod.

"You ready to leave?"

She managed another. "Just…let me get a good look. I didn't before. I was too busy."

"Take as long as you need."

His arms slipped away, leaving her oddly bereft.

She chalked it up to the lingering sorrow and turned to face the chopper. It was easier this time. She even managed to look at the shattered remains as a pilot, automatically cataloguing the damage and calculating more fully what must have actually happened during the crash. The pilot's door was still dangling open, she swung it wider and leaned up into the cockpit to get a better look at the gauges.

She didn't expect much.

Nor did she get it. Most were cracked, melted or covered in soot. But as she reached out to move the stick, something fluttered against the copilot's seat.

Eve froze.

"What is it?"

"Probably nothing. Looks like a piece of paper or fabric." Still, whatever it was, it was strangely intact given the way the seat beneath had been seared down to its skeletal frame. Had the monkeys left it there? She stretched out her hands, but couldn't quite reach it.

"Could you give me a boost?"

Rick wrapped his hands around her waist and lifted her up. She reached over the control panel between the seats and snagged it. "Got it." She half expected the curl of sooty paper to disintegrate in her hand as he set her on her feet, but it didn't. She held on to the singed corner and unfurled the roughly three-by-three-inch sheet of paper— and immediately wished she hadn't.

*Sweet mercy.*

It was a photo of Carrie Evans and Bill Turner.

Arm-in-arm.

The Polaroid appeared to have been taken in a corner of some candlelit restaurant. She couldn't be sure. There was no mistaking the intimacy of their relationship, however. The camera had captured it perfectly. Bill and Carrie's passion for one another shone through more than just their eyes. It was in the way their arms were hooked possessively and yet reverently around each other. They were clearly in love. She raised her head, hoping against hope Rick hadn't seen it—

He had.

He tore his tortured stare from the photo.

She had no idea what to do, much less what to say. All this time spent concealing the truth and here she was, shoving the most damning piece of evidence right under his nose.

*Dammit, just ask.*

She'd never know otherwise.

She held on blindly to her hope and did. "Rick, we came here to figure out why my chopper crashed. No one has to know we found this, do they? I mean, they're dead. What purpose would it serve to ruin their records now? It's not as if—"

Oh, God, she was babbling.

She stopped. Breathed. Waited.

Prayed.

Her heart nearly ripped in two as his hands came up. But instead of taking the photo away, he closed her fingers over the picture and covered her hands with his. "I'm afraid I don't know what you're talking about. I don't see anything." His gaze met hers, dark and steady. Determined. "Do you?"

Gratitude seared through her. And something else.

Something she was afraid to label.

She shook her head quickly. "No, I don't."

He nodded. "Then I think it's time we found a spot to bivouac for the night, don't you?"

"I do."


The silence was back—and this time, it had locked in like a dead bolt. Rick picked up the packet of instant coffee Eve had passed over twenty minutes before and tapped it into his canteen cup. He could barely make out the murky liquid from the jungle shadows as he swished it around in the dark.

He could, however, hear Eve sigh.

He glanced up as she shifted against the trunk she'd claimed as hers in the four-foot alcove they'd commandeered for the night. Though he couldn't make out her eyes any better than he could his coffee, he could tell by the angle of her head that her attention was still carefully fused to her own tin cup. He thought about saying something. Anything.

But what?

And why?

He already knew what was on her mind. The same thing that was on his. The crash. The sorrow, the guilt.

The regret.

Though they were drawing on opposite sides of the same coin, there was no doubt in his mind that hers had paid out in anguish far more deeply than his. No matter what they discovered in that wreckage tomorrow, he would always have one more death on his conscious. Eve would have three. No amount of time spent rehashing events with an army chaplain or some shrink would ease that debt. It was the price of leadership.

Of surviving.

But payday had hit Eve especially hard.

Frankly he wasn't sure which had been worse, weathering his own grief as they'd come face-to-face with the remains of that chopper or the agony of watching Eve succumb to hers. Her tears had damned near ripped him apart. She might be sitting three feet away now, calmly staring into her cup, but he could still feel her sobbing uncontrollably in his arms and he could still see the utter desolation in her eyes.

He'd have given anything to ease her pain.

He still would.

He'd also do anything to make sure she got her wings back—because he'd seen more than desolation today.

He'd also seen the truth.

One desperate, pleading stare from those emerald eyes was all it had taken. Just like that, six weeks of suspicion and misconception had been shattered. He knew exactly what Eve was hiding—and she was right. The secret she'd been jealously guarding since that fateful day had nothing to do with the crash. But it had everything to do with her friend and his sergeant. From the shock that had exploded on Eve's face when she'd spied that singed photograph, she'd had no idea proof existed.

But he had.

He'd been sitting twenty feet away the night it had been taken. But for a camera's inopportune flash, he might have succeeded in maintaining his own personal *don't ask, don't tell* policy. That flash had changed it. Once Turner's gaze met his across that restaurant, he'd been forced to officially acknowledge his sergeant's relationship with Captain Evans.

He'd been forced to counsel them both.

For his sergeant's sake, he'd done it off the record.

Or so he'd thought.

Maybe Turner was right. His sergeant had accused him of being more interested in saving the man from his woman than saving a soldier for the Army. Of not wanting anyone else to have a real relationship with a woman because *he* didn't want one. Of course Rick had denied it at the time.

Now he wasn't so sure.

Rick swished his coffee once more before lifting the cup to down a mouthful of the cold sludge. Truth be known, his impromptu confession to Eve about his folks had him reexamining several other motivations as well. Like why he'd really gone Special Forces.

And why he'd stayed.

*"I was five."*

Eve winced as the contents of Rick's canteen cup sloshed over his hand, landing on his boots with a soft plop.

He didn't curse.

He simply transferred his cup to his left hand and carefully wiped his right on his jungle fatigues. She forced herself to relax as he took his time wiping the coffee from his boots as well. After all, she'd spent the last two hours collecting her thoughts and screwing up her courage, trying to figure out the best way to broach that dream.

She could allow him a few moments to collect his.

He finished wiping his boots and set his tin cup on the gnarled root beside him. She blessed the dark when he finally raised his head, because she couldn't actually see his eyes.

"You don't have to tell me."

She took a deep breath and nodded. "I know. But I want to." Amazingly, she did.

That alone should have terrified her.

But it didn't.

Nor did her growing need to explain her dreams to this man have anything to do with gratitude. Yes, she was grateful Rick had agreed to conceal Carrie's relationship with his sergeant. Deeply grateful. But it was more than that. How much more, she couldn't be sure. All she knew for certain was she'd barely begun and already her heart was hammering against her ribs. Evidently wanting to share her past and actually doing it were two completely different things.

Dammit, quit stalling.

*Ask.*

"So...what exactly did I...say?"

"Enough."

Despite two hours of preparation, she flinched.

Still, she was forced to appreciate his honesty. He could have denied everything or tried to smooth it over. Carrie had at first. They'd spent the next two weeks on eggshells.

Until she'd had the dream again.

She wrapped her fingers around her tin cup and stared into the cocoa within, fighting off the humiliation as she faked a smile. "Guess it's a good thing I fell in love with choppers, 'cause I'd have made a lousy spook. First sign of stress and I jabber in my sleep. As it is, I've just had to learn how to avoid sleepovers without offending—uh—" She flushed. "People."

Sleep, hell. She was jabbering on while she was awake. Again.

As if Rick really needed to know she'd yet to spend an entire night with a man. So much for keeping the humiliation at bay. She set the canteen cup on the gnarled root beside her and closed her eyes—and stiffened.

His motion startled her.

His touch startled her. His fingers seared her skin, cooking off several layers as he slipped them beneath her chin. *"Don't."*

She opened her eyes only to find herself staring straight into his. He was so close she could make out the dark brown of his irises despite the darker shroud of night. "I'm sorry, I—"

"Don't be ashamed, Eve. It's not your fault."

Wasn't it?

He claimed to have heard enough. Maybe he just thought he had. "You know my mother left me, don't you?"

"Yes."

"And you know he struck me."

The fingers beneath her chin tensed. "Yes."

For some reason she couldn't explain, she was driven to rub the ugliness in. To let him know how truly far apart their childhoods had been. "There were a lot of he's, Rick."

She heard him swallow.

"How many?"

"Too many." She shrugged. "And not nearly enough."

This time his entire body tensed.

She shifted her stare past his shoulder, well aware she was avoiding his gaze. "Have you ever been hungry, really hungry? So cold you thought your fingers would fall off?" She'd seen the white stitching on his Ranger patch the day they'd met. She knew he'd survived Ranger school in the winter. Still, he had to have known deep down the Army wouldn't kill him.

Dallas might be in Texas, but it dipped into the lower thirties in the winter. With some other kid's discarded blanket for a coat, the nights had felt a whole lot colder.

She swallowed the knot of memories clogging her throat.

Even so, her voice came out hoarse. "It's one thing to wonder *when* you'll eat or be warm again, quite another to wonder *if*." She scraped up the nerve to seek out his gaze. "It's amazing what a person will do when she's reduced to that type of hunger, that level of cold. And if she has a child?"

His eyes closed.

He opened them again, but now he was avoiding her.

Regret seared through her. She felt dirtier than she had in years. What had possessed her to be so damned honest?

Had she really wanted to repel him?

If so, she'd succeeded.

Why else had he said less than fifteen words since she'd started? She slid her gaze down to the silent working of his throat. "I'm sorry. I didn't intend to get maudlin. Most of the time I'm even okay about it now."

It was the truth.

It had taken a while. Years. A decade of listening to Father Francis and the nuns who ran St. Cecilia's orphanage. But eventually, the old priest's words had sunk in and she was able to put the demons to rest. "For a long time I thought my mother had abandoned me. She didn't. She gave me life. Not once, but twice. They found her body in a cardboard box on some street years later. I could have been beside her, but I wasn't. In her own way, she loved me enough to let me go. Anna helped me remember that last night, among other things. It's just...sometimes when I'm upset the dreams come back, you know?''

"I know.''

He did.

She stared into his eyes and saw his nightmares too. He dreamed of his mother and of his father. She shook her head, shook herself. "I don't know what's wrong with me. You must think I'm such a selfish—'' She broke off as he reached out and trailed his fingers down her cheek, tipped her chin.

"I think you are an amazing woman, Eve Paris.''

He might not be able to see her latest blush, but he must have felt it. Lord knew she could. "I doubt that. But thanks...for everything.'' His presence. The picture.

His silence.

His hand fell away as he nodded solemnly.

She stared at his scar. A scar she'd caused.

The visible one anyway.

Despite his grease paint she could tell exactly where it was because the skin around it puckered slightly. She reached up and traced its length. "I am *so* sorry.''

His fingers closed over hers as they had outside the chopper earlier that evening. But this time, there was no sooty picture. Her hand was empty.

And then it wasn't.

He lowered his head and brushed his lips across her fingertips, then gently pressed his mouth into the center of her palm. She sucked in her breath as desire ripped through her, desire so intense it left her breathless.

He left her breathless.

Wanting. Needing.

She closed her eyes and every other one of her senses

came alive, focused with crystal clarity. She could feel the silk of his lips, the rasp of the stubble covering his jaw. The seductive heat in his breath. She could smell his subtle woodsy scent. Her palm began to ache.

She began to ache.

How could one simple caress from this man be more erotic than full-body contact with any other man she'd ever known?

She opened her eyes and knew.

That kiss had aroused Rick, too.

For a moment she was terrified he was going to kiss her again, this time on the lips. And then she was terrified he wasn't. Her fear fled beneath searing anticipation as he released her hand and slipped his callused fingers behind her neck and pulled her close. But he didn't kiss her.

He guided her head to his chest instead.

It took her a moment to realize he'd leaned back against his tree, drawing her along with him. He'd even managed to adjust her torso in his arms, cradling her thighs within his, before she could think about stopping him.

But he wasn't coming on to her.

He didn't even seem to be aroused anymore.

Rather, he seemed intent on simply holding her. An inexplicable warmth spread through her as he combed his fingers through her hair and pressed her cheek to his T-shirt. She lay there for a good minute, her head resting atop the solid muscles of his chest, gradually lulled under by the deep, steady thudding of his heart.

"Get some sleep."

Against her will, her eyes drifted shut. Or maybe it was with her will. She couldn't be sure anymore. All she knew was that for the first time, she was falling asleep in a man's arms.

And she wasn't afraid to dream.

# Chapter 10

She could have slept another eight hours.

Eve slid her rifle and rucksack off her back and leaned them against Rick's before rolling the lingering stiffness from her shoulders. Two hours into the day and her T-shirt, fatigues and boots were already drenched in sweat. Still, despite the driving pace Rick had set that morning, she felt more rested than she had in weeks, even years.

She wished she could say the same for Rick.

He had to be exhausted.

Four packets of instant coffee and an hour's power nap were all that stood between the man and an endless night of leaning against the base of some tree with her neurotic body cradled in his arms. She'd managed to rouse herself several times, certain it was finally her turn to stand watch. But each time, Rick had eased her head back down to his chest and lulled her to sleep with the promise that he'd wake her soon.

He never had.

Guilt flooded her. No matter what he'd said, she was standing the first watch tonight—and it *would* be a double. But first, they'd have to survive the day. Eve tore her gaze from the gear at her boots and forced herself to stare through the thinning trees and into the clearing beyond. At her bird. After all these weeks of wondering, all that stood between her and the truth were five slender saplings and twenty feet of scorched earth.

And Rick.

Except he wasn't between her and anything anymore, he was beside her. Literally as well as figuratively.

No, she hadn't heard him.

Nor could she see him. He was too good at what he did. But she could sense him closing in somewhere amid the denser foliage off to her right. And then she felt him—or rather, she felt his steadying warmth as he stepped behind her.

"Ready?"

She opened her mouth automatically. She closed it just as quickly. They'd come too far for lies, even polite ones.

"No."

Unfortunately she didn't have much of a choice, did she? Not if she was holding out for another night's rest in this lifetime. She sighed and turned to bathe within those twin pools of dark, soothing concern. Much as she wanted to lose herself in those eyes, in those comforting arms, she couldn't. Nor was there any sense in delaying the inevitable.

"Let's do it."

Rick stood there for several moments, then nodded.

He snagged her rifle and slung it onto his shoulder alongside his, then grabbed both their rucks as he turned to lead the way through the remaining trees. She didn't bother arguing as they cleared the saplings. It might be easier facing the wreckage this time around, but each step still ripped through her heart.

At least she managed to hold on to her tears.

Barely.

They reached her bird all too soon. She ignored the burning in her heart and in her throat and studied the blackened remains as Rick dumped their rucks at their feet. Everything appeared to be exactly as they'd left it.

She wasn't surprised.

Rick would never have exposed them like this if he suspected the Córdobans had tracked them last night. Still, she had to wonder how long their luck would hold. Unwilling to press it now, she got down to work. She turned away as Rick leaned their rifles against the open belly of the bird and concentrated on removing supplies Anna had blessedly managed to obtain on such short notice.

"If you need anything—"

She nodded. "I'll ask."

She felt more than saw his answering nod as she culled several screwdrivers, regular and needle-nose pliers, a crescent wrench, a mini sledgehammer and her crowbar from the selection of tools and scooped them into her arms. Given the amount and extent of the damage she'd noted the evening before, she suspected she'd need the hammer and the crowbar more than the other tools combined—plus the mini oxyacetylene cutting torch. Rick was already snapping photographs of the shattered exterior as she stood, so she stepped away from the bird and waited.

They'd decided against a digital camera, opting instead for a 35 mm with two dozen rolls of good old-fashioned film. Film that could be presented to the investigation board undeveloped—and hence, unquestionably *not* tampered with. They'd also decided each roll of film should include a close-up of the chopper's data plate. Inclusion of the Black Hawk's official military UH-60L nomenclature combined with its unique serial number would anchor each separate loop of negatives to the specific chopper she'd signed out that fateful morning.

Rick finally moved in for a shot of the data plate.

It was time.

Eve swallowed the lump in her throat and climbed into the cockpit as Rick loaded a fresh roll of film and snapped an initial shot of the data plate. She spread her tools out on what was left of the central instrument panel. Memories crowded in, stifling her as she stared at the charred remains of the copilot's seat beyond. Haunting memories. She jerked her gaze up and concentrated on the breeze wafting through the gaping hole where the chopper's windows should have been.

It didn't help.

She could still hear the rasping gurgle in Carrie's chest...and her final tortured confession. Eve swung her head to the right only to come face-to-face with the ghost of her crew chief's eternal, unseeing stare. She closed her eyes, wondering for the thousandth time if Rick had been able to close Sergeant Lange's before he'd buried the man.

"Eve?"

"I'm...fine."

With his hand gently squeezing her arm, she was.

She swallowed firmly. "You should probably get a few close-ups of the broom closet before I crack it open."

He withdrew his hand and nodded.

She twisted around until she was facing the rear of the chopper. Rick leaned through the doorway as she braced her left hand against the central console. She locked her right to the pilot's door, carefully evading the nightmarish void beside her. A succession of rapid flashes, clicks and whirs filled the cockpit as she focused on Rick's shoulders instead.

"Done."

She reached for the set of screwdrivers as he straightened, then thought better of it as she studied the steel access plate that covered the broom closet behind the pilot's seat. The sheet metal was warped and buckled in spots. Alone, the damage was good because the gaps would give her several places to insert the claws on her crowbar if necessary. Unfortunately the screws had also melted into the surrounding steel.

That was bad.

If she fired up her cutting torch without knowing what lay beneath, she might accidentally destroy the very evidence that could exonerate her.

Or seal her fate.

She'd been over that crash a trillion times in her head. The only explanation she could come up with—hell, the only hope she could come up with—lay behind that warped panel. The broom closet housed the collective's control rod and auxiliary servo cylinders. Rick still believed he'd never felt her pull pitch. But she knew she had.

There was only one way they could both be right.

The collective rod must have snapped.

Given the high tensile strength of the steel rod, mechanical failure was rare enough. And when compared to the relatively low physiological strength in her puny arms, it was damned near unheard of. But *not* impossible. Stranger things had happened when adrenaline had been thrown into the mix—and hers had been churning at full throttle that day.

Unfortunately, it wasn't now.

Popping those melted screws by hand was out of the question. She'd have to come up with another way to remove the panel. She stared at the iron crowbar.

It was worth a shot.

She retrieved the bar and slipped the claw on the angled

end beneath the first buckled seam, putting everything she had into a quick, all-out heave.

Nothing.

She tacked on a fervent prayer as she attacked the other four buckled sections in turn.

Not a single one budged.

"Want me to try?"

She flicked her gaze to Rick's sinewy arms. Not even the grease paint smeared into his skin could conceal the thick, generous muscles beneath. No doubt about it, the man was significantly stronger than her. Perhaps too strong. Since the screws had melted, there was a good chance part of the warped panel had fused to the collective rod beneath. She didn't want to risk any more damage than was absolutely necessary.

"Not yet." She wiped the sweat from her brow and dried her hand on her T-shirt. "Let's try the torch first."

He nodded and turned to walk over to his own ruck. He hunkered down and sorted through the supplies they'd packed in his and grabbed the oxyacetylene pack. Rick must have used a torch before because he turned on the gas to both cylinders and used the lighter from his pocket to ignite the gas mixture streaming from the cutting tip. He adjusted the flame as he returned to her side, then passed the tip and a pair of safety glasses through the open door.

"Thanks."

He nodded as she donned the darkened protective lenses. Sparks showered into the cockpit as she carefully cut into the warped sheet metal, carving a tight circle around the first melted screw, then each of the others in turn.

"There."

He took the torch from her hand and turned off the gas as she picked up the crowbar and slipped the claw beneath the right seam of the access panel. This time the sheet popped off easily. Much too easily.

Her heart shot into her throat.

She wasn't ready. She'd spent the past two days preparing for this moment, but now that it was finally here—

Dammit, now was *not* the time to chicken out.

She shoved the warped panel aside, her eyes automatically picking out the collective rod from the others and tracing it as she dumped the panel into the copilot's seat. A split second later, she found what she'd been looking for.

She blinked. Stared.

Gasped.

Rick stiffened beside her. *"Son of a—"*

The rest was lost to the sudden, furious pounding in her chest, the thundering roar in her ears. It didn't matter.

She'd heard enough. She'd *seen* enough.

Rick's curse confirmed it.

The collective rod had snapped, all right. But not for the reason she'd suspected. She swallowed the bile threatening at the base of her throat and reached out to trace her fingertip across the raw ends of the steel rod.

Except, it wasn't raw.

At least, not all of it.

Over half the diameter of the collective rod had been severed with something finely serrated, straight and held damned near perpendicular to the length of the steel.

The rod had been deliberately *cut.*

It wouldn't have mattered if she'd pulled pitch or not that day. Even if the engine hadn't cut out, without collective she hadn't had a prayer in hell of maintaining control. Someone wanted her to crash her chopper.

Hard.

"I don't understand. *Why?*"

She tore her gaze from the rod and fused it to Rick's equally stunned stare on the slim, desperate hope that he had an answer. He didn't. But by the time he ripped his own gaze from the rod and met hers, the fury searing through those dark brown eyes had coalesced into chilling determination.

"I have no idea. But I will find out."

"It just doesn't make sense."

Rick returned the crowbar and torch to his ruck along with the last of their tools and glanced up. Eve was slumped against the side of her bird, the emerald fire in her gaze now as cold and exhausted as the empty blackened hulk behind her. It had been surprisingly difficult giving her the space she'd needed these past three hours as she ripped apart the remainder of the wreckage, but he was glad he had.

She'd needed it.

Earning her exoneration at the expense of her crew's lives had been a shallow victory.

She'd needed time to adjust.

Time to loosen her grip on guilt.

While he suspected she was still clinging to the final threads, she had at least moved on enough to begin thinking clearly again. Dispassionately. Her tentative statement proved it. Just as the tension in her gaze begged him to confirm it.

He closed the flap to his ruck and gave it.

"I agree. Nothing about this makes sense."

The tension in her eyes eased—but the exhaustion didn't.

She needed food. Sleep.

Hell, they both did if they were going to figure this out. This time, he didn't plan on traveling far. But he did intend on moving them into the trees. Far enough and deep enough to kill this hair-raising sensation of exposure. He swung his ruck up and hooked it on his right shoulder then did the same with both their rifles before he stooped down to grab the main strap to Eve's ruck as well.

"Let's go."

Fortunately, she was too tired to argue. She simply followed him into the tree line, as silently as he'd taught her six weeks before. He didn't get them as far away as he would have liked. He was just too damned tired. Near as he could figure, he'd slept four hours out of the last sixty. If he didn't get another hit of caffeine soon, he wouldn't be able to shuffle one boot in front of the other because he'd be lying face down on the jungle floor, dead to the world.

Where would Eve be then?

Unwilling to contemplate the answer, he stopped in the middle of a particularly dense section of foliage. He could feel the confusion radiating from Eve behind him as she stopped short as well. He stared up through the dark green fronds of the ferns, measuring, gauging. The trees anchoring either end were three feet apart. Still, it was completely shaded, enclosed. Cooler.

It would have to do.

He dropped their gear. "Let's eat." He winced as he realized the clipped voice that slapped into him was his own. He turned to apologize, to explain, only to discover he didn't have to. Eve evidently understood that his terseness stemmed from exhaustion because she was already kneeling down and opening her ruck. She pulled out two MREs, slit the outer pouches open and retrieved both instant coffee packets without being asked.

He accepted them gratefully.

He tore off the tops and tapped the granules straight into his mouth. She grimaced, but she must have seen it done in the field before because she had her canteen open and waiting as he finished. He accepted the water gratefully too, quickly washing the bitter dregs down his throat.

"Thanks." He passed the canteen back.

"You're welcome. Now eat. And then for God's sake, get some sleep. You look like hell."

He scowled. "You don't look so fresh yourself."

She actually smiled. "At least I can still stand."

Damned if she wasn't right.

Until that moment, he hadn't realized he was half-leaning, half-sliding down the trunk of the tree behind him. He caved into temptation and lowered himself the rest of the way, his T-shirt scraping and snagging into the bark as he settled in at the base.

"Besides, I'm the reason you're exhausted."

He shrugged. "You needed the rest."

She leaned forward and passed one of the MRE pouches over. "So do you."

Not any more.

Or rather, not as desperately as he had two minutes before. The caffeine was already pouring into his blood, pulsing into his brain. He could feel the dull ache ebbing from his muscles as they spoke, his brain sharpening. The rest of his senses followed. "I'm fine now."

Her sharp snort disagreed with him. "And I could find my way back to the border from here with my eyes closed."

Closed eyes.

Now there was a fantasy.

He swallowed his groan. "Haven't you heard? Sleep's for sissies and pilots. All a grunt needs is coffee."

"Until you crash for good."

The concern in her frown took the sting out of the taunt. "Don't worry. I'll crash soon enough. But first, we need to talk." He leaned the MRE pouch against his right thigh and pulled out the cocoa packet to toss it back to her.

She caught it neatly.

He was jealous. Given the current, non-existent edge to his reflexes he'd have fumbled it—if he'd caught it at all. He watched her as she unscrewed the cap to her canteen and poured the water into her cup, wondering how hands

streaked with that much soot, sweat and grease paint could
be so slender and so graceful. The same thought had struck
him several times over the course of the morning as he
watched her rip that chopper apart panel-by-charred-panel.

*The chopper.*

The sabotage.

He rubbed his fingers into the muscles of his neck, mas-
saging the knots that had been tightening all morning as
she retrieved the cocoa packet and tapped the contents
down. "You do know you weren't the intended target,
don't you?"

She paused in midtear.

She looked up, hope swirling amid the guilt-ridden shadows of her eyes. "How can you be so sure?"

He lowered his hand and shrugged. "For one thing, you
were too new in country. For another, you may not remember, but on the ride from the hotel in Panama City to the
Huey you mentioned that other than Carrie, you'd yet to
run into anyone you knew. The level of tampering we doc-
umented today suggests a mature hatred or a professional
job. Both operate on more than a passing whim."

Personally, he was leaning toward a professional.

A mechanic, most likely.

Who else would have the security clearance necessary to
gain access to an army Black Hawk, in addition to intimate
knowledge of the UH-60's fuel sensors? Eve had said it
herself just an hour before—whoever tampered with the gas
gauge so that when the chopper's main fuel tank ran dry it
still registered as three-quarters full, had known what the
hell he or she had been doing. Especially since the external
fuel bladders had also failed to switch over.

As sabotages went, it had been bloody brilliant.

Despite 460 gallons of JP-5 in the external tanks, the
bird had simply run out of gas—in midair. Sawing halfway
through the collective rod should have ensured that no one

lived to tell about it. Facing that burned-out hulk again confirmed it. They'd been damned lucky to survive.

She had to be thinking the same thing.

"What about you? Could you have been the target?"

He swore he saw her hands shake as she swished the cocoa around in her cup. When she met his gaze, he knew he had.

His air bled out.

She was afraid. More so than she'd been when she'd thought she might have been the intended target. The fear had even succeeded in crowding out the guilt in her eyes. It was in the slender grime-streaked fingers biting into her cup. Eve was honest-to-God terrified someone was gunning for him.

The realization caused his heart to hammer painfully against his chest. And damned if the worry burning in her gaze didn't sear off the remainder of his exhaustion.

He reached out and tipped the curve of her sooty chin. "Relax. You told me yourself, that collective rod had to have been filed down in the privacy of the hangar. Same with the tampering on the fuel sensors. That pushes the time of sabotage back to the evening before the crash, maybe earlier. My briefing was a last-minute rescheduling—one that I suggested. Even I didn't know I'd be on any chopper, much less yours, until that morning."

That cleared his platoon sergeant from the list, too.

She searched his gaze for several moments, then nodded.

He could feel the tension pouring out of her as he lowered his hand and leaned back against his tree. He reached down as she took a sip from her tin cup and snagged his MRE pouch. He rooted through the contents. Hungry as he was, even turkey loaf didn't appeal to him. What he wouldn't give for a twelve-ounce sirloin cut from a side of Nebraska corn-fed beef about now. Yeah, right. That was as likely as him figuring out this mess before he managed a four-hour stretch of sleep—at least.

He sighed. "What about Carrie?"

Eve stiffened.

"Wh-what do you mean?"

He jerked his head up. Panic? That was the last emotion he'd expected. He must have been mistaken. His brain was becoming fogged again. The infusion of caffeine couldn't keep up. "The sabotage?"

Yeah, he'd been mistaken.

Her gaze was clear, steady. But worried.

And stunned.

"You think someone was trying to kill Carrie? That's insane. Carrie was open and honest. Okay, so she liked men more than she should have. But she also truly loved all people and people loved her. She was one of the good folks."

"She's also dead."

Eve flinched.

*Damn.* "I'm sorry. I didn't mean—"

"It's okay. She is dead. But she wasn't the intended target. She couldn't have been. She was just in the wrong place at the wrong time."

He froze.

"What is it?" She swung her head around and stared frantically into the jungle beyond. "Did you hear—"

He reached out and grabbed her hand. "Say that again."

"What?" She shook her head. "Say what? That Carrie wasn't the intended target?"

"After that."

"She was in the wrong place at—"

"*The wrong time.*"

Bloody hell.

He was so stupid. He'd spent the last several hours going over every single thing Sergeant Turner had ever told him about Carrie Evans. Trying to figure out why someone would want to kill her, only to wonder if he wasn't tracking down the wrong trail. That maybe Eve's crew chief had been the intended target all along.

Neither of them were.

"Ernesto."

"What?"

He released her hand. "Not what, *who*. Remember that platoon of native San Sebastián soldiers you dropped off at the LZ right before you picked me up?"

"Of course."

"Ernesto Torres was leading them."

"The president's son?"

"Yes."

She slumped against her tree.

He on the other hand, stood. Paced.

Or rather, he tried to.

He stared into the foliage, dismissing the adult boa constrictor that was looped around a thick, low-lying branch two trees away. He could only hope Eve hadn't seen it, because he was too busy to mention it. The facts were falling into place too quickly. So quickly his exhausted brain was having trouble cataloguing them. But they all led to the same conclusion.

His buddy was in danger.

"Rick, you're talking about an attempted assassination."

He swung around. "I am."

"But who would want to kill the man. Why?"

"Why was Kennedy assassinated? Lincoln? Or more appropriately in this case—Martin Luther King?"

"His views?"

"Exactly. It's no secret at the presidential palace that Ernesto was the driving force behind his father's initial request to bring our Special Forces in to help train theirs. He and his older brother, Miguel, fought about the proposal for two years before their father finally agreed.''

She gasped, then stood. "And now their father is sick."

"He's more than sick, Eve. The man is dying."

"I'm sorry." Her fingers closed over his arm. He stared at them. At her. "It's obvious you respect the man."

He did. "I've known him a long time. We met through his son. Ernie and I survived Ranger school together. He was an exchange officer. His father's a good man." In a lot of ways, Guillermo Torres reminded Rick of his own father.

"You think Miguel could be behind it?"

"I don't know. The night before the crash, I'd have said no. I've never trusted the man, but I also thought we were making progress. That given time, Miguel would have come around. I do know we'd managed to impress him lately. But there are others. Advisors to Miguel and his father who will never come around. And with Ernie out of the way?"

"By U.S. Army hands, no less."

He nodded. "You have to admit, an assassination disguised as a training accident would have provided an airtight cover."

"More than you realize."

Something in her voice told him she'd made a connection. "What is it?"

"The day before we went down, I noticed several locals hanging around the airstrip. I didn't think much of it because they were in uniform and accompanied by our own mechanics."

"It's a place to start."

Records had to have been kept. Names, ranks and unit designators logged. Clearances recorded.

Tomorrow.

They were supposed to check in with their Huey pilot

this evening. He'd arrange for their extraction to take place in the morning. But tonight, after he'd bagged some serious sleep, they'd head to the crash site one more time and carve off a damning chunk of that collective rod. By dawn, they'd be on their way to San Sebastián, Ernesto, and those logs.

What if it wasn't soon enough?

The hand on his arm pulled him back to the present.

Eve's hand.

She cupped his jaw. He closed his eyes against the touch. Her touch.

It didn't help. He was too damned tired for his body not to respond to this woman. Bloody hell. Even with two solid days of exertion soaked into their T-shirts and trousers, he could still smell her unique scent hovering beneath.

Soft, smooth.

Welcoming.

It was a scent that would haunt him into eternity.

He opened his eyes—but he didn't dare stare into hers.

"Don't worry, Rick. We'll get to your friend in time. Whoever is behind this, they can't risk striking again so soon. It would lead to questions."

He stared into that dark emerald gaze then—and hid his own private terror. The hell with questions.

He wanted answers.

Eve might not have been the initial intended target in the crash. But if whoever tampered with that chopper found out she'd been here and examined it, she would become one.

# Chapter 11

The jungle was much too dark.

Rick shifted his legs and massaged the charley horse in his upper left thigh that had managed to rouse him from sleep—a chore Eve had failed to accomplish as she'd promised. Though they were three feet apart, she didn't seem to notice he'd woken on his own. No doubt because she couldn't actually see him. Hell, he could barely make out her blond curls in the shifting shadows, shadows that weren't normally formed until the sun had traveled well past the afternoon and into the night.

How far into night, he couldn't be sure.

He couldn't see enough stars for the dense foliage and he didn't dare light the dial on his watch.

Because Eve was crying.

Once he'd cleared the sleep-induced fog from his brain, he'd realized why he could make out so many of her curls despite the fact that her body was facing his. Her head was buried in her knees. And her shoulders were quaking.

Silently.

He thought about clearing his throat. Even saying something. But he didn't. He shouldn't. If Eve had wanted his comfort and his ear, surely she wouldn't have held on to her grief until she knew he was unconscious to the world before giving in to it? Frankly, he could take a hint.

His mind could anyway.

Evidently, his heart couldn't. "Need a shoulder?"

She stiffened.

Several seconds passed before her head came up. She wiped her hands across her eyes and cheeks as she pressed her head against the tree behind her. He knew, because he could see the pale flashes of her hands and her face in the dark. She'd cleaned the grease paint and grime from her face while he'd been sleeping. Her ragged sigh filled the tiny alcove.

"I didn't...realize you were awake."

Obviously. She hadn't answered his question either.

He swallowed the surge of disappointment.

"Yes."

He blinked.

"I mean, if you meant it. Then, yes, I really could use a shoulder. But if you didn't, then it's okay. Because— Oh, hell. I'm yammering again." Her voice broke on the last word.

His heart broke.

He leaned forward without thinking and slid his hands beneath her arms, pulling her up and toward him in one smooth motion. She gasped softly as he settled against his tree and adjusted her on his lap and in his arms.

She hiccuped. "I guess you—"

"—meant it." He nodded firmly.

For some reason, that caused her tears to flow again. He guided her head to his chest as the sobs overtook her. This time, they weren't silent. Still, he didn't have the heart to interrupt her grief long enough to hush her. He just pressed her cheek deeper into the dampness spreading across his T-shirt and stroked his fingers through her curls over and over. He managed to catch himself a split second before his lips connected with the soft silk.

That brand of comfort, he couldn't afford.

A week ago, perhaps.

But not now. They'd come too far.

He'd come too far.

His arms trembled from the force of holding back, from fighting so bloody hard to hold his heart apart from hers. She must have felt the battle, because her sobs eased, then subsided altogether. She raised her head and stared into his eyes. This close, he could see the toll today had taken.

Her reddened eyes and flushed forehead.

Her tear-stained cheeks.

He could even make out the narrow slash of grease paint she'd missed beside her swollen lips.

For some reason, that green slash mesmerized him.

So much so, he had to clench his fist to keep from reaching out to wipe it himself. He forced himself to exhale. Unfortunately, his air came out in a single, audible whoosh.

She stiffened in his arms.

He made out her sudden blush, but only because the tide evened out her coloring. "I don't know what's wrong with me. I swear I haven't cried this much in years." She drew a shaky breath. "But lately, I can't seem to stop."

"Guilt."

For a second, he thought she was going to deny it. But then she nodded. "You're right. It is guilt. I thought I'd feel better, you know? But I don't. Especially after what we discovered. I just keep thinking, it didn't need to be."

She drew another breath. This one was slower, deeper. Resigned.

"You must think I'm so weak."

He succumbed to temptation and reached up. He smoothed his fingers along the smear of grease paint, gently erasing the slash from the curve of her silken skin. "I told you last night what I thought and I meant it. You are an amazing woman, Eve Paris. You're also strong. Much stronger than I am."

The corner of her mouth bumped into his fingers as she smiled softly. "Nice try, Super Soldier."

He smiled back. But it was true.

She was stronger than he.

Braver, too.

They'd both suffered painful losses in their lives. How she'd dealt with hers said so much more about the strength of her character than how he'd dealt with his. He'd run away. Not to the circus, but to the jungle. He was still running. He'd been running so damned long, he didn't know how to stop.

But Eve did.

Eve had.

She'd turned around and faced her demons. She'd stayed in life, fighting them every step of the way. She was still fighting. Hell, she'd risked what was left of her career, not to mention her life, to travel back to Córdoba and confront the ghosts in that chopper. Maybe it was time to learn from her. Maybe it was time to stop running for once and for all.

God knew he wanted to.

He just didn't know how.

He used to think he belonged in the jungle. That he needed the peace and the solitude that came at the end of each day as he'd wander off and hunker down to absorb the night. He wasn't so sure anymore. Something had changed.

He was beginning to think he'd changed.

Why else did the mere thought of being in the jungle without Eve feel so damned empty?

Lonely.

Was this the feeling that had finally driven his brother to take a chance at married life? Or was it what had driven their father to end his?

He didn't know.

All he knew was that this feeling was dangerous. He'd learned the lesson the previous night, as he'd held Eve in his arms the first time, comforting her as she slept. Pretending, fantasizing. Not about making love to her. Okay, partly about making love to her. But mostly about just loving her.

Until he'd remembered it couldn't be.

"Rick?"

Until that moment, he hadn't realized he'd been staring so intently into her eyes. He dropped his gaze to her mouth. Heat surged through him as the tip of her tongue slid across her bottom lip almost nervously, heat that had nothing to do with the humid night. He reached up without thinking and touched the center of the wet, tantalizing trail left behind. Fire exploded within his groin as her tongue slid out again, this time to lick the tip of his finger.

He groaned.

She smiled.

And, God help him, he lowered his head.

The darkened jungle faded away as he captured her lips with his and delved slowly, carefully, between. He was ready, prepared for the raw, greedy desire that ripped through him as her tongue met his. He wasn't worried. Unlike their first kiss not far from this very spot, unlike their second out on that dance floor in Panama City, he could control this.

For a full five seconds, he did.

And then the hunger set in.

Deep and reckless, it lashed at him as it had before. But this time, it cut deeper. Burned hotter. Until, suddenly, it was dangerously close to spiraling out of control.

And so was he.

He anchored his hands to her curls, turning her head in order to gain better access to her mouth. For a split second, he was afraid he'd been too rough—until she moaned. The low keening in her throat that followed stoked the fire in his groin to a raging inferno. Desperate to douse it, he tore his mouth from hers and razed his lips down her throat. He found the source of the sound and covered it, desperately trying to absorb the vibrations through her flesh.

The keening deepened.

His hunger swelled.

He returned to her mouth and consumed another low, throaty moan. He was dimly aware of her hands at his waist, tugging at his T-shirt, sliding beneath, caressing his sweat-dampened flesh. He tried to pull away, to warn her.

He was filthy.

Saturated with more than two days of near non-stop exertion. But she didn't seem to care.

Nor would she release him.

If anything, she pulled him closer, kneading her fingers into the muscles of his chest, scraping her nails across his nipples. He groaned as his brain took the suggestion to heart.

His hands immediately followed.

One moment, her T-shirt lay between them and the next, it didn't. He abandoned it, bunched up somewhere above her bra, and tugged his hands down and around her back to complete the mission. He located the clasp with his left and tugged it open, claiming the generous swells that spilled out with his right. This time, they moaned together. He'd fantasized about this moment for far too long. Despite the dark, he was driven to memorize as much as he could.

He tore his mouth from hers and forced his night vision to its very limits as he focused on the creamy silk splayed out in his palms. He flicked his thumbs across her nipples and then covered them, groaning because she felt so damned *good* in his hands.

His hands.

He stared at them. His sweat-stained, filthy hands.

And realized where he was.

What he was doing.

What he should *not* be doing. Not with Eve. She deserved a man who cared enough to shower first. A man who would make love to her for the first time in a soft bed on dry sheets and not on some hard jungle floor crawling with insects, beetles and lizards. A man who would pull her close and hold her afterwards. A man who would continue to hold her while she slept. A man who would be there when she woke.

For the rest of her life.

Much as he wanted to be that man, he wasn't.

He pulled her bra down and carefully latched the ends of the straps behind her. It took three tries on this end of the operation as opposed to one heated rip on the other, but she sat there calmly, patiently, her chest heaving with less and less force as the passion began to ebb. He tugged her shirt down next and smoothed it into the waist of her trousers.

He did the same to his own.

"Bad timing, huh?"

The worst.

He nodded anyway as he cleansed his own remaining passion from his lungs with a deep sigh. He reached up and tipped her chin. How did he say this?

"Eve, I…"

She smiled softly, sadly. "I know. You wouldn't have

joined the Army and escaped into the jungle years ago, much less still be here, if you could."

She'd nailed it so cleanly, he didn't know what to say.

So he just held her in the dark, breathing, feeling.

Regretting.

When he found the nerve to seek out her gaze again, he swore he could make out compassion. Understanding.

He didn't deserve it.

"We need to go. We should have been gone hours ago."

She shrugged. "You needed the sleep."

He couldn't argue with that. But he should have.

Their situation had changed.

He had a whole lot more to worry about than some roving squad of Córdobans. Whoever had sabotaged that chopper had to be searching for it. They'd need to make sure that the evidence of their tampering hadn't survived the crash as well as he and Eve had. He brought his hands to Eve's face and cupped her cheeks, smoothing his thumbs across the lingering evidence of her tears. Tears she'd shed for their fellow soldiers who hadn't survived.

"I know you miss her."

She nodded. "But it's more than that. It's more than them. When we found that picture, I thought maybe you knew, that maybe you were protecting them, too. But when we visited the graves I realized you didn't. You couldn't have. After everything we've been through, you would have said something. If only to me."

Regret blistered him.

It was now or never.

He sucked in his breath. "Eve, I did know. I should have come clean yesterday. I was at the restaurant when that photo was taken. I counseled Turner afterwards, then I spoke to Carrie. I don't mean to offend you, but you said it yourself. Carrie liked men. A lot. But this time she was in danger of damaging more than her reputation. I warned her to break it off before someone else found out and she lost her career.''

Eve sighed. "I know. And you're right. But it wouldn't have mattered. She was about to turn in her wings."

There was no way he could respond to that.

Not without hurting her.

He'd learned firsthand in Panama City that Eve could be blinded by friendship and loyalty, at least as far as her sorority sisters were concerned. Look at Anna Shale. Even so, he couldn't fault her for it. Given her childhood, he understood it, even respected her for it. Unlike her mother, Eve would never abandon someone she cared about.

It sure as hell wasn't his place to make her try.

She grabbed his arm. "You don't believe me, do you? You think Carrie was just using your sergeant. Well, you're wrong. She would have married the man if he'd asked her."

Her precise conditional wording of that last part slammed into his face with the force of a percussion grenade. He tried shaking his head, tried shaking it off. He couldn't. A good ten seconds later, his ears were still ringing. And he still refused to believe it. Eve was wrong. She had to be.

But what if she wasn't?

The tension in her grip told him he'd better push it. He swallowed hard. "Carrie...told you that?"

Her eyes glistened as she shook her head slowly. A tear slipped free, coursing down her cheek, shimmering in the sliver of starlight as she pulled her hand away and sighed. "She didn't have to. She was pregnant."

*A baby?*

The hell with a percussion grenade.

Rick sucked in his breath as the bombshell effectively drop-kicked him out of the back of a C-130 troop transport three hundred miles above the ground. He flailed around, struggling to find the ripcord to a parachute that just wasn't there. He closed his eyes and tried to slow his spinning brain. It didn't help. He could still hear the air whooshing past his ears as he careened straight for the ground.

But as he crash-landed, Eve was there. Staring up at him, worry in the furrow of her brow, in her touch, as she cupped the side of his jaw. "You didn't know, did you?"

No.

And neither had Turner.

If his sergeant had, the man would never have let Carrie fly. Rick closed his eyes again and scrubbed at his own bitter tears. He no longer had one death on his conscience.

He had three.

Something was wrong.

Very wrong.

Eve could feel it humming in her blood. She couldn't put her finger on it, but when she heard the sudden catch in Rick's breath two feet behind her, she knew he felt it too.

"Hurry."

She didn't bother glancing over her shoulder. She hooked her hands on the charred frame of the cockpit door and pulled herself into the wreckage instead. She twisted around in the dark and reached out, automatically locating the access panel before Rick could illuminate it for her. "Forget the flashlight. Get the cutting torch. I swear I just heard a—"

*"Chopper."*

She and Rick stiffened simultaneously. This time the thunder of distant—but incoming—blades was unmistakable.

"It's a Huey."

Unlike six weeks ago, Rick didn't ask if she was sure. He grabbed his ruck with one hand, her right arm with his other, hauling her out of the cockpit in one smooth motion before practically dragging her across the clearing and into the tree line beyond. She grunted as a thick vine smacked against the side of her jaw. Two seconds later, she stumbled over another.

Rick didn't even slow down.

He just tightened his grip and dragged her faster. He sealed his mouth to her ear as they reached the rest of their gear. *"Stay down."*

She nodded.

A soft click followed as he switched off the AK-47's safety. His breath filled her ear a second time as he tucked the rifle into her right hand, his K-Bar into her left. "It's set on automatic."

She nodded again.

It took a full ten seconds to realize Rick hadn't just left her side, he'd left her section of the jungle. She had no idea how long she sat there in the dark, nervously fingering the serrated edge of the K-Bar, but it felt like an eternity. If anything, the blood-letting groove running down the flat of the blade underscored the bizarre shift to her priorities. Five minutes before, she'd have given anything to understand the silent, brooding wall Rick had slowly but surely erected between them over the past two hours—and how to blast through it. The tension had gotten so bad, she'd reapplied her camouflage paint and suggested they return to the crash site in the dead of night to slice off a chunk of the tampered rod. And now, because of that blasted Huey thundering overhead, she didn't even have that.

All she had were more questions.

Like *who* was flying that damned bird?

She'd called Anna's pilot herself earlier that evening while Rick slept. The man wasn't due to arrive until dawn. It was still a good hour until midnight, dammit. Had he sold them out to the Córdobans? Had Anna's cousin?

And where the hell was Rick?

A Huey could carry twelve men easily. The thought of Rick confronting a reinforced squad armed with God only knew what by himself scared at least that many years off her life.

"*It's me.*"

His warm breath in her ear tripled the loss.

"Sorry. Needed to recon the immediate area." Rick retrieved his K-Bar from her nerveless fingers and tucked it into the nylon scabbard at his waist as he stood. He donned his ruck and grabbed hers before latching on to her again. This time he half led, half dragged her by her hand. "Follow my lead no matter what, understood?"

To where?

And to whom?

She nodded anyway, feeling every inch the bobbing dog. But at least her head was still firmly attached to her body.

For the moment.

Seconds later, she received part of her answer. They were headed back toward the crash site. Straight toward the Huey. She could feel the leading edge of the breeze kicked up by the rotor's downwash, the earth vibrating beneath their boots, as the bird closed in on the same clearing she'd have willingly given her wings to have safely landed in all those weeks before. Another few steps and the jungle thinned enough for her to see the chopper as well. Definitely a Huey. Those running lights proved it.

They reached the tree line as the Huey touched down.

Rick clamped his hand on her shoulder and nudged her firmly down into the concealing foliage. "Stay low."

Not a problem.

"Where are you going?"

"Nowhere. Yet."

He pulled the nine-round magazine out of his rifle and locked in a thirty-round banana clip as the pilot powered down the Huey's engine. Six men in fatigues vaulted out from the chopper's gaping belly. Rick sighted in on the leading man.

"Captain Bishop! It's Colonel Arista! Ernesto Torres sent me!"

Rick lowered the barrel a fraction of an inch.

"Ernesto says to tell you, you never could hold your milk!"

The rifle fell away. "I'll strangle the son-of-a-bitch."

From the shock on Rick's face as well as his voice, there was one hell of a story behind that pass phrase. However, now wasn't the time to ask about it. Eve studied the soldiers as they spread out around the Huey. The chopper's running lights glinted off several rifles. The barrels were drawn low, non-threatening. "Who is that man? Who are they?"

"The president's personal guard."

She blinked. Not bad. Ernesto must be some friend for Rick to rate this particular escort. She flicked her gaze to the later model Huey.

And in style, no less.

"Don't let it go to your head. Arista can't stand me. The feeling's mutual."

"Oh."

"Wait here. I'll do the talking."

"At least you're talking to someone."

He stiffened.

She shrugged. "Let's just say I'm beginning to see why you fit in so well around here."

"Eve—"

"Apology accepted. But I will hear the rest of it and soon." For a moment, she thought he was going to deny it—the tension, the silence.

Until he nodded.

Rick carried his AK-47 with him as he stepped out of the trees, but kept the barrel low. Meanwhile, she kept her hands locked to her own rifle, the barrel high as he ap-

proached the San Sebastián contingent. Backlit by the
Huey's lights, Rick and Arista greeted each other as old
friends, complete with hands clapped across the other's
shoulders.

*Love thine enemy.*

She waited until she was sure both men intended to carry
out the charade to its natural conclusion before she lowered
her barrel slightly to study the rest of the men still maintaining their informal guard. Not a one wandered over toward the wreckage less than twenty yards away.

Shouldn't they at least be curious?

Or had they been ordered to stand off for a reason?

She shifted her gaze just in time to see Rick and Arista
shake hands. Another compulsory session of shoulder clap-
ping followed. Rick turned and waved her out as he approached. He slung his rifle over his arm as he reached the
tree line and pulled her close—intimately close.

Darkness or not, she stiffened.

"Relax. We're lovers."

Panama.

*"Anna?"* She couldn't believe it. She wouldn't.

There was no way Anna would betray their presence in
Córdoba to Ernesto, or anyone else.

He leaned down to press his lips to her temple. "Not the
woman, just the game. It was the best I could come up
with."

*Unbelievable.*

She offers herself to the man on a silver platter and he
refuses. Then he all but ignores her for the next two hours,
and now he wants her to let the entire world think he can't
stay out of her pants?

Men.

"Let me guess. You didn't mention the photos."

"Or the sabotage. I told him I brought you back so you

could mourn your friend and bury the ring I mistakenly took from her hand.''

She snorted. ''Guess I'm better in bed than I thought.''

Fire seared into her cheeks as she realized she'd actually said it out loud. It flared hotter as he murmured something suspiciously close to *you have no idea*.

''So—ah—what's his excuse?''

''Arista claims human intelligence filtered up to him a couple of hours ago. He says a squad of Córdoban democratic rebels located the wreckage this afternoon. Arista also claims that as soon as the rebels got word to him about the crash site, he told Ernesto he intended to retrieve the bodies.''

''That's quite a claim.''

Especially since they'd spent the majority of that very same afternoon tearing the wreckage apart bolt-by-bolt as she searched for further evidence of sabotage. Arista must have tracked the signal from the call she'd made to their own Huey pilot earlier that night. How else had he known he'd need that cryptic pass phrase? Rick must have been thinking the same thing, because he nodded.

''I told you I don't trust the man.''

''But your friend does.''

Rick shrugged. ''Ernesto was raised trusting him. I suspect he's about to learn differently.''

Now there was a loaded statement.

''What about you? Are you willing to trust him enough to get us to San Sebastián in one piece?''

''For the moment.''

Two loaded statements in a row. She could only hope neither blew up in their faces.

He snagged the straps to her ruck. ''Ready?''

Why not? He'd come this far on her instincts.

It was time to follow his.

She nodded. ''Let's do it.''

# Chapter 12

"You will, of course, stay the night."

Despite the fact that Miguel Torres was standing two feet in front of her in his private office in the San Sebastián presidential palace, staring into her eyes, Eve knew damned well the decree was intended solely for Rick.

Evidently, so did he.

"Of course."

Ernesto stepped forward and clapped Rick on the shoulder, drawing him from her side before either of them could protest. "Excellent. And now, Señorita Paris—" The man flashed his easy grin in her direction. "If you will allow us a moment or two to catch up, I promise to send him along shortly. *Mama!*"

Eve winced as Ernesto waved the subdued woman to his side. She felt bad enough knowing Carlotta Torres had been roused from her husband's sickbed to help roll out the red carpet at a quarter to midnight, she certainly didn't expect her to—

"Please escort Señorita Paris to her room."

"It would be my pleasure. Señorita…?"

Given the cultural climate, Eve deferred to Rick. The look he shot her told her to go. Much as it grated, she was forced to agree. Rick had warned her earlier that evening that even with a chunk of the Black Hawk's collective rod in hand, it would be difficult convincing Ernesto that the sabotage had been directed at him. Without that proof, it would be doubly so. Given the men's long-standing friendship, not to mention Ernesto's patronizing affection for the women in his life, including his stepmother, Rick would fare better without her.

She returned the woman's weary smile with one of her own. "Thank you. Just let me get my—"

"Rosa will bring it."

As if on cue, Rosa did. Eve felt sorry for the maid as she struggled to heft and balance the sixty-pound ruck.

Obviously Carlotta didn't.

Before Eve could steady the girl, much less grab the ruck herself, Ernesto's stepmother turned, her sensible heels sinking into the dark-green carpet of her son's study as she crossed the room. Moments later, those far-too-energetic heels clipped out onto the tiles of the shadowy hallway beyond, with Rosa and Eve trailing haphazardly behind.

Eve breathed easier as Rosa steadied her grip.

Frankly, she wasn't sure she could have helped the girl if she'd wanted to. Every last ounce of adrenaline had drained from her blood during the Huey flight, leaving nothing but bone-weary exhaustion behind as they landed. By the time Carlotta and Rosa reached the end of the first hall, she had to work to keep up with both women's shorter, stockier legs.

Hope kept her going after the second turn.

If she was lucky, there was a shower at the end of this dimly lit hall. A bed.

What there was, was another blasted hall.

And another.

Surely there was one tiny, unoccupied bed behind any one of these enormous mahogany doors? Heck, she'd be willing to turn around and curl up on any one of the cushioned benches they'd passed along the way. Just when she was about to give up hope altogether, those too-cheery heels stopped short.

Carlotta shoved open the slab of wood in front of them and stepped inside to flick on the lights. ''Your room, *Señorita.*''

Eve followed the women through the doorway and froze. This wasn't a room, it was another blasted bridal suite. If anything, the pristine feather coverlet made the four-poster at the far wall seem even more intimate, more inviting than the bed in Panama had been. Eve winced as Rosa dumped her grimy ruck onto the edge of the coverlet. Her nylon web belt followed, the flap to her holster falling open as it hit the bedpost. Eve winced harder as her 9 mm fell onto the carpet.

Nothing like a loaded pistol to make a hostess feel safe.

Eve turned around to find Carlotta staring at the 9 mm—and then her. Curiosity warred with disapproval.

She wasn't surprised.

She doubted many of Ernesto's friends showed up in the dead of night with a bedraggled, camouflaged, pistol-packing woman in tow. She could only hope Colonel Arista had kept his mouth shut regarding her supposed personal relationship with Rick. It was bad enough that everyone knew her wings had been stripped. San Sebastián was unabashedly Catholic. She didn't need the woman fearing her stepson would be seduced into violating the Church's doctrine on premarital sex.

From the in-country briefing she'd received weeks before, Eve knew that San Sebastián society tended to pat the

studly man on the back with one hand—while using the
other to stone the scarlet woman.

Arista must have talked.

Because she felt very much the scarlet woman beneath
that faint frown. "Is something wrong, Señora Torres?"

The woman's frown smoothed into a polite smile. "Not
at all. In the bath you will find several towels and a robe,
as well as a selection of soaps and shampoos."

*Use them.* The woman might as well have issued the
command aloud.

Eve fully intended to. "Thank you."

Carlotta nodded and turned to the door. There she
stopped to snap her fingers once. Rosa ceased gaping at the
9 mm on the floor and whirled around to follow her mistress out. Eve closed the door behind them and turned to
face the room. It would have been sinfully easy to crawl
into that bed, but somehow she didn't think Señora Torres
would approve. Besides, she really did want that bath. She
caught her reflection in the freestanding mirror across the
room and grimaced.

She needed it.

She headed for her ruck and retrieved the plastic bag of
alcohol wipes from the front pouch, tucking the 9 mm in
its place. She pulled out two wipes and started in with one
hand on the grease paint she'd reapplied hours before, as
she opened and closed doors with her other. The first re-
vealed a walk-in closet. The second led to a small sitting
room.

She hit pay dirt with the third.

The bathroom.

More importantly, a tub. A glorious claw-footed porce-
lain tub big enough to swim in—and she would. Eve
dumped the grimy wipes into the trash and shut the bathroom door behind her before crossing the blue-and-white
tiles to start the water. Stooping low, she grabbed the first

bottle her fingers hit inside the basket of bath beads, powders and soaps and added some of its contents to the stream.

Two minutes later she was naked, her grimy fatigues dumped atop her jungle boots at the foot of the tub as she stepped over the side. Her groan filled the room as she slipped into the steaming bubbles, no longer offended at being left out of the discussion in Ernesto's study. If the little woman was too delicate to join in, who was she to argue? She'd choose clean over insulted any day. She might even give in to the exhaustion dragging down her eyelids while she waited.

Why not?

The door was locked. Rick had announced to the entire world that he was her protector.

What could possibly happen?

"She will be fine, my friend. Mama will see to it."

Rick turned away from Eve's retreating form and faced his buddy's all-too-knowing eyes. He could have sworn he'd hidden his thoughts better. That wry grin proved he hadn't. Ernesto's deep chuckle added insult to injury as the man threw his arm around his shoulders and guided him down the opposite end of the dimly lit corridor toward his own study.

"Come, let us drink to your safe return."

Rick flashed a grin back at him. "Why not? It's been a damned long couple of days." There'd be time enough to change his mind—once they were firmly out of Miguel's earshot.

He and Miguel had never seen eye-to-eye.

Dealing with the man professionally had only exacerbated his dislike. Watching the man ogle Eve just now, despite her obvious exhaustion, sure as heck hadn't improved it. He could practically see the lothario plotting to get her alone. Bloody hell, Miguel wouldn't even let her bathe first.

He never should have brought her here.

He wouldn't have, except here was where Ernesto was.

Ernesto tightened his arm as they turned the corner and nudged at the side of his head with his knuckles as if they were kids. "You do have it bad, Ricardo. Very bad. *Relax.* Mama is wise to Miguel's ways. She will place her as far from the family's rooms as possible."

That was what he was afraid of.

Unfortunately, it was too late to turn back now because they'd reached his buddy's leather-bound study. Ernesto shoved the door wide with his free hand and guided Rick through with the other. The moment the door closed, Rick spun around and cut to the chase.

"Someone tried to kill you."

Ernesto held onto the knob for a good five seconds, and then he threw back his head and laughed. And laughed.

And laughed.

By the time the worst of the great booming guffaws faded, tears were streaking from his friend's eyes all the way down into his neatly trimmed mustache.

It must have been his delivery.

Ernesto was still chuckling as he crossed the study and sank into the leather chair behind his desk. Tears were still streaming down his cheeks as he pulled the handkerchief from his suit-jacket pocket and wiped his brow. He finally leaned back in his chair and sighed.

Rick just stood there.

Ernesto stared.

Then frowned.

And then, "You are serious."

"Deadly."

He straightened in his chair. "Ricardo, please tell me you did not come all this way to walk into my home and tell me this without some kind of proof. Even from you I must have—''

"Part of it's back in Córdoba.''

"*Córdoba? Jesucristo,* surely you are not suggesting that I go—''

Rick retrieved one of the plastic vials from his cargo pocket and stepped up to the desk. He checked the annotation he'd inked onto the base of the container, then carefully set the vial on the edge of his buddy's blotter.

"What is that?''

"Film.''

Ernesto frowned. "That, I can see.''

"Get it developed. You'll be hard-pressed to miss the rest.''

"And what, my friend, is 'the rest'?''

"Evidence of sabotage.''

Ernesto leaned forward, his attention clearly captured now. "Sabotage? Arista tracked you to the crash site. Are you suggesting that someone sabotaged your lady's chopper?''

"She's not my lady.'' *Liar.* He pushed on regardless. "Nor am I suggesting anything. I'm stating it. Someone sabotaged that Black Hawk. I saw it myself. The fuel sensors were tampered with and so was the collective rod.''

"And, naturally, you think I was the intended victim?''

Rick braced his knuckles on the edge of the desk and leaned forward, making a point of invading his buddy's personal space. "You can't tell me the thought didn't cross your mind when that chopper went down that it could have been you.''

The knot in Ernesto's throat shifted as he swallowed.

Evidently, not.

Hell, he probably would have thought the same thing himself if he hadn't spent the past two months fighting his

202 Crossing the Line

growing attraction to Eve, as well as a growing case of guilt over his own involvement in his sergeant's death.

A case growing worse by the day.

By the hour.

As usual, his friend seemed to tune in to his thoughts.

"What about you? Why is it I only hear about this suspicion of yours now, seven weeks after the crash?"

"I was distracted. But the fact is, I should have thought about it. And so should you. While you still have the chance." Rick jerked his chin to the plastic vial between his fists. "See it for yourself. Surely a man with your spot in the presidential pecking order can get it developed discreetly?"

They both knew he could.

Just as he knew Ernesto would do it.

"While you're waiting for the prints, I need a favor. I'd prefer you didn't mention it to Eve." He snagged the man's gold pen from its stand and scratched out a name down the side of the blotter. As expected, Ernesto's brow shot up at the rank and branch of service, not to mention both nationalities he scrawled beneath.

"May I inquire—"

"I'd rather you didn't."

Ernesto inclined his head. "What is it you need?"

"Whatever you can find out. I'd do it myself, but you have the connections and, frankly, I need the sleep."

Ernesto glanced at the smear of dirt, sweat and dark-green cammo paint he'd left on the blotter and grinned. "You need more than sleep, my friend."

"Then you'll do it?"

"Of course."

He straightened. "Thank you. For the hospitality and the timely extraction, too. I owe you."

"*Carajó*. It is I who owes you and you know it. But if

you insist on repaying me, there is the matter of a lady who appears not to be yours…"

"Don't even think about it."

Ernesto's chuckle dogged him as he turned and headed across the room. Hell, he could still hear it as he stepped into the hall and closed the door behind him. Ten paces down the corridor stood the girl who'd carted Eve's ruck out of Miguel's study. She had his beside her now as well as both AK-47s, magazines still locked in, leaning against the wall.

"I'll take those."

She smiled gratefully as he lifted the ruck and slung it over his right shoulder. He snagged the rifles next.

"Where is Señorita Paris?"

"In the white room. But I am to escort you to the—"

"Where is this white room?"

The girl appeared to weigh her mistress's displeasure against his own. She finally shrugged and pointed down the hall. "Take the last right, then another right, then a left. Four doors down at the end."

"*Gracias.*"

"*De nada.*" She smiled. It was above average. But unlike Eve's, it didn't sear straight through his gut.

Ernesto was right. He had it bad.

*Damn.*

He nodded and headed down the hallway to the first turn, feeling the noose tightening about his neck—his heart—with every stride of his boots. He knew darn well what that maid was thinking. He was thinking it too.

But he wasn't doing it.

They wouldn't be doing it.

Not tonight. Not ever.

He just had to figure out a way to let Eve know without hurting her. While he was at it, he'd search for a way to let his body know, too. Unfortunately, just thinking about

Eve's body had his own thrumming in hopeful anticipation. After that heavy petting session in the jungle this evening, it was going to be damned difficult, even knowing what he now did.

A baby.

Bloody hell.

Which of course, was precisely where he was headed. Only his would be lined with satin sheets. He knew she was hoping he'd change his mind. He suspected she'd even accept a purely sexual relationship with him—for a while. Unfortunately, he couldn't. If this was just about having sex with Eve he'd have taken it in a heartbeat and he knew it.

But it wasn't.

It was about making love.

Yesterday he might have been able to cross that line, to take that step. But not now. Not after what he'd learned today. He could never have her now. Loving Eve Paris might well be heaven on earth. But making love to her would also earn him a one-way ticket to hell.

He turned the final corner and steeled his resolve.

His hope.

It was after midnight. Eve had taken the last watch—a double no less. She had to be exhausted. She was probably sleeping. He nudged the door open and stepped inside.

She wasn't sleeping.

Other than her ruck and web gear, the bed was empty. So was the room. Where the hell was she?

*Miguel.*

He slugged the panic down.

"Eve?"

His bellow echoed through the room as he dropped his gear and opened the door on his right. It led to a darkened sitting room.

"Eve?"

A closet.

*"Eve?"*

Bloody hell. Locked.

He slammed his palm into the third door. Hard. "Eve!"

Nothing but chilling silence.

Images flashed through his mind. The chopper, shattered. The cockpit baked almost beyond recognition. A sawed-down collective. A tub, filled with water. Eve inside it.

Dead.

Panic rocked through him again. This time, he didn't bother knocking it down. He used it. He yanked his right boot up and smashed his heel straight into the door with all his might. The edge of the wood splintered as it crashed open.

"What— Who— *Rick?*"

Eve scrambled to her feet so quickly, she slipped.

He shot into the room and grabbed her by her arms before she could fall. Her wet, glistening arms. Her wet, glistening body. Bubbles? In some far corner of his panic-seared brain, it actually made sense. Or…it had. A moment ago.

Maybe.

"I'm sorry. I thought—"

What had he thought?

He sure as hell couldn't seem to think now.

The amusement lurking in those deep-emerald eyes burned off his confusion. A second later, humiliation burned into his skin. He swore his face was at least as pink as her steam-flushed cheeks. At least she wasn't nude.

Well, not completely.

Unfortunately, though the froths of tiny white bubbles clinging to her curves were making a valiant effort to hang on, they were slowly but surely losing ground. Any second now the thinning froth sliding down her breasts was going to go.

*Cover her.*

With what?

Himself?

He blinked. He could swear her lips were moving. But he couldn't hear anything. "Sorry, I didn't—"

"A towel. Could you please hand me a towel?" She pointed behind him, to her left. He turned around and spotted the stack of plush white towels beside the sink. He also spotted Eve again, reflected in the mirror behind them.

The bubbles.

He reached out and grabbed the top three towels off the stack and turned to thrust them at her.

It was too late.

The froth slid off her breasts at exactly the same moment, plopping softly into the water below. Good God, the shadowy jungle had *not* done her justice. He ripped his gaze up only to face a simmering reflection of his own desire in hers. She reached out and took the top towel from his hands and shook it out before carefully wrapping the white terry around her torso and tucking the trailing end in at her breasts. He knew it was for the best, but he still swallowed a groan as those mesmerizing curves disappeared from his view.

"Thank you."

He reached out, automatically assisting her over the lip of the tub only to stand mutely, stupidly, behind as she crossed the blue and white tiles. She snagged one of the matching robes from the row of hooks beside the bathroom door, tossing it over her shoulder as she stepped over the splinters of wood that had fallen down into the doorway. She turned, stared at the still-steaming bath beside him, and smiled.

Spoke.

"It's all yours. If you want it."

He knew damned well she wasn't talking about the tub.

* * *

She loved him.

Eve smiled to herself as she headed to the bed.

The realization didn't cause her to stumble or even force her to catch her breath. Heck, her pulse didn't even pick up its pace. Instead, the knowledge seemed to spread through her on a warm steady wave of healing contentment. It was as if her heart had known forever that Rick Bishop was the man for her and had simply been waiting for her brain to catch up.

It finally had.

She really did love him.

Her heart had left so many clues these past few days. So many unexpected turns in her thoughts and in her actions. Or so she'd thought. They all made sense now. She made sense. Why else had she trusted Rick with so much of herself?

With so much of Carrie?

Rick would never betray her confidence. She knew it just as surely as she knew that he was also in love with her.

She just wasn't sure he'd realized it yet.

She suspected he might.

Maybe that's why he was fighting so hard, fighting them. Why he'd withdrawn from her after they'd kissed in the jungle.

If so, it was okay. He needed time.

Time she planned to give him.

It was the least she could do after he'd given so much of himself to her. Eve pulled her ruck and web gear from the bed and set it on the floor beside Rick's, then crossed the room to lock the door. She thought about waiting for Rick to finish his shower, then decided against it. When he was ready to talk about them or what had happened with Ernesto, he would.

Until then, she was tired. They both were.

They needed sleep.

The shower spray ceased as she drew the feather coverlet to the foot of the bed. She padded across the room once more and flicked off the lights, doing her best to ignore the sliver shining through the crack in the door where the lock had been. Then she slipped beneath the gloriously dry comfortable sheets. The moment she closed her eyes, she felt him.

As usual, Rick made no sound as he approached the bed.

She was halfway to convincing herself she could fall asleep anyway when she felt the side of the bed dip.

Her side.

She opened her eyes and peered through the shadows.

She could make out a white terry robe that matched the one she wore, as well as the damp sheen to his freshly washed hair. From the darker shadow on his jaw, she didn't think he'd had a chance to shave. But the grease paint was gone.

And he smelled wonderful.

Still she waited, as silent as he.

It was odd. She could almost hear him trying to form the words. Whatever was on his mind, he didn't seem to know how to say it. A chill shot down her spine as he drew his breath in cautiously, as if he was trying to steel himself. But why? After everything they'd been through, how bad could it be?

"Rick?"

"I killed them."

The words just hung there.

She didn't know what to say, what to think. She finally forced out the only word she could. "Who?" Fear snaked through her as she waited. Fear of the unknown.

Fear of knowing.

"Carrie. Turner. The baby. Their baby."

The fear gave way to utter confusion as she pushed herself up on the bed until she was sitting against the headboard. "I don't understand. I was there, remember? *In* the pilot's seat. If anyone is responsible, it's me."

"You're right, you don't understand. There's no way you could. But I do. Eve, Turner shouldn't have been there. Hell, if it wasn't for me, Carrie wouldn't have been there either."

*Sweet Mother in Heaven.*

The way Rick had grown more and more distant earlier tonight in the jungle, the wall she swore she'd felt erected brick-by-brick after she finally told him about the baby.

"You *knew* she was pregnant?"

"No. And I don't think Turner did either."

"Then I really don't understand. Why—"

"Because he wanted out. Out as in out of the Army. Out as in, 'Captain Bishop, I've never asked you for anything, but I'm asking you now. Man to man. *Tear up my paperwork.*'"

"Oh my God, he asked her to marry him."

Rick shook his head slowly, regretfully. "But he was going to." He sighed. "Turner had sixteen years in. His enlistment extension was set to expire the moment our C-130 touched down in the States. Two months ago, he was good to go for four more years—just enough to take him to retirement. But he also wanted to retake the oath in the jungle." He shrugged. "It happens in SF. Even did it myself when I was enlisted. So I swore him in and bagged the paperwork. Told him I'd turn it in to Admin when we got back to Fort Campbell. Then he comes to me, two weeks before the crash, and—" His voice caught.

She waited.

When he swallowed, she knew he needed her to finish it. "And he asked you to tear it up. I bet he'd already cleared it with the soldier who witnessed his oath, too. Turner told you no one would ever know. A favor for a man who'd saved your ass in the line of fire once. Or maybe twice."

He bowed his head. "Yeah."

There was a bank vault's worth of guilt in that one word. And he was clinging to every penny.

"Don't own it. It's not yours."

His head shot up. He knew exactly what she meant and he was pissed. But not with her. "Then you tell me, whose is it? Carrie's? You told me yourself she would have said yes. I sat on that paperwork for two goddamned weeks after Turner came to me. If I hadn't, he'd have asked her to marry him well before that crash. She'd have told him about the baby. You're right about Turner saving my ass. I knew the man well. If he'd known Carrie was pregnant, he *never* would have let her fly."

"Rick, it wasn't his choice."

"Well it wasn't mine either, was it? Militarily, maybe. But as a man? We argued the night before the crash, you know. Turner accused me of screwing with his life because I was too bloody chicken to go out and find one of my own."

The bitterness in his laugh ripped into her.

"He had no idea how right he was. The worst of it is, Turner didn't even need to be on that chopper. I'd been doing the briefings alone for weeks. But I ordered him along. I'd planned to sandbag him with names, dates, an entire list of officers Carrie had slept with. I told myself if he could survive a no-holds-barred discussion of the woman's reputation and he still wanted to marry her, fine. He could have the damned paperwork. I'd take the heat and deny administering the oath myself." He raked his fingers through his hair, then dug them into his shoulder as he sighed. "Christ, I wish I'd given him the papers the first time he asked."

It tore her up to see him wracked with so much pain,

tortured by so much doubt. Especially when it wasn't valid, no matter how much his heart and his conscience might be telling him it was. She knew that better than he could.

Just as she knew Carrie better than he ever would.

"Rick, the fact is, you didn't give them back. And I can honestly say, I wouldn't have either. Not then, not given his extenuating circumstances—and trust me, Carrie and I have been best friends for years. I have no illusions as to just how many *extenuating circumstances* she had stuffed in her closet and in her bed. If our positions had been reversed, I would have done my damnedest to convince Turner to stay in the Army. That's a commander's job and we both know it. We look out for the needs of our soldiers, yes. But we also have a duty to our country to look out for the needs of her Army."

His hand fell down to his lap.

She hadn't convinced him...because it shook.

She watched him link his fingers together and clamp down tight enough to make the shaking stop. The blood in his fingers bled off so far the white of his knuckles blended in with his robe. She knew he didn't want her touching him, but she couldn't take it any longer. She couldn't take his torment any longer. She leaned forward and reached out.

He flinched.

Her heart shattered.

"Rick?"

He finally faced her full on. She sucked in her breath as the light from the bathroom reflected off his cheeks.

Off his tears.

"Eve, make no mistake, I want it. I want you. More than you'll ever know. But I can't. Ever. Can you understand that?"

"No. I can't give up on you. Don't ask me to. I won't."

"You don't have a choice."

Yes, she did.

"Rick, I love you."

He nodded slowly. "I know. But don't you see? I have no right to this. To you. I denied Bill Turner the very thing I now crave. But it's not mine. *You* are not mine. It can't be."

He was so wrong.

But he wasn't ready to see it. And he certainly wasn't ready to hear it. He might never be.

So she did the only thing she could.

She reached out once more and pushed the covers away from her body, then she wrapped her arms around him. He stiffened. It didn't matter. She drew him down onto the bed anyway, onto her chest, and cradled him close.

It took a while.

But gradually, his breathing slowed. Deepened.

He fell asleep.

And this time, she held him.

# Chapter 13

He woke on the first tap.

*The door.*

Rick extricated himself as quickly and as smoothly as he could from Eve's arms. He pressed his lips to her forehead, soothing the furrow between her brows as well as her sleepy protest and stood. By the second tap, he'd tightened the belt to his robe and crept halfway across the room, stopping only to retrieve his 9 mm from his holster and chamber a round. He rested the pistol against the wall and cracked the door open on the third knock.

Ernesto's weary mustache greeted.

"I believe you."

Rick nodded and pulled the door wider. "I'm sorry."

His buddy shrugged.

"What do you plan to do about it?"

"Strangle the *bastardo* with my bare hands. But first, I will need to uncover who he is. We shall begin where you two have left off. Can you be ready to return to Córdoba by dawn?"

"Yes."

What time was it?

Rick glanced at his watch. It was missing. He'd left it in the bathroom. He turned toward the bed, skimming past Eve's slumbering body and tousled curls as he searched the night stand for a clock. Two hours before dawn.

Two hours before he had to leave Eve.

"Naturally, I shall require the piloting services of your lady as well."

Rick scowled—and not because of the request.

"I'll ask her."

"She says yes."

Rick stiffened as Eve's voice floated across the dimly lit room. So much for not rousing her. Fortunately, Ernesto was too good a friend to stare past the arm Rick had hooked to the door.

*"Gracias."*

"You're welcome."

"Is that all?"

Ernesto held up a folded square of paper. "A gift."

Rick took the square and slipped it into the pocket of his robe. "By the way, sorry about the bathroom door. Let's just say, I had trouble holding my milk." With that, he closed the bedroom door in his buddy's face.

Eve was sitting up when he returned to the bed.

"What was that all about?"

"Ernesto wants to examine the wreckage for himself."

She shook her head.

*Damn.*

"The milk?"

She shook her head again—and stared at his pocket.

Double damn.

Must be that blasted pilot's vision. He retrieved the square of paper from his robe and opened it, tipping the sheet toward the sliver of light shining in from the bathroom as he scanned Ernesto's scrawl.

Bloody hell.

He placed the sheet in her outstretched hand.

She glanced down and then up. "Nice try. Perhaps you'd care to translate?"

It wouldn't be his first choice, no.

He sighed. "I asked Ernesto to run a check on a name."

"A name? Why would you try to hide—" She stiffened. *"Anna?"*

He nodded. "Lieutenant Anna Shale, U.S. Navy. Except, she's not in the Navy. Not anymore. Several months ago, her commission was terminated. Reason—suspicion of treason. The charges were dropped, but it's common knowledge in Naval Intelligence circles that she was guilty as hell."

"I don't believe it. Ernesto is wrong. His information is wrong. Maybe he had the wrong name, the wrong contacts—"

"Ernesto was an exchange cadet at West Point. He has the right contacts. Some of the same contacts I would have used. He also had the right name. I wrote it down myself." Only now, he wished to God he hadn't. He crumpled up the sheet of paper and shoved it into his pocket, then lowered himself onto the side of the bed to try and draw her close.

She refused to budge.

"Eve—"

"Dammit, no! You're wrong. You're both wrong. Anna is innocent. I know her. She would never have sold out. Never."

"Then why has she been targeted by Delta Force?"

*"What?"*

Rick nodded. "I saw the operative. Hell, I know the

operative. He was in the restaurant. *On the job.* Surely you noticed she was on edge?''

She had.

He could see it in her eyes. He could feel it in the tremor that swept through her body. He slipped his arms around her again and pulled her close. This time, she didn't resist. He pulled her closer and brushed his lips against her temple. ''It's okay. We'll figure this out.''

''H-how? C-Carrie is dead. Anna's branded a t-traitor. My wings are stripped. Wh-what's happening to us? To the S-Sisters?'' His heart constricted as another tremor struck, and then another. She was shaking, freezing.

Shock.

She'd had too damned many of them lately. But this one was directly due to him. Why the hell couldn't he have kept his mouth shut? He rubbed his hands up and down her back, but it didn't help. He pulled Eve down into the bed with him and tugged the covers up over her shoulders.

She was still shaking.

Body heat.

He tugged his robe open, then hers, and pressed the length of her body to his. It took a good minute, but the tremors gradually ebbed until they finally stopped altogether. Still, he held her, stroked her hair, continued to murmur reassurances in her ear.

It was a mistake.

She stirred and the tremors began again.

In him.

He tried to halt them. But he was powerless against this much sensation from this woman full on. He could feel every one of her curves pressing into him, molding to his naked flesh. Every single, bare, *intimate* inch of him. Her soft breasts spilled onto his chest. Her smooth thighs nestled snugly into his. Her arms slid over the muscles of his chest as she reached up to guide her hands to his face.

He closed his eyes as she trailed her fingers across his whiskered cheeks, but it only made it worse.

Without sight, the rest of his senses took over.

He could hear her breathing quicken. Smell her natural fragrance mingling with the bubbles that had clung to her flesh earlier. He could feel her nipples as they tightened and pressed into his skin. He could feel the soft silk of her golden curls on her head...and lower. She lifted her face and a moment later, he could feel the warmth of her breath on his lips. He recognized the hint of mint from the toothpaste in the bathroom, because he'd used it too.

And then he could taste it.

He could taste her.

But before he could capture her mouth and return her brief searing kiss, she slipped away, staring deep into his eyes as her sultry whisper filled his ears, filled him. "Take me over the edge, Rick, please. Make me forget. Carrie, Anna, the crash, the sabotage, everything. Everything but you."

It was the last word that did it.

He shuddered.

Then groaned as her tongue slipped between his lips again, incinerating the last of his resolve and the very air from his lungs along with it. He barely had time to fill them again before her hands slid to his chest, tugging the robe from his shoulders and peeling it off his body.

*Yes.* He wanted this.

He wanted Eve.

He captured her mouth and delved deeply, drawing on her love and on her courage. Showing her with his lips and his tongue what he could never say with his heart. He didn't yet know how he would manage the coming years without her, but he did know he would never be able to face them without the memory of tonight. She seemed to understand, to forgive him, even as he sealed the length of her body to his, turning them in one smooth motion until she was tucked firmly beneath him.

He groaned as she arched into him, exposing the slender column of her neck for his kiss. He claimed it, claimed her, razing his mouth down her throat, his breath coming hoarse and ragged as he consumed every inch of exposed flesh he could find. He finally reached the throbbing pulse at the base. Still, he wasn't satisfied.

Nor was he anywhere near sated.

He peeled her robe down her shoulders and used the sleeves to trap her arms behind her back with one hand while he caressed and fondled her mesmerizing breasts with the other. He palmed each in turn, taking his sweet time as he rolled the plump nipples between his fingers, plucking at them over and over until she gasped. He waited until he could stand the anticipation no longer before he finally bent low and replaced his hands with his mouth and tongue.

He groaned.

And she gasped.

"Rick, please. I want—I *need* to touch you."

He raised his head and captured her smoky stare, reveling in her driving, frantic need. "Soon, sweetheart. Soon."

For now, he was too close to the edge.

If they had protection, he would have caved into her pleading in a heartbeat. A condom would have dulled the sensation enough to help him hang on.

But they didn't have one.

So she couldn't.

He groaned as she found a way to thwart him, bucking up against him to rub her thighs against his erection, luring him dangerously closer to the edge.

It was time.

Time to give her something that would occupy her body and her mind and give her the release she sought without damning him to hell in the process. He smoothed his hand up those warm silky thighs. She wanted to forget?

He'd make her forget.

When he was done, she'd be lucky if she remembered her *name*.

Eve sucked in her breath as she stared into the smoldering passion in Rick's gaze. No man had ever looked at her quite like that before. Coming from him, it was an overwhelmingly heady sight. The fierce determination swirling amid the desire, however, gave her pause.

What the devil was Rick planning?

Apprehension skimmed up her stomach, straight to her throat. Rick's calluscd palms and teasing fingers followed close behind, but they stopped a bit shorter—at the base of her ribs. She sucked in her breath as he sent her one last fiery look before he shifted his body and bent down low. When he slipped his hands between her thighs and parted them, she knew exactly what he was up to.

*Oh, my…*

Her lids slammed down instinctively as she arched into his intimate kiss, her breath hissing out long after she should have died from pleasure. When she recovered from the initial shock, she tried to protest, to shift, to draw him up. But he wouldn't budge. He simply locked her thighs in place and ignited a swirling inferno inside her core that threatened to consume her. In the mindless moments that followed, she couldn't move, couldn't talk. All she could do was gasp and sigh, over and over. All that existed was his seeking mouth, his knowing tongue. Her entire world was so drenched she couldn't begin to understand how she could be so on fire.

But she was.

The flames of his passion licked at her again and again, alternating between soothing, teasing and stabbing. And then he started all over. Every now and then he latched on with his lips and tugged insistently until she couldn't even sigh anymore. All she could do was moan.

She was close, so close all she had to do was let go and she'd be there. But she couldn't. She didn't want to.

It wasn't right.

Rick wasn't there with her.

She tried tugging at his hair, pulling at the muscles of his shoulders. When that didn't work, she begged. Pleaded. Shamelessly.

Dammit, she needed him. Now.

*Inside* her.

Suddenly, he was above her, looming over her—and then he was ramming into her so hard and so deep that for one brief delirious moment, she was filled to the brim. In that moment, her entire world was absolutely perfect.

Then he moved.

And it got even better.

She locked her arms around his chest and held on for dear life, reveling in the rock-hard muscle covering every inch of her as he thrust into her again and again. Unable to rein in her voice or her heart any longer, she poured out her pleasure and her love into his ear as her world converged on that single glorious sensation. She was dimly aware of his voice answering her back, ragged and raw. Her name, over and over, and then something else. As if it had been ripped from his throat.

She tried to concentrate, tried to understand.

But it was impossible.

Because he was still moving, still grinding into her, each thrust harder and deeper than the last. She was wound so tight, every sensation so intense, she was terrified that any moment she was going to shatter into a million tiny pieces.

And then she did.

A moment later Rick stiffened, shouting her name one

last time before he followed. But as what was left of them floated down to the bed, she realized what he'd said.

*He loved her.*

What should have been one of the most precious moments of her life had turned into one of intense agony.

Of shame.

Eve closed her eyes against the band of light shining through the bathroom doorway, against an even harsher pain. She didn't need to catch a second glimpse of Rick slumped against the edge of the marble sink, staring intently into his clenched hands, to know he was desperately trying to figure out how to get out of their room without offending her. She could feel it. Just as she'd felt him pulling away from her twenty minutes before—before their passion had even begun to ebb—retreating behind that damned stoned wall of his, this time shoring it up with a vengeance.

The worst part was, this was all her fault.

She'd sworn she would wait. That she would give Rick the time he needed to deal with his conscience and his fears.

Well, she'd blown that resolution, hadn't she?

She gotten so used to turning to Rick these past few days, so used to leaning on him, she just assumed he'd be there whenever she needed him. The irony was, he had been there. But because of it, because of her, there was a very real chance that he might not be coming back.

Ever.

Eve froze as she heard the bathroom door swing wide. Hope surged in her heart, only to falter as she caught the soft rustle of fabric that followed, not at the side of the bed, but somewhere past the foot. Her hope died out altogether at the solid twin thumps that followed.

Boots.

Rick was leaving.

She opened her eyes carefully, studying him as he pulled a not-so-fresh set of camouflage fatigues from his ruck and silently donned them. She slammed her lids back down as he turned to retrieve a sheet of paper and a pen from the small writing desk beside the door that led to the sitting room. The rip in her heart deepened with each soft scratch of the pen. He finally folded the sheet. She knew darn well they'd spent too much time together over the past week for him to ever believe she was asleep as he crossed the room.

She kept her eyes sealed shut anyway.

She thought it would be easier.

It probably was—for him.

She, however, would never forget the agony of lying motionless while the man she loved more than flying itself gently pressed his lips to her temple and whispered his regret before he turned, retrieved his boots and quietly slipped out of their room, locking the door firmly behind him.

Just like that, the fantasy was gone.

Like her mom. Like Carrie and her unborn baby.

Like Turner and her crew chief.

Like her single, blinding moment of joy in Rick's arms.

She opened her eyes and stared at the sheet of paper. Even as she reached out and lifted it, she knew what it said. The excuses it held. She didn't doubt that Rick needed to meet with Ernesto, to plan for their flight. But the rest was a lie. She didn't have an hour left before it was time to leave. The clock had already run out.

Because Rick had chosen to give up.

Again.


"Am I to blame?"

Rick tore his stare from the section of gold curls visible through what was left of the Black Hawk's cockpit window thirty feet away. It took him a couple of seconds to process his friend's question. He finally shook his head and turned to shove the evidence case containing the fingerprints he and Ernesto had just spent the past hour meticulously lifting from the Black Hawk's wreckage into the belly of the waiting Huey. "No, Ernie. You didn't cause any of this."

Ernesto reached inside the bird and snagged his thermos. He poured the steaming coffee into his waiting cup. "You are sure? You would not try to spare me, given—" He waved the cup toward the wreckage. "—this."

He understood his friend's concern, but it was unfounded. The information Ernesto had provided concerning Anna Shale might have triggered what had happened between him and Eve, but it wasn't the cause.

He was.

He and his lack of self-control.

Rick had never claimed to be a Boy Scout. Though he hadn't made a practice of it, he'd had sex without a condom before. He knew the temptation and he knew the risks. He just thought he could handle them. He wasn't supposed to have entered Eve at all. Even when passion changed his mind for him, he still thought he could chance a few searing moments inside her body without a damned inner tube dulling the sensations. He'd been so certain he could pull out in time.

He was wrong.

He'd felt himself losing the battle from the moment he'd entered Eve. But when she'd clamped down on him in the throes of her release? That was the precise moment he'd lost the war.

"You love her."

Rick glanced up and took the steaming mug of coffee from Ernesto's outstretched hand. "Thanks." He left the statement lying there. They both knew it was true. Unfortunately, he also knew it wouldn't make a bit of difference.

If anything, it complicated matters.

His friend waited as he searched for the words.

Rick took a sip of the coffee when the words refused to come and searched again. He leaned forward, delaying the inevitable as long as he possibly could as he sought out those gold curls and tracked them until they disappeared deeper into the wreckage. He sat down inside the Huey and sighed.

"I screwed up, Ernie. Bad."

His buddy's brow rose, but he remained silent.

He was grateful. This was hard enough. He stared into his cup. "She could be pregnant." He didn't need to see that brow to know that this time it shot all the way to his hairline.

"Your lady is…worried for her career?"

Christ, he hadn't even thought of that.

Just went to show what a selfish bastard he really was.

"Yes—no. Probably." He sighed. "Hell, I don't know for sure. Neither does she. I won't know for a month or more, if she'd even tell me after what I did this morning. But I do know I can't afford to hang around until she finds out."

*"Ahhh."*

That single sound grated through him. In Ernesto's own annoying way, he'd said more than most shrinks could say in a lifetime of couch sessions. He waited for the rest.

"We have come to the real problem, yes?" Ernesto set his coffee cup on the Huey's floor and pushed it aside.

Not good.

Bloody hell. He should have known better than to confide in Ernesto Torres. Then again, maybe he had. It wasn't as if he'd been doing so well on his own. Rick sucked in his breath and just did it. He hit the highlights in two minutes. Turner, Carrie and the baby. By the time he finished, he felt like a guest on some cheesy self-help talk show. He must have sounded like one too, because Ernesto's low whistle filled the Huey.

"You should have come to me sooner, Ricardo. I may not have been able to help you, but you could have helped me."

"How so?"

He shrugged. "You could have taken my place in the confessional. At least you would have done the penance justice."

What the hell?

Rick stiffened—until it hit him. He forced himself to relax, to lean against the side of the Huey.

Ernesto nodded sagely. "Take off the sackcloth, my friend. You will find your burdens easier to bear without it. Especially when they are not truly yours."

Rick frowned. "That's what Eve said."

"She is wise."

She was, but that wasn't the point. Rick took a sip from his mug and scowled into it. "She's wrong. So are you."

"Am I?"

"Yes, dammit."

His buddy tossed off another one of those damned Latin shrugs. "If you say so."

"Hell, why not come out and just call me a liar?"

"Because you are not. But you are set in your ways. You have been for many years. Far too many, I think." He reached down and retrieved his coffee. "Tell me, if your positions were reversed and you had sworn your oath to your country and then died in much the same manner, leaving your sergeant behind, would you wish him to deny his desires and his future, simply because you had chosen to go back on your word?"

He refused to answer that one.

He couldn't.

Despite his silence, Ernesto nodded. "I thought not. Just

as I also suspect that beyond the obvious, your turmoil has little to do with what happened here seven weeks ago. I bid you to look farther back, into your past. Tell me what you see. No, tell yourself. And then, go to your lady and tell her.'' With that, Ernesto stood up. He took a sip from his coffee, then tossed the rest into the grass. ''And now, while you think on what I have said, I shall go and see what remains to be done so that we can leave.'' He stared off into the trees for a moment, then shook his head. ''The sooner we leave this place of death, the better, I think. For all of us.''

Rick took the mug from Ernesto's hand and set it beside the thermos, watching his buddy as he snagged his rifle and slung it on his shoulder before strolling off. For a man who knew someone was out to kill him, not to mention that his father was dying, his step was remarkably light.

*His father.*

Not Ernesto's, his own.

His past.

Rick glanced up in time to see his friend join Eve before they both disappeared behind the far side of the wreckage. He didn't call Ernesto back. He'd already figured out what the man had been trying to tell him. What Eve had tried to tell him the day before when he'd broken off their love-making not far from this very spot.

He was running again.

He was using Turner the way he'd used the jungle and the Army. Once again, he was trying to escape.

The fear, the uncertainty.

The twin shaft of pain that came right along with love.

He'd long since figured out that if he wanted one, he'd have to accept the potential for the other. Did he? Could he? In his heart he knew Eve would never set out to hurt him deliberately. But his mother hadn't set out to destroy his father either, had she?

Yet she had.

Ernesto was right. This wasn't about Turner and Carrie and a baby that would never be. It was about him and it was about Eve—about the baby that deep down, he wanted to have with her. If not now, then someday. Someday soon. The question was, would he be able to put the past in its place and forge a future with Eve?

He didn't know.

But he knew he had to try.

The breeze picked up as Rick dumped his coffee out into the clearing beside Ernesto's. A split second later, the hair on the back of his neck snapped to attention. Whatever vibes his friend had picked up on, he felt them too.

Strange.

He hadn't noticed them before.

But then, he'd been preoccupied. Ernesto was right. It was time to gather the remains that he and Eve had been forced to leave behind the first time—and get the hell out of here. Maybe after Carrie and Turner and Eve's crew chief had been laid to rest, he and Eve would be ready to move on. If he was lucky and she forgave him for walking out on her this morning, it would be together.

He shoved the mug beside the thermos and grabbed his rifle as he stood. Ten paces across the clearing, the wind shifted and he froze. Sniffed. That breeze was definitely off.

The jungle was off.

Once again, the telltale hairs on his neck snapped to attention. This time, they refused to relax. Especially when he realized the birds and insects on the far side of the clearing had gone mute. He inhaled again, deeply. There was something in the air all right, and it wasn't good. The lingering hint of smoke, melted steel and cooked fuel had masked it earlier. He placed it now.

Sweat. Exertion.

Ernesto's, Eve's...and someone else's.

Bloody hell. Not some*one*.

Many.

He hit the tree line in three seconds flat, battling the urge to scream Eve's name across the clearing like some raw, day-old recruit as the horror in his mind raced against the sudden terror wracking his heart. He tightened his grip on his rifle and continued his advance, pushing past more than a decade of training until he was drawing on pure instinct alone. Seconds ticked away.

Minutes.

Goddamn it, how many did he have?

How many did *Eve* have?

He refused to believe it was already too late.

And then, finally, mercifully, he was *there*.

Rick scanned the wreckage quickly, noting anything and everything that was in or out of place. Eve's ruck was still resting alongside the four-foot section of rotor blade that had been sheared off during the crash. The cutting torch was leaning against the ruck, as if she'd set it down a moment before. Her rifle was propped up against the dangling cockpit door. Ernesto's lay in the scorched grass two feet away. He forced his stare to double back, scanning even more slowly as he prayed. His heart slammed into his throat as he was finally forced to acknowledge the truth.

Eve was gone.

So was Ernesto. It was as if they'd simply vanished.

Impossible!

He scanned the wreckage once more, narrowing his field of vision during this pass, widening his criteria, not knowing what the hell he was searching for until he found it.

And then he did.

Three feet away from the ruck. A tiny spot of red.

*Blood?*

His heart slammed back up his throat. This time, he

couldn't knock it down. He choked on the blinding panic. The enforced inertia. The need to move. Examine.

Search.

But if he moved before he heard nature's all clear, he could be risking his one chance at tracking Eve undetected—

*There.*

The second the insects and birds resumed their song, he was off like a surface-to-air missile. Rick snagged the red and kept moving, not opening his hand until he was covered by the shattered steel of the chopper. He stared at the meticulously whittled, ceremoniously stained sliver of wood in his palm, the gleaming needle at the end.

A traditional Córdoban war dart.

He knew exactly who owned the blowgun the wooden dart had been fired from. What he didn't know was who the dart had struck, much less if the tip had been dipped in poison designed to paralyze—or to kill.

# Chapter 14

She was dreaming.

She had to be.

But this dream was unlike any other she'd ever had. For one thing, the world was upside down—and it was moving. For another, it smelled. Scratch that, it stunk. Like the time Carrie's first Greek geek left his socks and running shoes in her dorm-room closet their freshman year—for the entire Spring Break. Eve peeled her lids open. Trees, vines, ferns, all upside down. She might be woozy, but she wasn't dreaming. Someone was carrying her...and it wasn't Rick.

"What the devil's going on?"

And where *was* Rick?

"*¡Idiota!* I told you to gag her."

"She was asleep."

"Well she is awake now. Do it! If you had taken all three as you were *ordered* to, we would be done with this."

All three?

Then Rick was safe?

Eve prayed even as she blinked her eyes against the fog still swirling through her brain. She strained to stare around the massive, sweaty back beneath her cheek—to find that voice. The one up ahead. She knew that voice.

"Colonel Arista?"

She should have kept her mouth shut, because the next thing she knew, someone shut it for her—with a solid smack from the butt of a rifle. Her face smashed into that filthy shirt before she had a chance to discover who'd wielded it.

A moment later, the world went black.

When Eve came to, she was lying on her side with a grimy gag stuffed half-way down her throat. She could only hope the bastard who'd carried her hadn't used his sock. She could hear men arguing some distance away. Unfortunately, she had no idea what they were arguing about. They were speaking Spanish.

She tested the gag.

Loose.

Thank God.

She clamped down on her bile and slowly pushed the flat of her tongue against the fabric, nudging the filthy rag far enough out of her mouth so that she could hook it over her bottom lip. She could always pull it into place if she needed to. Between the midday heat, her bound arms, and the gag now riding her upper chin, she still couldn't breathe comfortably, but at least she wasn't eating some thug's sweat.

So where was she?

Where was Rick?

Please God, don't let him be—

*No.* She refused to think it. Rick was fine.

Somewhere.

She had to believe that. Just as she had to stay alive until he found her.

Grass tickled her face and throat.

She lifted her head slightly and eased her throbbing jaw to the right. She couldn't see far. Eight, maybe ten feet. She definitely appeared to be in a clearing.

But which one?

She lowered her head and rested her jaw against the ground. Her hands were drawn so tightly behind her back she swore her shoulder sockets were about to rip loose. She thought about shifting, trying to get more comfortable, but she didn't. She'd learned her lesson the first time. She curled her fingers up instead, attempting to gauge the strength and material of whatever was binding her wrists.

Her blunt nails scratched skin.

*"Eve?"*

She froze. Waited a beat. Prayed. She finally returned the muffled whisper. "Ernesto?"

*"Sí."*

Relief seared through her. "Where's Rick?"

"Tracking us, I hope."

Oh, God. So did she.

She closed her eyes against the other sight. The one still tormenting her no matter how many times she'd ordered it from her head. Dammit, Rick was *fine*. Probably headed this way, just as Ernesto said.

But what if he wasn't?

"Good, you have woken."

She groaned as Arista grabbed her bound wrists and hauled her up and over Ernesto's prone body before she could re-seat the gag. The rag dropped to her neck as Arista did his best to dislocate her arms by dragging her several feet backwards before he shoved her up against the side of a chopper.

*Chopper?*

She ignored the colonel's swarthy frown, twisting her head to the right before he could stop her. He rewarded her with a stinging slap—directly over the bruise on her jaw. She swallowed her groan easily. Hell, she'd survived worse beatings by the time she was five.

For the first time, she was actually grateful.

The skills she'd learned then just might keep her from revealing how truly terrified she was now. Nor did she need to draw on her army POW training to know that she had nothing to gain if Arista discovered he'd gotten to her—and everything to lose. She swung her head to the left, toward the dormant tail rotor. "Nice Huey. Does it fly?"

"Not for you, woman." He grabbed her neck and wrenched her head forward, then slammed her shoulders into the bird.

White-hot pain ripped out across her back and down her arms and spine. She drew in her breath slowly. Despite her screaming shoulder sockets, she managed a soft *tsk* as she exhaled. "That's a bad case of chauvinism you've got there. You should get it taken care of before you get hurt."

"*¡Silencio, puta!*"

She blinked. "Sorry, I don't speak Spanish. Must be the woman in me. Too dumb to learn."

Arista raised his hand again, this time fisting it, but before it could fly, Ernesto shouted something in their native tongue. Something with Rick's name in it. She understood that much, at least. Arista just threw back his head and laughed.

"I hope he comes for me, *El Bastardo Pequeño,* I truly hope he does. For it would make my job all the easier." With that, he strolled halfway across the clearing to his men.

Including Arista, there were three.

Evidently four of the seven men who'd picked them up last night at the crash site were on the level.

She hoped.

Eve skimmed the remainder of the forty-foot clearing but couldn't find any sign of the missing men. Just enough open space to land a bird in. She could only pray the men weren't tracking Rick. She shifted her aching shoulders against the Huey so she could face Ernesto and gasped. He was lying on the ground, facing her. From the raw, seeping cuts and purple bruises darkening his forehead, cheeks and jaw, he must have put up quite a struggle when he came to. But the pain in Ernesto's eyes told her his heart had absorbed a blow far worse than those that had been leveled against his body.

Rick was right.

Ernesto's trust had been shattered today as well.

"I'm so sorry."

He shook his head. "Do not be. I am the one who should apologize. I led you and Ricardo back to this place." He jerked his swollen jaw to Arista. "Back to him."

"Why did he call you little bastard?"

Ernesto managed a wry grin. "You learn quickly…for a woman." Like her, Ernesto was doing his damnedest to hold it together.

She shrugged, swallowing another groan as her left shoulder socket popped in protest. "I had two years in college. ROTC scholarship requirement. Unlike Rick, all I remember are the basics. You know, the naughty words."

That earned her a half-hearted, wheezing chuckle.

Despite his efforts, Ernesto didn't sound good. He looked even worse. Lord, did she need Rick.

Alive.

"We're not going to get out of this, are we?" She hated the fear that had finally crept into her voice. But at least she'd been able to keep it from Arista.

Ernesto sighed. "I do not know. I must be honest with you. Arista and my mother intend to see that we don't."

His *mother?*

Her shock must have been visible enough to penetrate even those swollen lids because he nodded. "*Sí, mí madre.* Well, not my birth mother. Though I did pretend when I was young."

She knew the feeling. She'd been guilty of a fantasy or two growing up herself. But his mother? As bad as she'd had it, she couldn't conceive of this. "Why would your mother—Carlotta—try to kill you?"

Unfortunately, Arista arrived in time to answer for him. "Because Ernesto's father has gone *loco.* Crazy. Why else would he decide to name an impostor as his heir?" Eve flinched as the colonel's hand cupped the back of her neck. When he leaned down to rub his fingers beneath the collar of her T-shirt suggestively, she realized he'd shifted tactics.

Brute force hadn't worked.

Evidently the threat of rape was next.

She refused to be cowed by either. She even managed to hold down her stomach as his hot breath filled her ear. "Shall I tell you what you want to know now? Or should we wait until there is more..." He slid his hands up her breasts and squeezed hard. "...privacy?"

"Now will do."

He chuckled. And stood.

She eased out her breath as Arista left her side—until he turned. She flinched as the bastard kicked Ernesto squarely in the ribs just for the hell of it. She recognized the stark note in Ernesto's groan just before he faded.

His ribs were broken.

He wouldn't be able to handle much more abuse.

Arista hunkered down and slapped his cheeks smartly, bringing Ernesto around, only to lift his head by the roots of his hair before slamming his skull back into the ground. "Shall I tell her what she wishes to know? Shall I describe how your whore of a mother serviced your father and then gave you up for a handful of pesos? Shall I tell her how Señora Torres was forced to take you in and raise you as her own because the president's first seed destroyed her womb? Shall I tell her how your father betrayed her loyalty to him after all these years by confessing in his delirium that he intended to strip her own child of his birthright and name a *bastardo* as his heir?" Arista punctuated each sentence with a slam, then stood and kicked his right boot directly into Ernesto's ribs again.

This time, Ernesto passed out completely.

Eve sent up a silent prayer of thanks as Arista abandoned Ernesto's side—even when he stopped in front of her.

"You must admit, it was most clever. By laying the blame at the feet of the great and powerful American army, we manage to—how do you say it—kill two birds with one stone?"

She smiled just to piss him off. "But it didn't work, did it? You won't be able to blame us for his death now."

She wasn't so sure when Arista returned her smile with one even more smug. "Ah, but we can and we will. You see, I will not be the death of you." He shook his head. "You were murdered by a band of those dastardly Córdoban rebels. I am sure you have heard of them, no? After all, your own CIA is providing their weapons." He snapped his fingers. "Pablo!"

One of the men tossed him a rifle.

Arista held it out. "You see?"

She did.

An M-16. Made in the good ol' U.S. of A. Though she suspected this particular M-16 had come from a San Sebastián armory. Not that anyone would be the wiser. Not after Arista bagged and tagged the weapon's expended distinctive shell casings and then filed down the serial number on the rifle.

If he hadn't already.

She and Ernesto were doomed.

Why else had the colonel offered detailed evidence that could convict him? Arista didn't intend to let them live. The worst of it was, this clearing was too far away from Rick or anyone else for her to call for help. The gags proved it. Hers had been down around her neck since she woke. Ernesto's lay beside his battered and unconscious face.

Arista didn't even care.

She stared at the M-16.

It was loaded.

If she could get Arista furious, he just might try to smack her with that rifle again. Wrestling it from him with her hands tied behind her back might seem impossible. But the odds were a heck of a lot more attractive than waiting around to die. She spat at his boots, aiming for—and marring—the buffed toes. "So what are you waiting for?"

As expected, his fist flew.

To her shock, so did a bullet. It tore straight through Pablo's meaty neck, taking half the man's windpipe with it before it pinged into the steel skin of the Huey six inches from Arista's head.

*Rick.*

Arista's arm shot out before she realized his intent. He grabbed her hair by the roots and hauled her to her feet, shielding his body with hers. His putrid breath poured into her ear as he shoved a 9 mm pistol into the flesh beneath her jaw and coldly chambered a round. "That is what I am waiting for, *puta.* Your lover."

Her nerves shrieked as she stared into the jungle.

Where was he?

Eve twisted her head to the right as best she could, scanning the tree line before Arista jerked her face toward his. She couldn't see Rick. Not that she'd expected to. But she could feel him—and she had spied the other thugs slipping into the sheltering belly of the Huey.

The colonel plus two.

Three-to-one odds?

No way. Arista might be a criminal, but he was not criminally insane.

The missing men. She knew where they were now.

"Rick, it's a trap! He's got four men hiding in the surrounding tree—" Arista's fist cracked into her jaw. The force of the punch smashed her skull into the chopper behind them. She tried like hell to hold back this groan.

She failed.

Another round flew, this one landing with a soft, telling thwack inside the Huey. One of the men staggered out through the doorway, clutching at the dark stain spreading across his chest. He pitched face-first into the ground with a solid thud three feet from the colonel's boots.

Arista bellowed into her ear, enraged now.

"Let me guess, that was your pilot."

This time, he bypassed his fist and bashed the side of her skull straight into the Huey. Stars exploded before her eyes as a third round took down the next stooge.

Only Arista remained.

And his hidden men.

She opened her mouth again—

"One word, *puta,* and Ernesto Torres dies before your very eyes. I may even let you help pull the trigger. The choice is yours." Arista shifted the barrel of the 9 mm to the man's limp body. The pistol was rock-steady.

The bastard meant it.

"*Fine.*" For now.

He gripped her hair tighter, ripping chunks from her scalp as he used the tangles to haul her around with him as he faced the shadowy trees, still using her as his shield as he crammed the pistol's barrel beneath her jaw once again. "Captain Bishop! I give you one warning and one warning only! I shall count to five. If I reach the final number and you are not standing directly in front of me, unarmed, I will kill her. Understood?"

Silence.

Arista waited a full two seconds and then shrugged.

"One."

"Two."

"Three."

She caught the rustle in the leaves.

"N—"

"I meant it, *puta*. You will help me pull the trigger."

Dammit, he'd said it was her choice, hadn't he?

Rick or Ernesto?

If she saved Rick, he would never forgive her. But if she saved Ernesto, she would lose the man she loved. Not that she'd ever really had him. Dammit, this wasn't a choice, it was a nightmare! Worse than any she'd ever dreamed, worse than every one she'd ever lived. "I choose *both*." She gathered her strength and prepared to launch herself backwards into Arista and hopefully knock him off balance.

*"Eve."*

She froze. "Rick?"

Her heart was pounding so fast she barely felt the hair tearing from her scalp as Arista whipped her body around with his, careful to keep her in front. She was still dimly aware of the barrel of the 9 mm crammed beneath her jaw—but she was piercingly aware of Rick as his camouflaged form slowly separated from the trees. His hands might be carefully folded atop his head, but he was smiling at her gently. He was telling her with his eyes and with his confident, easy pace that everything would be okay.

*Relax.* She would be fine.

He would take care of her.

She didn't doubt it for a second. Not with him fifteen

feet away, walking steadily toward her. But what about him? Good God, why wouldn't he stop? She'd lost too many people she cared about already. But she loved him most of all.

"Rick, please, *don't*."

Even the grease paint couldn't disguise those gorgeous dimples as they caved in deep and low, carving a hole straight through her heart. "I have to, sweetheart. I love you."

Arista grinned. "Four."

Rick took another step.

"Five."

Rick stopped, three feet away.

"Excellent, Captain. Now, drop the knife."

Rick opened his hands, but kept them at his head. To her horror, his K-Bar fell beside the heels of his boots.

It was stained with blood.

Whose? How many of Arista's men had Rick managed to kill before he'd announced his presence?

How many still lived?

Arista glanced at the knife and chuckled. "Why am I not surprised, Captain?"

The corner of Rick's mouth lifted slightly. "Because you know me." The lift faded. "Now, release my woman so we can settle this like men."

"But I am not a man, agreed? What was it you called me a mere eight months ago? Ah, yes. A monster." Eve swallowed her terror as Arista crammed the 9 mm deeper into her neck. He grabbed her breasts with his free hand and leaned down to run his tongue up the side of her jaw and into her ear. She couldn't stop the shiver of revulsion that coursed through her as he followed it with a cruder grope. Arista just laughed. "I hope you enjoyed the tender hands of your lover last night, Señorita. For they will fade beneath mine as we make love."

"You don't make love, Arista. You maul."

Arista clucked his tongue. "But the village girl was mine to maul, was she not? Just as this one will be." He dragged his hand from her breast and fitted his fingers around her neck, cutting her air supply in half as he squeezed firmly. "Perhaps when I am done, I shall leave her staked out for the Córdobans, yes?"

"Over my dead body."

"That, my dear Captain Courageous, is precisely what has already been arranged." He jerked his head toward the Huey. "Now, if you would be so kind as to—"

"*Arista.*"

Eve stiffened—not so much at the fury in Ernesto's gasp, but that the man had spoken at all. She could have sworn he was still unconscious. From the shock on Arista's face as Ernesto twisted his entire body before jerking his bound hands beneath his boots as he jackknifed up, so had Arista.

But Rick hadn't. He *moved.*

A split second later, so did the 9 mm at her jaw.

Eve screamed.

Arista's arm fell to her shoulders with a thump. A moment later, it was his body and not Rick's that landed at her feet with a sickening thud. She stared down at the screwdriver buried up to the hilt in the colonel's neck. Blood pooled out, seeping into the earth beneath Arista's shoulders and his head. He stared up at them, gurgled once, and then he was dead.

Eve threw herself into Rick's arms.

She shuddered as he gathered her as closely as he had days before when he'd helped her confront the remains of her chopper, not even caring that her shoulder sockets strained and popped as he crushed her to him. He pressed his lips to her brow fervently, over and over, before he finally released her enough to smooth his shaking hands down her back. His fingers worked the knotted ropes at her

wrists as he shifted his lips to her hair and murmured reassurances in her ear.

This time, she knew exactly what he was saying.

The same thing he'd confessed that moment in bed at
the presidential palace hours before, the same thing he'd
said a minute ago when Arista had been holding a gun to
her head.

Rick had told her he loved her three times now.

But each admission had been elicited under duress.

She refused to bind him to any of them.

If she did, he would only end up leaving her as he had
earlier this morning. And being abandoned by Rick had
hurt more deeply than all the other leavings combined. She
stanched the pain in her heart and drew herself up straight,
stepping away as the ropes fell from her wrists.

"Eve?"

She shook her head, unable to speak. Rick reached out,
but before he could touch her, Ernesto coughed, then
hacked. They turned in unison, shoving confusion and pain
aside as they vaulted forward together to free Ernesto from
his bindings. Rick's hand closed over hers as she reached
out.

"I've got him. You go fire up that bird."

She stared up at him and then nodded.

He was right.

It was time to collect her crew and get the hell out of
this godforsaken country. She'd figure out how to say goodbye later, after Rick hefted his friend into the Huey behind
them—and she got them airborne. Because unless Rick
came to her willingly by the time they reburied the bodies
in the States, she would be returning to Panama to get to
the bottom of the accusations against Anna Shale.

Alone.

"You look like hell." Rick closed the door to his
friend's office, hoping his grin took the insult from his

words as Ernesto crossed the room to greet him. From the twist to the man's own split purple lips, it had.

"True, but already the ladies have begun to descend upon my humble form, eager to nurse me back to health." His buddy used his unwrapped wrist and hand to gesture toward the leather armchair beside his desk. "Sit, please. I would join you, but truth be told, my ribs hurt too damned much."

Rick hooked a thigh on the edge of the desk instead, bringing his head down to Ernesto's level. He stared into his friend's eyes as the twist to the man's lips faded—and the pain set in. "Everything under control?"

"*Sí.* And you? Have you finished with the bodies?"

Rick nodded. Hours ago, in fact.

He'd spent the latter part of the afternoon ensuring that the remains of Carrie Evans, Bill Turner and Sergeant Lange were properly secured in the San Sebastián morgue until arrangements could be made to return them to American soil. While Eve hadn't been thrilled with his suggestion that she head to the room to shower and rest long enough to give the pain medication she'd been prescribed a chance to kick in, she had agreed.

"And the film?"

Again, Rick nodded. "I just got back from turning the rolls over to General Gage." The task had taken longer than he'd expected, but it couldn't be helped. Not if he and Eve hoped to salvage their careers. Unfortunately, the sun would be setting soon. He was anxious to return to the room, to Eve.

To talk.

Among other things.

"Then what are you waiting for?"

Rick wasn't surprised that Ernesto had read his mind. Nor was he surprised at his friend's attempt to run him off.

But today had been one hell of a day. That was precisely why he'd stopped here first. According to the doctor who'd examined Eve and Ernesto hours before, the man's cracked ribs, sprained wrist and bruised kidney would heal soon enough.

As for his heart?

That was anyone's guess.

In less than twenty-four hours Ernesto's world had been tossed upside down and then shredded. His stepmother had been arrested. A man he'd known and trusted most of his life was dead. His brother blamed him for getting bumped down in the pecking order and his father had been weaned far enough off his morphine to name him for a job he never wanted in the first place. Yeah, the man was doing just swell.

The stark pain in his eyes confirmed it.

"I am fine, my friend, or I shall be. If you do not go soon, however, you may suffer another fate."

"What you talking about? General Gage assured me—"

"I was not referring to your career, but your lady. She stopped by ten minutes ago. In fact, she may already be gone."

Gone?

Eve should be sleeping by now.

Then again, he should have returned to their room three hours ago. Still, she had to have assumed he'd been held up, had to know he'd be back for her. But something in Ernesto's stance said not. And then there was the way Eve had pulled away from him after he'd eliminated Arista and his men—and had been oddly distant since. Granted, not many women could deal with the reality of what he'd done that day, and how he'd accomplished it. But he was sure she could.

All he had to do was picture Arista's hands on her body to know he'd do it again.

But would she?

"Ernie, what happened?"

"She stopped by, asked how I was doing, noted that the Huey was still in the courtyard—and then asked for permission to take it up."

"Why the devil would she want to fly now?"

Unfortunately, his friend shrugged. "After all that has happened today, I did not ask."

Suddenly, he wasn't sure of anything anymore.

He was also scared.

Even if the pain medication had kicked in, she couldn't have gotten enough sleep. She was too tired to fly, dammit. Much less at night. And if she was upset…

"I gotta go."

By the time the door slammed behind him, he was halfway down the corridor. It took far too long to wind his way out through the familiar hallways. By the time he reached the last turn his boots were hitting the blood-red tiles at a double-time. He forced himself to stop short just shy of the courtyard door and draw air into his lungs, to calm his pounding heart.

He couldn't hear blades on the other side.

Either he had time—or it was already too late.

He nodded to the presidential guard and shoved the door open—and breathed easier. Until he spied Eve.

Her fully loaded rucksack.

His heart began pounding again.

Painfully.

He crossed the cobblestones silently, waiting until he was four feet behind her before he cleared his throat. "I thought running was *my* standard operating procedure."

He held his breath as Eve stiffened.

A second later, she dropped her ruck. It slid off the

Huey's skid and landed on the cobblestones at her boots. The moment she drew in a deep, shaky breath and turned, he knew he was right. She was running.

Damn, but it stung.

Not that he didn't deserve the slap. After all, Eve had taught him how to love. All he'd done was teach her how to turn tail and retreat. Ernie might not know where she was headed, but he did. She planned on returning the Huey to the hangars it shared with the wing of American Black Hawks on the outskirts of town. She obviously hoped to grab a cot in the barracks with her unit and log her first full night's sleep in weeks—without him.

"Well?"

The word hung between them for so long, he could feel the awkward silence settling in around it. Around them. After everything they'd shared it just plain hurt.

But so did she.

He could see it in her gaze, in the way she struggled to keep it focused on his. That hurt even more than her running.

The tip of her tongue darted out to wet her lips. "I…guess I should have waited, but it'll be dark soon. I wanted to have the bird home by then." She paused as if she expected him to say something.

What? Goodbye?

The hell he would.

Her gaze finally fled from his. "Well, um, thanks again for everything. I'll…see you sometime." She turned to the Huey and reached for her ruck. He snagged it before she could and held it suspended between them, determined not to let it go. Not to let her go.

"I blew it, didn't I?"

For several horrifying moments he was afraid she wasn't going to answer. She finally turned back, staring up at him as she shook her head slowly. "No. If anyone blew it, it was me. I never should have asked for more than you were willing to give.'' She reached for her ruck again. ''I'm sorry.''

''I'm not.''

Her hands fell to her sides.

He watched as the shock of his words ignited the emerald flame in her eyes. Hope followed.

It stoked his own.

He tightened his hands on the ruck before she could try to claim it again and tossed it behind her—well away from the chopper. ''You were right. Ernie was right. Hell, so was Turner. I was running. Fast. For a long time, from life. But lately, from you too. But then I began wondering if maybe I could handle what I felt for you...until last night proved I couldn't. But I want to. God, I want to. Eve, I love you.''

He heard her breath catch, watched those beautiful green eyes glisten. He waited for what seemed like eons.

But she didn't speak.

''Sweetheart? Say something. Please.''

The tears just flowed harder.

''Honey, you're scaring me. I admit it took me a while, but I finally realized I might have helped restore your wings only to ground you again, at least temporarily. I'll make it up to you. I swear it.'' He'd take a damned desk job if that's what it took. ''Just tell me you want this baby.''

She found her voice then. ''You think I'm *pregnant?*''

He winced as her words echoed across the courtyard. Even the pair of loyal presidential guardsmen loitering a discreet distance away stiffened. The moment the brunt of her shock ripped through his panic, so did he. ''You're not? I mean, it's probably too soon to tell, but—''

''It's not. I'm not. Oh, God.'' She turned and slumped down into the side of the Huey. ''I can't believe this. Just once I'd like to hear the words without something besides sex or fear or adrenaline driving them.'' She stared up at him and shook her head as he stood in front of her, bemused. ''Rick, I finished my cycle when we left Panama. I'm not ovulating. I know that's not a guarantee, but it would be a pretty long, long shot. I guess I should have told you last night, but I wasn't thinking clearly beforehand. And afterward…'' She didn't finish. He knew why.

He hunkered down in front of her knees and tipped her chin. ''And after, I behaved like an ass.''

*''Yeah.''*

He combed his fingers into her curls, still damp from her bath and smoothed them from her face. ''Would it help to know the only running I plan on doing from now on is to you?''

He didn't deserve the fresh set of tears that slipped down, but he took them.

Cherished them.

Deep in his soul he knew that these were a precious gift. He caught them with his thumbs as he'd been driven to the day of the crash. Then he leaned forward and smoothed them from her soft skin with his lips. When he'd dried every last one of them, he eased his mouth over her bruised jaw and whispered the rest in her ear. ''I don't have a ring on me, honey, but I do have my heart. Please take it. I love you, Eve. Marry me. I'm ready to come out of the jungle now. I want to come home.''

He wasn't glossing over his sergeant, the past or the crash. He knew damn well he still had a lot of healing to do.

They both did.

They could heal together. He cupped his hands to her face and waited. The tears streamed down again, then finally ebbed.

And then she nodded.

Smiled.

"I already have a ring, Rick, and three more Sisters. What I don't have—what I desperately need—is you."

His heart swelled until it damn near exploded with joy. He couldn't help it, he scooped her up into his arms with a whoop that reverberated throughout the courtyard. He turned his back on the chopper and Eve's gear, leaving both to the presidential guard as he struck out across the cobblestones and into the palace, ignoring her protests all the way.

"Rick, the Huey! Someone has to—"

He covered her lips with his and swallowed the rest as he turned down the first corridor, deepening the kiss as he turned down the second, and the third. The hell with that blasted chopper. Ernesto could find his own damned pilot. This one was his. He turned down the final corridor and kicked the door at the end open, slamming it firmly shut behind them and throwing the lock before he strode across the carpet. He reached out and snapped the white bedspread to the foot board with one hand.

"Tired?"

Amusement quirked her lips and her brow as she stared up at him, still in his arms. He tossed her onto the sheets in lieu of an answer, stripping off his T-shirt and his jungle boots—and then finally his trousers, his skivvies and socks in one final sweep before he crawled in after her.

Precisely three seconds later, she moaned.

By then, Eve knew he had no intention of sleeping.

Not for a very, *very* long time.

\* \* \* \* \*

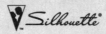

If you enjoyed what you just read,
then we've got an offer you can't resist!

# Take 2 bestselling
# love stories FREE!
# Plus get a FREE surprise gift!

# $ Saving Money $ Has Never Been This Easy!

Just fill out and send in this form from any October, November and December 2002 books and we will send you a coupon booklet worth a total savings of $20.00 off future purchases of Harlequin and Silhouette books in 2003.

## Yes! It's that easy!

I accept your incredible offer!
Please send me a coupon booklet:

Name (PLEASE PRINT)

Address                                                        Apt. #

City                        State/Prov.                   Zip/Postal Code

In a typical month, how many
Harlequin and Silhouette novels do you read?

❏ 0-2                             ❏ 3+

097KJKDNC7                                                    097KJKDNDP

**Please send this form to:**
In the U.S.: Harlequin Books, P.O. Box 9071, Buffalo, NY 14269-9071
In Canada: Harlequin Books, P.O. Box 609, Fort Erie, Ontario  L2A 5X3

Allow 4-6 weeks for delivery. Limit one coupon booklet per household. Must be postmarked no later than January 15, 2003.

HARLEQUIN®
*Makes any time special*®

*Silhouette*®
*Where love comes alive*™

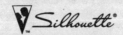

**Silhouette**

# COMING NEXT MONTH

SIMCNM1002